After Luke

After Luke

Published by The Conrad Press Ltd. in the United Kingdom 2022

Tel: +44(0)1227 472 874
www.theconradpress.com
info@theconradpress.com

ISBN 978-1-914913-77-8

Printed and bound in Great Britain by Clays Ltd, Elcograf S.p.A

Typesetting and Cover Design by The Book Typesetters
www.thebooktypesetters.com

The Conrad Press logo was designed by Maria Priestley.

After Luke

KERRY-LEE DELPORT

Chapter 1

Staring out over a rainy New York City skyline, my heart felt as heavy as the thick grey clouds looming over the city and I wondered for the umpteenth time if I was making the right choice.

New York had been my home, our home, for the past ten years and I would miss so much about it.

I'd miss the late-night pizza runs and early morning coffee shop visits after a run in Central Park.

I would miss our friends and going out for dinner to our favourite restaurants, but mostly, I would miss the memories this city held for me.

So many wonderful, happy years, developing into snippets of blissful memories over the years.

It was only recently that the city had felt less like home and those once happy memories now haunted my every turn.

I felt my eyes burning, at the thought of the latter and suddenly felt my chest tighten and my breath caught in my throat.

What was I thinking? I was leaving our home, the place we had built a life together, where his memory lived on.

Even though those memories hurt so much sometimes

that I was certain they would break me in half, I couldn't leave. It would be like leaving him behind.

I wasn't ready for that. Not yet. Maybe not ever.

Raking in another shaky breath, I sat on the window ledge, my vision blurring.

'Sophie, are you ok? Breath, just breath,' Kaitlyn soothed, squeezing my hand and rubbing my back.

Kaitlyn; my best friend and my anchor.

The one thing holding me in place, keeping me from drifting into an abyss of darkness.

I don't know what I would have done without her these past two years.

She had let me lean on her for strength, support and just about anything else I needed her for, and I loved her dearly for it.

I also felt like a burden.

One she hadn't asked for and certainly one she didn't need, but despite my numerous protests, she had been by my side through it all.

'We're family. It's what family does,' she had told me so many times I'd lost count.

We met in kindergarten and had been inseparable ever since.

If truth be told, I don't think I could have survived this long without her. She was the sister I never had.

In fact, most people usually mistook us for sisters.

I could understand why; at first glance there were some similarities, with us both having Mediterranean complexions and sandy blonde hair, along with being similar height (although Kaitlyn liked to tease me that she was an inch taller than my five-foot-six frame).

It was only upon closer inspection, our subtle differences showed; Kaitlyn had the biggest, kindest, hazel eyes, whereas mine were a deep turquoise and although we were both slim, Kaitlyn had a far more delicate bone structure. She could have easily been a ballerina.

I, on the other hand, wasn't quite so delicate, showing just a hint of curves.

It was one of the things Luke said he loved most about me, that I wasn't a stick insect, he used to say.

The thought made me want to cry, again.

So, I refocused and pulled myself together. Something I had almost perfected lately.

Almost…

Kaitlyn handed me a glass of water and the anxiety pills I had been prescribed, snapping me back to the present.

I hated taking them, but what I hated even more was the fact that I still needed them at all, especially after all this time.

I'd never been one for taking pills, of any kind, but every so often an anxiety attack (which is what the doctors had diagnosed me with) would strike and I needed to take them.

Swallowing the pills down, I closed my eyes.

Taking another deep breath in and slowly letting it out, just like I'd learned in yoga, I felt my heart rate slowly creep down to an acceptable pace, instead of the sledge hammer that had just been trying to break free from my chest.

'Better?' Kaitlyn asked gently.

She was one of the most caring people I'd ever known. Never quick to judge anyone, which made me all the more grateful for her.

She was always there, never losing patience with me.

'Yes, thank you,' I squeezed her hand tightly. 'I'm sorry. I know it's silly. I was just thinking about leaving the city and… I don't know, I feel like I'm leaving him behind.' I twirled the two wedding bands I always wore on a thin chain around my neck.

One was Luke's, the other my own.

I had continued wearing my wedding ring after his funeral, until it became too difficult to talk about with new people I met, who would clock the ring on my finger and inevitably ask after my husband, so I had added mine to the chain which already held Luke's and I now wore them both close to my heart, always.

'Oh honey, he's with you wherever you go. He'll always be with you, he's in your heart and soul for all of time and he'll always be watching over you,' Kaitlyn assured me.

I couldn't respond for the lump in my throat.

The day Luke had collapsed in this very apartment had been the worst days of my life.

Or so I'd thought – the days that followed had been far, far worse.

We were about to have dinner – it was Luke's twenty seventh birthday and we were meeting our friends for drinks later that night.

We never made it.

Luke never made it home from the hospital and I lost my husband, my best friend, my whole life, in one night.

The doctors had worked for hours to save his life, but in the end it just wasn't enough and when one of the doctors had walked into the waiting room, I knew right away from the look on his face that Luke was gone.

My world came crumbling down around me in an instant. I shattered into a million tiny pieces, with Kaitlyn by my side, holding onto me as though she was trying to put me back together, but it was no use.

I would never be the same again after that night.

How could this be happening? It must be a nightmare. That was all I kept thinking.

Luke and I had always been health conscious. Almost everything we ate was natural and homemade and we worked out at least five or six times a week.

We loved to go running in Central Park, something we did together most weekends.

But according to the doctors, it had nothing to do with our healthy lifestyle.

Luke had a rare type of brain tumour, which had gone undetected.

Until that fatal night.

The guilt of this still eats away at me to this day.

I was his wife! I should have seen the signs. I should have known something was wrong! We always looked after each another and I had failed him in the worst possible way.

I was now paying the price.

I would never look into the depths of his chocolate brown eyes again. Or run my fingers through his thick, lustrous, dark hair. Or roll my eyes at one of his ridiculous jokes.

It didn't matter how much the doctors (or anyone else for that matter) had tried to convince me it wasn't my fault. Or that there was nothing I could have done, or that there are no warning signs in these instances.

I would always hold myself responsible.

I should have known something was wrong and now I'd never get the chance to tell him how sorry I was, or how much I miss him. And Lord knows I miss him, every single day.

That had been two years ago today, yet it still weighed down on me like it was yesterday.

I lost half of myself that day and I'd never gotten it back.

I've been drifting through life since then, numbly, simply existing, no longer truly living, but as life goes, it likes to kick you while you're already down.

A few weeks ago, I received a call that no daughter ever wanted to get.

My dad was in hospital, after suffering a heart-attack and had to undergo surgery there and then.

Thankfully he was on the road to recovery now, but after losing Luke, the thought of losing anyone else was just too much.

So, I'd made the decision to pack up my life and move back to my picturesque hometown of Beaufort, North Caroline, to be closer to my parents and help with anything they needed while dad recuperated.

Of course they had said there was no need for all the fuss

and I should stay in New York, it was, after all, where my job and all my friends were, but my friends could visit and I could write from anywhere in the world – one of the perks of being a novelist.

So, here I am, my whole life packed into the back of a removal van, heading home to live with my parents.

Well, initially anyway.

That would be short lived because, according to my dad, the most important thing to him was that I take his place working at Willow Farm Sanctuary – a local animal sanctuary on the outskirts of Beaufort.

This wasn't ideal, given the whole point of me going home was to be under the same roof as them, at least until I could find myself a place to rent (or buy – I hadn't really planned that far ahead yet), but I wasn't in any place to argue.

I wanted to help in whatever way I could, and if this is what he wanted me to do, then I would happily do it.

Doctors' orders had been for Dad to relax as much as possible, so I figured if he knew I was taking care of his job at the sanctuary, it would be one less thing for him to worry about.

I only hoped that the country air could clear away some of my own troubles in the process.

'Call me the minute you get there ok,' Kaitlyn hugged me tightly.

We were at the airport, since I'd opted to fly rather than drive the ten or so hours home.

It was too long a drive and in my current state, if I'm

being completely honest, I didn't trust myself to be behind the wheel that long, especially since I'd had to take my pills this morning, which usually made my brain feel as foggy as the gloomy day around me.

'I will. Thank you for everything. Promise you'll come visit as soon as you can?' I tried not to sound like a whiny child and failed miserably.

'Of course. I'm not leaving my favourite girl alone in a one-horse town for long, don't you worry.'

I smiled at Kaitlyn's description of Beaufort.

It was small compared to New York, of course, but I grew up there, so it shouldn't come as too much of a shock to the system.

I hoped.

After living in the city that never sleeps for the past ten years, I wasn't so sure how I'd cope being home again, but by the sound of it, I was going to have my hands full with the sanctuary and helping my parents, which I could only hope was exactly what I needed.

A few hours later the plane touched down in New Bern, where I'd arranged for my car to be delivered.

At the very least I needed my own transportation out here, this wasn't New York after all, I couldn't just hail a cab, or hop on the subway.

And there she sat, my new (to me) shiny white Range Rover.

Ok, so I'd splurged a little, but I was entitled to treat myself now and then, and after the sale of the apartment, which had gone far better than I could have anticipated, I had more than a little extra cash, so I figured I might as well, at the very least, drive in comfort going back and forth between my parents and the sanctuary.

And anyway, it wasn't one of the super flashy, chunky Range Rovers that celebrities drove, this was a slightly smaller version and it was perfect.

After collecting the keys and stowing my suitcase in the trunk (and dropping Kaitlyn a quick text to say I'd landed and would call her when I got to my parents) I cranked the aircon – thank heavens for small mercies.

I'd forgotten how humid North Carolina could be in the summertime. Even though it was only early June, I could already feel my long sleek waves starting to frizz in the heat.

Ignoring the cries of help from my hair for now, I hit the road, putting even more distance between my old life.

All the while, wondered what lay ahead.

It wasn't a long drive to my parents' house.

The roads weren't particularly busy, well, not by New York standards anyway.

About an hour later I pulled onto my parents' drive and looked up at the house I'd grown up in.

It looked exactly as I remembered it.

White picket fence surrounding the front lawn with big old oak trees towering above the house, casting shadows across the lawn, where numerous flowers I didn't know the names of, grew beautifully (my mom was an avid gardener).

I, on the other hand, hadn't inherited her green thumb.

I managed to kill a cactus garden for goodness sake – the

one thing that grows in possibly the harshest climate and yet I somehow managed to kill it.

Something Luke had found hilarious.

Two rocking chairs still sat nestled together on the porch. The swing seat nestled in the far corner, where my parents usually found me as a child, curled up with a book.

My mind drifted back to a summer, years ago, when Luke and I had visited.

I couldn't wait to show him my childhood home and the quaint little town I'd grown up in.

I wasn't sure which he had loved more, my enthusiasm, or Beaufort.

We had dreamed of moving back here one day, having a few kids and starting our own little family. I had wanted a boy and girl, just like my brother and I, who, as much as he drove me crazy growing up, I loved dearly.

My brother, Paul, who was 9 years older than me (and always used to tease me about being the oops child, given our age gap), also lived in Beaufort with his wife, Sarah.

They were expecting their first baby early next year.

He had tried to convince me that he could handle things here, but it wasn't fair, it was too much to put on one person.

Taking care of his own family, while looking after Mom and Dad, all the while running the family business – which he'd only recently fully taken over, after years of working with our dad, would have been too much for anyone.

Dad had always been smart with his money and from a young age he'd started up a boat charter business, slowly bringing in more and more business over the years, until it was a booming company, owning a dozen or so boats, offering everything from private cruising to adventure and sunset tours.

Paul was in the process of expanding the business. He wanted to add boat B&B to the addition and although I admired his drive, I worried he was taking on too much.

Then again, once my brother put his mind to something, there was no stopping him – a trait that seemed to run in our family.

'Honey, you're home,' my mom's voice pulled me from my reverie, and I jumped out of the car.

'Hi, Mom,' I pulled her into a great big bear hug and held on for what felt like a lifetime.

A mother's hug was one of life's most precious gifts. It was that one sure thing that could cure almost any ailment or heartache.

In my case, it only eased the pain somewhat.

'How's Dad?' I asked, when I finally let her go.

'Oh, you know your dad, tough as old boots that one,' Mom chuckled. 'He'll be fine honey, don't you worry. Now, come on in, he'll be so glad you're finally here, he hasn't stopped going on about it all week.'

After retrieving my suitcase from the trunk, I followed Mom inside, where I found my dad in the living room looking very sorry for himself.

He brightened when he saw me, and my heart warmed. It really was good to be home, I'd missed them both a lot more than I realised.

'Hi, Dad,' I hugged him gently, suddenly worried about breaking him, which was such a disconcerting notion.

My dad has always been this indestructible superhero figure to me, who could never get hurt. This was a stark reminder that life was precious and fleeting. Something I already knew all too well.

'Hi, honey, how are you? You look thin. Are you eating properly?'

Trust my dad to be fussing over me when he'd just suffered a heart-attack.

'I'm fine, Dad. More importantly, how are you feeling?'

We sat back down, just as Mom re-appeared with her famous sweet tea, Dad sighing, grateful for any distraction to take the spotlight off him.

I waited patiently for an answer.

Another sigh, this time defeated, knowing I wasn't going to let it drop.

'I feel fine, honestly, I don't know what all the fuss is about.'

My dad, as I suspected was the case with most dad's, didn't enjoy being fussed over or feeling like an invalid.

'It's life telling you to slow down, George,' Mom tutted.

My parents were in their late fifties, but they both looked great for their respective ages.

They could easily pass for early fifties, even late forties at a push, but dad was supposed to be winding down, hence handing over the family business to my brother, even though he still helped Paul on a fairly regular basis, I was quite certain.

Not to mention working at the sanctuary. He clearly

didn't understand the meaning of winding down. Not that Mom was much better.

Jane Preston was a force to be reckoned with and was just as well known and loved around Beaufort as Dad was.

She was heavily involved in a wide variety of charities, as well as being a member of the Beaufort council and of course her favourite pastime, gardening.

Mom worked part time as a landscape designer, and I was pretty sure she'd had a hand in most of the gardens around our small town.

'Pfft,' Dad huffed in response to Mom's comment, but I think deep down he knew it was true. And I was here to make sure he listened and started to wind down – they both did.

They had both worked hard over the years and it was time they started to relax and live for themselves. Travel, try new foods, see the world. Do all the things they've ever wanted to.

They had earned the right to retire earlier than some, so it was high time they took advantage of it.

After spending the afternoon catching up, the three of us enjoying a delicious meal together – nothing can beat a mama's home cooking.

It took me right back to my childhood.

Mom was a great cook and still volunteered at a local shelter, cooking warm meals for anyone who needed them.

She'd never let the fact that she'd gone to culinary school in Paris and owned her own restaurant (which she still owned, but thankfully had a great manager to run the place for her) go to her head.

It's one of the many things I loved so much about both of my parents; they were humble and down to earth, despite their successes in life. They never forgot where they came from.

They had seen difficult times as well as good, and then difficult times again, but through it all they had taught Paul and I the meaning of family; sticking together and working together to get through the tough times and enjoy the good times.

It's one of the reasons I felt we were still so close.

And as I sat on the porch later that day, soaking up the last of the sun's rays, filtering through the trees, I sighed deeply, content, happy, and for the first time in a very long time, I felt lighter.

There truly was no place like home.

Chapter 2

The smell of bacon and coffee woke me the following morning and it took me a moment to realise where I was.

Blinking, I looked around my old room.

Not much had changed; a small desk and chair were still against the wall opposite my bed, surrounded by a floor to ceiling bookshelf that Dad had made me – I'd always been a book worm.

A small dresser, adorned with make-up and jewellery sat against the far wall, while beachy paintings hung on my walls, draped with warm fairy lights, which hung around most of the room, but my favourite feature was the balcony that overlooked the water.

Getting up, I grabbed my dressing gown and stepped onto the deck, blinking in the morning sunshine.

It truly was beautiful out here, I thought, looking out over the water, watching the gulls waiting patiently for their breakfast.

I always loved the way the sunlight shimmered across the surface of the water and filtered through the trees like streams of gold dust descending onto the earth.

I desperately wanted to unpack my camera and get a few

shots, but my stomach had other plans. It rumbled rather loudly, so I padded downstairs to find my parents at the breakfast table in the kitchen.

'Good morning honey, how did you sleep?' Mom asked, pouring me a cup of coffee before topping up their tea.

'Better than I have in a while,' I told her honestly.

I'd had a great night's sleep.

No nightmares or waking up in a cold sweat, just a sound, dreamless night's sleep. Something I had taken for granted a few years ago.

'That's good dear,' I could hear my mom's underlying concern.

They knew how badly I'd handled losing Luke and I knew how much they worried about it, about me.

'Help yourself to some breakfast,' Mom added.

'Thanks, Mom. This smells amazing, but should Dad be eating bacon?' I asked, spooning a mountain of scrambled eggs and rashers onto my plate.

'That's not bacon,' Dad grumbled.

'They're lean turkey rashers, it's the next best thing,' Mom said, giving Dad the look.

I suppressed a giggle.

'I don't even get proper scrambled eggs anymore, they're mostly egg whites,' Dad continued, sipping his tea.

'There are loads of heart healthy recipes I'd be happy to try, that I think you'd like, and I can guarantee you won't even notice the difference,' I offered.

I'd gotten my healthy eating habits, not only from living in a warm climate, so generally all you wanted were salads (or in my case seafood), but also from my parents, which is also why the heart-attack came as such a shock – although it shouldn't have, given my experience – there was no discriminating when it came to health, but my dad sure did like his egg and bacon breakfasts and I could tell he wasn't impressed with the alternative.

'That would be wonderful honey,' Mom said enthusiastically.

Dad didn't look convinced, but I would bring him around.

'I was going to run into town this morning, to get a few things and stop in to see Paul. Is there anything I can do while I'm there? Just put me to work,' I smiled, popping a forkful of egg into my mouth.

'Oh, if you could run a few errands for us, that would be great?' Mom asked hesitantly.

I guess it must be difficult for parents to ask their children for help, or to have to rely on them, not that I minded in the slightest, after all my parents had done for Paul and I, providing a happy, loving home and making sure we never went without, it was the very least I could do.

'Of course, that's what I'm here for, anything you need.'

They both gave me warm, grateful smiles and we finished our breakfast, chatting about everything and nothing.

'Sophie Hamilton, I was about to send out a search party!'

I was on my way into town and I had Kaitlyn on loudspeaker in the car.

'I'm so sorry, I got so caught up catching up with my parents and then I just crashed. Do you forgive me?' I asked with a smile.

I hadn't meant to worry her. I hadn't even heard my phone ring last night.

'Of course. You know I can't stay mad at you! So, what's it like being home?'

'So far so good. My dad seems well, although he's not impressed with some of his new food changes, but he'll have to get used to them. My mom's good. You know her, she's always happy go lucky. I'm just heading into town now to see Paul,' I explained.

'That's great and I'm glad to hear your dad's ok, but Soph, I meant how are YOU doing?'

I knew what she'd meant.

'Honestly, I don't know. It's great being home, of course, and wonderful seeing my parents, but a part of me is missing New York. And our apartment. What if I start forgetting him out here?'

As the thought occurred to me, I felt the all too familiar chill run through my body, causing my hands to tremble.

Breath Sophie, just breath.

'You won't. Your parents wouldn't let you and neither will I. I'll be out there as soon as I can, ok? Just hang on in there until then. Keep busy and keep your mind occupied.'

'Yes, Doctor Miller, or should I call you Obi-Wan Kenobi?' I heard Kaitlyn stifle a laugh and thankfully she let the topic drop.

We continued chatting until I got to town and Kaitlyn promised to call me tomorrow.

She had a crazy day of photo shoots, which included high maintenance models, who often drew shoots out longer than they needed to be.

Kaitlyn was an up and coming photographer for Cosmopolitan magazine and although she loved what she did, it was sometimes far more stressful than necessary.

I knew she would have loved taking pictures out here, this was way more up her street, but Cosmo paid the bills, as she always said.

'Excuse me, one of your boats appears to be sinking.'

My brother whipped around, face turning as white as a ghost and I burst out laughing.

I just couldn't help myself. As kids we'd constantly pranked one another, always trying to outdo the last.

'Little sis,' he grinned.

Thankfully, he was too happy to see me to be pissed, and gathered me up in a great big hug, spinning me around the office.

'Welcome home,' he said, placing me safely back on the ground.

'Thanks, it's good to be home. How are things? How's Sarah feeling? I cannot believe you're going to be a dad! I'm going to be an aunt!' I squealed with excitement.

'Ok, calm down before you scare the customers. Come on back and I'll put a pot of coffee on.'

'So, how are you, really?' Paul asked once we were seated in his office.

It was a room that held so many of my childhood memories. I'd always been the one here with dad, saying I would take over one day.

It's funny how life has other plans for us.

'I'm ok. There are good days and bad days, you know,' I replied honestly.

Only, he didn't know.

This was always the hardest part, talking to people who couldn't possibly relate to what you'd been through.

'For what it's worth, I think you've done the right thing, moving home. New York is no place to heal, but out here, this is God's land, He heals all wounds.' My brother squeezed my hand and I smiled.

It was something our dad had said for as long as I could remember, and I don't think I ever really understood it until now.

I'd been having a hard time with my beliefs these past two years.

Our parents had raised us as good Christian children, attending church every Sunday, saying our prayers before bed, and I'd never once questioned my faith, until that fateful day.

Deep down I didn't exactly blame God for Luke's death, but I think I blamed him for not giving me more time with him.

He took him too soon and I had resented Him for it for a long time, but somehow, being home, I felt closer to Him again and I hoped he could forgive my unjust blame.

Paul and I spent the next hour catching up. Reminiscing about when we were kids, sneaking onto the boats with our friends at the weekend and spending endless summers on the water.

We had no idea back then how easy we had it. How simple life was.

Which is exactly how a childhood should be; simple, carefree.

'Tell Sarah I send my love and I'll see her soon. And give my niece or nephew a cuddle from me,' I instructed as we hugged, saying our goodbyes.

I took a slow walk back to the car, taking in the waterfront, watching the fisherman sitting along the pier, laughing together and sharing stories, I imagined, about their youth and the good old days.

Children excitedly carried their fishing nets and buckets, while their parents trailed behind.

All of this was exactly why Luke and I had wanted to raise a family here, instead of New York. We wanted our kids having the same childhood we'd experienced growing up.

Not that New York wasn't a great place to raise children, it just wasn't what we wanted for ours.

We were both from small towns and had both been fortunate enough to have happy childhoods, so naturally, we wanted exactly that for our children.

I didn't want to dwell on this thought for too long, so picking up the pace back, I headed back to my car and drove the short distance to my parents' house.

Things never stood still for long in the Preston household – something I was determined to change.

The following morning my dad was driving me out to the Danvers sanctuary (well, I was driving, dad was directing).

He wanted to introduce me to everyone himself and said

he knew a slightly shorter route, making the drive out there just under an hour.

It was a good drive and great to have a little time alone with my dad. I wanted to know how he was really feeling.

'Mostly just tired. I guess the old ticker isn't what it used to be 'eh kiddo,' Dad smiled, but I sensed his underlying apprehension.

'You're going to be just fine, Dad,' I reached over to squeeze his hand.

'Oh, I know honey,' he squeezed back.

'Then what is it? I know something's bothering you.'

'It's called being a parent,' he chuckled. 'I pray that one day you'll know what it feels like, although it can be exhausting and scary and worrying, but being a parent is one of life's greatest gifts and you will make such a wonderful mother someday. But as a parent, no matter how old your children get, even when they have lives of their own, you always worry about them.'

'You're worried about Paul,' I guessed.

'Not just Paul,' I could feel my dad eyeing me knowingly.

'Dad, I'm f-'

'Sophie, I'm your dad and dads know when their little girls aren't ok. You've done a great job holding it together for everyone, but you've been holding on so tightly I'm afraid you haven't been able to let go or move on. It was a terrible thing that happened, and Lord knows we all miss Luke, but honey, at some point you have to try move forward, stop holding onto the past. No one would think any less of you.'

I didn't know what to say, or if I could even find my voice to say anything.

I hadn't been holding on for everyone else, I had been holding on for me, because Luke was my everything and letting go feels like letting go of all our memories, our life together, his memory, and that just didn't seem right.

He deserves more than that, better than that. His memory deserves to live on forever and if I wasn't the one to do it, then who?

'Just think about it. I know it's difficult and no one is saying you need to forget Luke,' my dad continued, as if reading my thoughts. 'He was the love of your life, he'll always be a part of you, but he wouldn't want you living half a life and you know I'm right. If he were here, he would be telling you the same thing, to go and live your life, to travel, to write again, find love or at the very least go on a date.'

I choked out a laugh, I could hear Luke saying exactly that.

'I'm not saying any of this to upset you, honey, I hope you know that. I'm only telling you because I love you. We all love you so much, as did Luke, and we all want what's best for you,' my dad added.

'I know, thanks, Dad.'

I could feel my eyes welling up and I really wanted to change the subject before I was a weeping puddle on the floor of the car.

Thankfully we weren't far from the sanctuary and dad had to switch back to being my own personal navigation system.

It wasn't long before we reached the entrance, where I turned onto a long winding road, lined on each side with grand old oak trees, forming sweeping arches over the road, made even more dramatic by the wispy Spanish moss hanging delicately from their branches.

When we pulled up to the farmhouse, the first thing I noticed was the beautiful garden in front of the house, surrounded by a low white picket fence, with a cobblestone walkway down the middle, leading toward the house.

Even if my dad hadn't mentioned that Mom had helped Rosie with the garden, I would have known my mom's handiwork anywhere.

The house itself was beautiful, with a porch wrapping all around the lower level and the top floor having its own balcony along the entire front section.

The shutters were painted grey, which contrasted perfectly against the pale yellow of the rest of the house. It was exactly the right backdrop to the colourful garden out front.

'George, you made it,' someone suddenly exited the front door – Rosie, I assumed. 'This must be the lovely Sophie. We've heard so much about you,' I was embraced in a typical mom hug before I could even consider objecting.

'Oh, hi,' was all I could splutter.

I'd clearly lived in New York too long – forgetting how welcoming and friendly people were in the country.

'Soph, this is Rosie. Rosie, this is my baby girl, Sophie,' Dad beamed proudly, and I couldn't help but grin.

'It's so nice to meet you, my dad has told me all about

the sanctuary. It's a wonderful thing you do here.'

I meant every word. I'd always loved animals, so the fact that I would be helping at a place like this, had me feeling excited about something for the first time in a long time.

'Well, we're just happy your old man is ok and we're even happier for the extra pair of hands. We can use all the help we can get these days. Come on, I'll give you the grand tour,' Rosie looped her arm through mine as though we'd known each other our whole lives, putting me instantly at ease.

Before we could get too far we heard yelling and a second later, just as we were about to round the big red barn that sat off to the side of the main house, a blur of black and long legs went flying passed us.

'Get back here, Beast!' Someone shouted, before appearing.

Ok, so I might be a hot mess; completely emotionally and physically unavailable, still grieving the loss of her husband (even though it had been two years), but I wasn't blind and I could still appreciate God's artwork, even if that was all it was, simply appreciating a fine piece of artwork from a distance, with no emotion or risk of getting pulled in.

Case in point; the extremely handsome, very rugged, tall, shoulders for miles, man standing before us, puffing.

Rosie chuckled, 'Stop calling him that,' she scolded.

'That's exactly what he is. He's a beast who cannot, and will not, be tamed,' the gorgeous man replied.

This I could relate to. Luke often referred to me as his

wild palomino (mainly due to my hair colour), but that wasn't the only reason.

I used to be so adventurous, game for anything, the first one to suggest sky diving or rock climbing, and I was never one for conformity, a free spirit and all that hippie, tree hugging stuff. But lately I had become the one thing I never thought possible – subdued, tame. A shadow of my old self.

'Sophie, this is my son, Caleb. Caleb, this is George's daughter, Sophie,' Rosie introduced us.

'It's nice to meet you,' I offered a polite smile.

'Ah, so this is the prodigal daughter,' Caleb laughed, a deep, hearty laugh that made me smile a little wider. 'Your dad doesn't stop talking about you. It's always "Sophie this" and "Sophie that" and "you should read her novels." I'm afraid I haven't, by the way, not much of a crime thriller type. Come to think of it, I'm not much of a reader of any kind.' Caleb shrugged, nonchalant.

I was too ashamed to admit I hadn't written anything these past two years, so I changed the subject.

'What's his deal?' I asked Caleb, nodding in the direction of the horse, that was no longer in site.

'Oh, he's just a stubborn young stallion. He's our most recent rescue and well, he's still a little skittish around people, I guess.' Caleb wiped sweat from his brow, looking tired.

'Sophie, perhaps you could help Caleb bring him in, I just need to run over a few things with your dad,' Rosie suggested.

'Sure, if that's ok?' I asked Caleb, not wanting to get in

the way.

'Absolutely. Can you ride? We're best taking the other horses out after him, it'll take too long to find him on foot.'

It had been a while, but I was sure I could remember the basics, so I nodded.

Turns out, the saying 'just like riding a bike' could also be said for riding a horse, much to my relief! As soon as I was in the saddle, it all came flooding back and it felt incredible.

As my confidence grew, so did our speed. The world flew by in a blur while the wind caressed my face and sent my hair whipping wildly behind me.

'Whoa, slow down there, missy,' Caleb called, racing alongside us.

I gently pulled on the reins and the beautiful chestnut horse Caleb had paired me with slowed down.

'I'm sorry. I haven't ridden in ages and that was just-' I couldn't find the right word.

'Exhilarating,' Caleb suggested with a lazy lopsided grin.

'Yes, exactly. Exhilarating,' I breathed.

I felt free and wild, just like the stallion. The stallion that suddenly appeared in my peripheral vision.

'There he is,' I whispered to Caleb.

'Well spotted,' Caleb complimented.

Slowing our horses, we came to a gradual stop.

'What do we do?' I asked as we dismounted and tied our horses' rains to a nearby tree.

We seemed to be in a sort of clearing, surrounded by trees, except for an almost perfect circle where the tall grass swayed gently in the breeze, along with the array of wildflowers.

It was beautiful.

'We wait, and hope he comes to us. Get down low and move towards him, slowly. Stay close in case he spooks,' Caleb instructed in a low voice.

Kneeling down, we simply watched him for a minute.

He'd already picked up our scent and huffed unhappily at being found, but he didn't move, standing his ground. I already liked him.

We crept towards him, slowly, inch by inch. It felt like it had taken us forever just to make it halfway, when our horses whinnying caught our attention.

'Damn, something must have spooked them. It'll send Beast running again if they don't stop soon,' Caleb whispered.

'I'm ok here. Why don't you go see to them and I'll keep going,' I told Caleb almost absentmindedly, too focused on the young stallion.

'Are you sure? I don't want to have to tell my mom I let you get trampled on your first day,' Caleb joked, but I could sense genuine concern. It was sweet, but unnecessary.

'I'll be fine, honestly.'

After a moment's hesitation, Caleb looked at Beast as if to say, 'don't even think about it', before heading back in the direction we'd just come from, still bent down, going as slow as he could.

I continued towards the beautiful stallion, who's ears were pricked and was still huffing unhappily, but he still made no move to run.

I wasn't that far from him now and I started whispering reassuringly, trying not to spook him.

'It's ok boy, I'm not going to hurt you. Come on now, just a little closer, you can do it.'

Another few minutes and I was within arm's reach.

As I'd gotten closer, the stallion had stilled, keeping his eyes on me, but so far it didn't seem like he was going to bolt again.

Then again, what did I know. Still, I kept his gaze and continued hedging closer.

As slowly as I possibly could, I plucked a handful of grass and reached it out towards him. So slowly it barely looked like I was moving at all, but he picked up on every movement.

'That's a good boy, you can do it. Come on now, it's ok,' I soothed.

I had no idea what I was doing, or if I was going to make things better or worse, I was simply running on instinct and hoping for the best.

To my complete and utter shock and amazement, he actually took it. He took the grass from my hand, ate it, and then continued munching the grass around me as if I wasn't even there.

I sat there, frozen, for what felt like the longest time, too scared to move for fear of scaring him off, but equally, simply taking in this moment.

Feeling a connection to this incredible creature.

Eventually, when my legs started to go numb and I needed to move, I slowly straightened, once again just inching up as slowly as possible, but this time, the stallion seemed happy enough with my presence and only briefly flinched at my initial movement and then, as if sensing there was no danger, continued to enjoy the grass and wild flowers.

Was I pushing my luck, trying to get the reins Caleb had left behind around the young stallion's neck? Of course I was, but I'd gotten this far.

So, taking a long slow deep breath in and let it out even more slowly, I took a tiny step towards him.

He looked up and our eyes locked.

I'd always loved horses, especially their eyes. They were such gentle creatures and I'd always felt as though you could see the depths of their souls when you looked in their eyes.

This was no different. It was as though I could see the hurt and pain that he'd endured, but also the hope and trust that lay beneath, wanting to surface, but not knowing if he could trust me enough to let them bubble up.

I offered my hand as a sort of sign, to tell him he could trust me, as the most incredible thing happened. He walked up to me, nuzzled my hand and let me place the reins around his long elegant neck.

I couldn't find any words, so I simply stroked his neck before he continued grazing.

'Ladies and gentlemen, we have ourselves a horse whisperer,' Caleb announced when we arrived back at the barn.

After I'd managed to get the reins on Beast (I really

didn't like that name), he had started to pull back and whinny when Caleb had approached.

Apparently, he was only happy to let me close, so we'd taken a slow walk back to the barn, while Caleb trotted ahead of us.

I hadn't minded, I enjoyed my time with the stallion. I felt like it bonded us further.

'What happened?' Rosie looked up in surprise.

'He let Sophie close enough to, not only touch him, but get the reins on him. Something none of us have been able to do, by the way,' Caleb added for my benefit.

'Perhaps he just prefers women?' I suggested modestly.

It could be the case, especially if he was ill treated by a man.

'Then why couldn't my mom get near him either?' Caleb asked, raising an eyebrow.

Ok, he had me there.

'That's my girl. I knew you'd be the perfect fit here,' my dad said and as much as I appreciated their praise, I wanted the spotlight off me.

'Dad, shouldn't we be getting you home, it's getting late, and you need to rest.'

'That's right George, you need to listen to your daughter,' Rosie scolded playfully.

'Oh, don't you start too! But yes, I suppose we should be getting home. Your mother will be wondering what's happened to us,' Dad chuckled, knowing full well that Mom wouldn't expect us back anytime soon.

'I'll be back first thing tomorrow morning,' I promised Rosie and Caleb.

'About that, your dad and I were talking, and there's no obligation, of course, but we have a small cottage on the property that you are more than welcome to use, so that you don't have to keep driving back and forth every day. You could stay a few nights, or full time, or split your time between the sanctuary and your parents, it's entirely up to you. Sleep on it and you can let me know anytime what you decide,' Rosie smiled, and it touched her warm blue eyes.

'That's very kind of you, thank you. I'll chat to Mom and Dad tonight and let you know soon.'

We said our goodbyes shortly after and made our way home.

'You should consider Rosie's offer honey,' Mom said during dinner. 'It makes sense for you to stay with them while you're working on the farm, your dad occasionally stayed the night, if he ended up working late.'

'I appreciate their offer, but the whole point of me moving home was to be here for you and Dad. To help out around here too.'

'You already are. The sanctuary has become a huge part of our lives, and knowing you'll be taking over my responsibilities on the farm is a huge relief for both of us,' Dad reassured me, but I needed time to think it over.

'Let's just see how it goes for a while. I mean, what if I can't do it or don't enjoy working there?'

No one seemed to have considered either of these possibilities.

'After seeing you today, I doubt either of those will be

the case. You should have seen her Jane, she was practically glowing when they got back with the young stallion.'

My parents were looking at me like I was a science experiment.

'Ok guys, you're creeping me out, stop looking at me like that,' I got up, clearing the table.

Granted, everything about today had felt amazing, but that didn't mean I'd enjoy every other day, or that I'd manage it. Today could have been a total fluke, or the Danvers' might decide I wasn't the right fit.

Still, when I remembered how wonderful it had felt being on horseback again, and being with Beast, I couldn't help but smile while washing the dishes.

After saying goodnight to my parents, I took my cup of camomile tea upstairs where I gave Kaitlyn a quick call, before sitting in my deck chair, sipping my tea, watching the world go by. At snails' pace.

I forgot how slow time moved out here. It was the opposite of New York in every way, but I was starting to get the distinct feeling that this was exactly what I needed.

Chapter 3

'Good morning, horse whisperer.' I was greeted by a man who I guessed to be in his sixties.

Should I know who he was? I wondered, as I made my way over to the main house, trying not to yawn.

Just before I got out of my car, I noticed the clock on the dashboard blinking seven am.

Ugh! I was barely awake and suddenly the idea of staying here on the farm seemed far more appealing than commuting every day at this ungodly hour.

'Good morning….' I trailed off, not knowing who he was.

'Where are my manners, I'm Sam Danvers. I hear you met my wife and son yesterday. I also hear you made quite the impression with Beast,' Sam offered me his hand.

'Mr Danvers, hi, it's nice to meet you,' I took his large warm, calloused hand and firmly squeezed – my dad always said you could tell a lot about a person from their handshake.

Mr Danvers had been out of town yesterday with their eldest son, so I probably should have realised who he was, knowing he'd be back today.

I blamed it on the early hour and my fuzzy, half asleep brain.

'Please, call me Sam. Mr Danvers makes me feel so old,' he chuckled. 'Come on in Sophie, Rosie's just put a fresh pot of coffee on,' Sam ushered me along before I could object.

Although I'm not sure I would have, the allure of fresh coffee was far too tempting.

'Sophie, good morning, would you like a cup of coffee?' Rosie greeted me cheerily.

They were morning people. I groaned internally.

'That would be great, thank you,' I replied, stifling a yawn.

'There she is. Back for more huh?' A far too cheery Caleb greeted me as he walked into the kitchen.

He already had beads of sweat forming on his forehead, clearly hard at work already.

'I'd love to see what else Sophie can do with Beast,' Caleb said to his dad, while helping himself to a cup of coffee.

'About that, since you managed to wrangle him yesterday, you get to give him an official name. If you'd like?' Sam asked eagerly.

I could only assume he wasn't fond of the current name either.

'Really? I'd love to. I might need some time to come up with something, but I'd love to see him again?' I asked hesitantly.

'Ok, but you two be careful. Caleb, you keep a close watch,' Sam instructed.

'Yes, sir,' Caleb replied to his dad, before turning to me, 'Why don't you head on out to the barn, Beast is in the far left stable. Just don't go in yet, I need to grab a few things first, then I'll be right out.'

'Ok.' I took my last sip of coffee, feeling like a kid on Christmas morning, only this time it wasn't a toy pony, it was the real thing.

'Thank you for the coffee, Rosie.' I placed my cup in the sink, eager to see Beast again.

'I'll come by to check on you later, but you be careful. Beast sure does have a wild streak in him,' Sam warned gently.

'Thanks, Sam, I will,' I replied as I rushed out the front door.

I half ran to the barn, heading straight to the far end, just as Caleb had instructed and sure enough, there he was, just as beautiful as I remembered.

His sleek black coat shimmering in the early morning light that streamed into the barn.

I wasn't sure if it was simply that he sensed movement, or if he sensed me (I liked to think it was the latter), but he started huffing and stomping his hoof against the floor, as though he was itching to be let out.

Soon boy, I thought as I approached, slowly, cautiously.

As I got closer, he calmed down somewhat, just as he had yesterday in the meadow. Perhaps he did remember me after all.

I was once again within arm's reach and I slowly reached out.

'Good morning boy, did you miss me?' I whispered gently and reassuringly to him.

My hand was mere inches from his nose, when suddenly I was being yanked backwards, almost sending me flailing to the floor.

But strong hands gripped my arms to stop me from falling.

'Are you insane? You don't just come waltzing in here unaccompanied, petting the wild stallion like he's your pet Labrador,' a deep voice rumbled from behind me and I squirmed out of his iron grip to spin around and face him, noting Beast's unhappy sounds in the background.

This must be the other brother, I thought, facing him, trying to get my bearings, while feeling incredibly off centre by his brooding presence and stormy ice blue eyes – Grayson Danvers.

As much as I hated to admit it, he was even more ruggedly handsome than his younger brother. They had the same warm chestnut brown hair and piercing blue eyes, yet this brothers' eyes were tainted with something familiar that I couldn't quite put my finger on.

Their builds were much the same; tall and lean, broad shoulders, narrowing down at the waist, except Grayson seemed more solid, stronger somehow.

His muscular arms and death grip were a clear sign of years working the farm, as were the way his jeans hugged his hips.

That didn't give him any right to man-handle me, however.

'I wasn't about to "pet" him, I was being careful and for your information, I was the one who brought him back after he bolted yesterday,' I finally responded indignantly.

'So, what? You think that makes you some kind of expert? You're a New Yorker, but please enlighten me about your extensive experience with horses?' He folded his arms over his chest, distracting me momentarily as the muscles on his long arms bulge.

'I never said I was an expert, I simply-'

'Gray, there you are, I've been looking for you everywhere man,' Caleb's timing was impeccable. 'I see you've met Sophie. Whoa what's up your as-, I mean, butt, this morning?' Caleb was also clearly intuitive when it came to his brother.

'Nothing. You better keep a leash on this one before she loses a finger.'

And with that the whirlwind that was Grayson Danvers turned around and left as quickly as he had arrived.

'Charming,' I muttered irritably.

'Oh, just ignore Grayson, the rest of us do. Now, are you ready to get started?' Caleb's infectious enthusiasm was hard not to latch onto.

Pushing thoughts of Grayson out of my mind, I turned my attention back to the task at hand.

What was the task at hand exactly? I suddenly wondered.

And then wished I hadn't.

'You want me to go in there with him? While he's all,' I motioned my hands around in wild circles, implying Beast was all kinds of crazy this morning, bucking and kicking and neighing angrily.

'Yeah. I saw what you did yesterday. You connected with him, he'll react differently to you, better. I think you calm him down,' Caleb explained.

'You think? You want me to go in there on a hunch?'

'I'm not usually wrong about my hunches if it helps?' Caleb winked.

Ok, so suddenly that infections enthusiasm was far less appealing.

Come on Sophie, you can do this, I tried to convince myself. Taking a deep breath in and thinking I had officially lost my mind, I stepped into the paddock.

When Beast didn't appear to be stopping any time soon, I froze, feeling afraid for the first time in a long time.

It was strange to feel anything after being numb for the longest time.

Apparently, I wasn't good at hiding what I was feeling.

'Relax, he'll sense it if you're afraid,' Caleb whispered from the other side of the paddock.

Ok, breath. He didn't hurt you yesterday, he won't hurt you today, I reminded myself.

After a few more steadying breaths I took a step forward, towards Beast, and then another and another.

He began calming down, so I continued the slow steady pace towards him.

I could hear voices behind me, but I didn't take my eyes off Beast for a second. He watched me intently in return, as I approached, but didn't appear to be getting ready to trample me, I thought with a sigh of relief.

'That's a good boy. I've got something for you,' I knelt down, just like I had yesterday in the meadow and opened my hand, letting the scent of the apple Caleb had given me, just before I'd entered the paddock, drift towards him.

I watched in fascination as his nostrils flared, huffing

once again, and I guessed he wanted it, but didn't want to come and get it.

That's ok, I could wait. And I did.

I waited as the seconds ticked by, wanting desperately to prove that he could trust people again.

My patience paid off when Beast started hedging gradually closer to me and finally, as if the temptation was too much for him, he closed the small gap between us and took the apple right out of my hand.

I wanted to, quite literally, jump for joy. I could have done a happy dance right there and then in the paddock, but I stayed as still as possible.

Once he finished the apple, he sniffed my shoulder, almost nuzzling my neck, looking for more deliciously sweet treats. Damn! I didn't have any more but made a mental note to stock up on apples and carrots.

Feeling braver than perhaps I ought to, I started to straighten up and just like yesterday he let me stroke his long neck briefly, before trotting off.

Watching him walk off for a brief moment, enjoying my success, I slowly turned around to beam at Caleb, just as movement near the barn caught my eye and I could have sworn I saw the back of Grayson, briefly, before he disappeared into the barn.

Had he been watching? I hoped not. I didn't need any more run ins with him while I was here.

The rest of the week went by in much the same way. Working with Beast – I had yet to think of a name for him.

Shadowing Caleb or Sam (successfully avoiding

Grayson, who was apparently away on business shortly after our first run in) and pretty much learning my way around the farm.

It was exhausting work! I had a whole new appreciation for anyone who worked a farm or ranch job. Scrap that, for anyone who did any form of manual labour for more than a few hours a day was a hero in my book.

As it turned out, I got weekends off from the sanctuary, which didn't seem fair, given that the work didn't stop, but I was grateful for the time off, wanting to make sure my parents were doing ok.

I felt like I'd hardly seen them this week, given that my days consisted of an early start, working on the farm, then practically face planting my bed almost as soon as I walked through the door each night.

For the first time in a long time, I actually felt like a city girl – something Caleb liked to tease me about, although I couldn't help feeling as though he was flirting. Just a little.

Having the weekends off also meant seeing Paul and Sarah for more than five minutes at a time.

'How are you feeling?' I asked my sister-in-law, noticing how she glowed.

I couldn't be happier for them both, they were going to make wonderful parents and I was going to make an even better aunt, naturally.

We sat in their garden, overlooking the water, while Paul and Dad grilled some steaks. Sarah, mom and I sipped our sweet teas while soaking up the sun.

'Better than I expected I would. I had a terrible bout of

morning sickness at the beginning, but I've been ok since then,' Sarah replied. 'Anyway, I'd much rather hear about your encounter with the illustrious Grayson Danvers,' Sarah asked excitedly.

It also turned out that our families are closer than I initially realised.

Not only were Caleb and Grayson good friends with Paul, but our parents were in near constant contact, so I could only assume news had travelled down the line to Sarah, about my run in with Grayson.

Sarah waited patiently for the juicy story. Sorry to disappoint you Sarah, I thought dryly.

'There isn't much to tell really, I got close to one of the newest members of the sanctuary, a young stallion, and Grayson pulled me back – almost knocking me to the ground, I might add, like a complete neanderthal. Even though I was perfectly fine. Beast would never hurt me.' I shuffled in my seat, annoyed at the sheer memory of Mr Moody Pants.

'Oh, how romantic! Trying to protect you,' Sarah was a goner, stars in her eyes and everything. 'He's a very eligible bachelor, you know. So is Caleb,' she added with a mischievous glint in her eyes.

'If you say so, he seemed more like the Grinch to me. What is his deal anyway?'

'Grayson?' She asked, I nodded.

'He just likes to keep to himself, isn't that right Sarah?' My mom interjected.

Sarah had been part of the family long enough to receive the 'mom look'. That look your mom gives you when she doesn't approve of something.

The look she was giving Sarah right now, which didn't surprise me. Mom didn't like gossip.

I'd have to get the scoop from Sarah later. Then again, did I really care?

Nope. Grayson Danvers was not my problem.

Just then, the boys announced the steaks were ready. My stomach rumbled in response.

It was a perfect day.

Lazy Sunday's in Beaufort were one of life's pleasures that everyone should get to experience at least once in their lives.

After having breakfast on the porch, I decided to take the ferry to the Shackleford Banks – one of my favourite places to visit as a child.

I loved watching the wild horses grazing, while building sandcastles on the shore, only for my brother to jump on them.

So, armed with my camera, I headed out.

It was only a short ferry trip, but I always loved being on the water.

Feeling the sun on my skin and the wind in my hair, and it had been forever since I'd felt the gentle crunch of sand beneath my bare feet.

I walked along the beach for the longest time, dipping my toes in and out of the cool water, stopping to take pictures of couples walking along the shore, kids playing in the sand, the wild horses grazing the long grass in the distance.

A day at the beach truly was good for the soul, I thought, sitting back in the sand.

I wished so much that Luke could be here. He would have loved a day like today.

I imagined us walking along the beach, hand in hand, splashing each other, and I could almost hear his laughter.

He would have taken me for lunch, knowing how much I love the seafood here, before having sundowners on the beach.

Despite the heat, I shivered, and suddenly didn't feel much like sitting on the beach alone anymore.

Getting up, dusting myself off, I strolled along the shore, in the direction of the ferry.

On the walk back, I stopped to snap a few more shots, mainly of the wild horses – even though I'd already taken more than enough.

I always ended up with far too many photos of the wild horses and today was no different.

Zooming in on them made me think about Beast, and I hoped he was doing ok without me.

He still didn't trust anyone else to get close enough to take him out.

Perhaps I should go over and check on him, I thought briefly, but before I could make my mind up, my camera landed on a familiar figure and I zoomed in a little further.

Caleb? I thought, squinting into the distance. It certainly looked like him.

'Caleb? What are you doing out here?' I called out with a smile, when I'd closed the distance between us.

'Sophie, hi,' he said a little too brightly. 'I volunteer out here. We come out and check on the wild horses from time to time.'

'I'm impressed,' I told him honestly. 'Working at the sanctuary and volunteering here too, that can't leave you much time for your own life?'

'I get by,' he smiled.

Caleb had such an easy way about him. Nothing was too much trouble.

'I was actually just finishing up here. Would you like to grab lunch?'

'Oh, um, I was just about to head home,' I replied hesitantly, caught off guard.

'Come on, I know a great beach bar. They serve the best fish tacos you'll ever eat.'

My stomach grumbled and my mouth watered at the thought of seafood.

'Is it ok for us to, um…' I didn't know how to put it, but in typical Caleb fashion, he just laughed.

'We're two co-workers grabbing a bite to eat, relax, Sophie. Come on.'

I laughed at myself for thinking it might be a date – something I was nowhere near ready for – and followed Caleb.

'Ok, you were right, they were amazing!' I sat back in my chair, so full I wasn't sure I could walk back to the ferry. Come to think of it, I might sink the ferry.

'I love this place. I'd actually love to have my own beach bar one day,' Caleb sighed happily.

'Really? I assumed you and Grayson would take over the

sanctuary?' I took a long sip of my drink, enjoying the cool liquid.

'I love the sanctuary and I adore the animals, of course, but it was never really my dream, it was more my dad's and Grayson's. I'm not sure I could leave though, they need all the help they can get.'

'That's very noble of you Caleb, but you also need to be true to you, and follow your own dreams.'

'What about you? Are you missing New York yet?' I didn't miss the change in subject, but I let it go, for now.

'Honestly, not as much as I thought.' It was true, I suddenly realised.

Of course I missed it, and I missed Kaitlyn terribly, but I felt more settled here somehow. Like I was where I should be, where I belonged.

'I'd hate living in a big city, or any city for that matter. Give me peace and quiet over traffic and smog any day,' Caleb wrinkled his nose in disgust.

I laughed at his description, which wasn't far off, but there was also so much more to big cities.

We spent the rest of the afternoon sharing stories about where we'd travelled and childhood memories. All light-hearted conversation and it felt really good.

I was amazed at how easy it was to laugh at the silly stories Caleb told, and become animated when I told Caleb what New Year's Eve was like in New York.

It felt good to simply be here, in this moment, enjoying good food and good company.

Of course, I did things just like this with Kaitlyn and our other friends, but this was different somehow.

Whether it was the change in scenery, or the fact that Caleb was like a blank canvas – not knowing anything about me, or my past, I wasn't sure, but I was enjoying the easy-going feel and free flowing conversation.

But all good things come to an end, and as the sun started to sink closer to the horizon, we decided it was time to go.

Reluctantly getting up, we walked back to where the ferry would pick us up, chatting all the while.

'Thank you for today, it was exactly what I needed,' I told Caleb meaningfully when we were back in Beaufort.

'Maybe we could do it again some time?' He asked hesitantly.

At the risk of making myself look like an idiot twice in one day, jumping to conclusions, I smiled and said, 'Sure,' hoping that he wasn't asking me out on a date this time.

'Great,' Caleb beamed, before adding, 'I'll check on Beast when I get back to the farm and text you.'

He'd agreed to check in, to save me the trip.

'See you in the morning,' Caleb smiled his easy-going grin and walked off to his car, leaving me wondering what I had gotten myself into.

Chapter 4

The following day on the farm was tough.

It must have been well over ninety degrees, and after spending the day on the beach yesterday, probably not drinking as much water as I should have, I felt a little dehydrated.

Not wanting Sam to think I couldn't cut it, I downed what was left of my water and carried on hammering the fence into the ground.

After spending a few hours with Beast that morning, I had offered to help Sam with the new fence for the sanctuary.

Rosie had received a call about a number of farm animals in desperate need of rehoming, after the farm owners had to sell, and the new owners had no interest in the animals.

So, it was full steam ahead. We needed to get the fence done fast.

Caleb and Grayson had driven out to the farm to assess things and were due back shortly, with hopes of collecting the animals tomorrow.

Sam and I worked well together, which made the job a lot easier and a lot quicker too, with only a few more posts to go.

Good thing too because the world was starting to turn on its axis.

'Sophie, are you ok?' Sam called out. Clearly nothing escaped him.

'I'm fine, but I think I'll go grab some more water, would you like anything?' I asked, wiping the back of my hand across my damp forehead.

'If you could top mine up too, that'd be great,' Sam tossed me his water bottle and I made my way to the main house, noting Grayson's truck was parked next to my car. They must be back already.

I knocked, even though Rosie kept telling me it wasn't necessary, and after a few moments when no one answered, I opened the door.

'Rosie?' I called out, but nothing.

I had to steady myself on the doorframe for a moment. I really had turned soft, Caleb was right, I was a city girl if I couldn't handle manual labour in the North Carolina heat.

Ok, no waiting around this time, I thought, walking into the kitchen and going straight to the tap, gulping water down as fast as I could.

'We have glasses you know,' an all too familiar voice rumbled behind me and I straightened up, slowly this time, to stop the world from spinning.

'Do you always creep up on people?' I asked, not wanting to do this again, not now.

Instead of looking at him, I began filling our water bottles. I didn't want to leave Sam out there for long.

'Look, I wanted to apologise. I know we got off on the

wrong foot before and I'm sorry.' His voice sounded sincere, but I wasn't buying it.

This time I turned to face him.

The look in his eyes was genuine, but I narrowed my eyes speculatively.

'You've been great with Beast and I should have realised that. I overreacted,' Grayson continued when I didn't say anything.

'Thank you,' I didn't know what else to say and I really needed to sit down, I was starting to see two of him, which may not have been such a bad thing, he was extremely good looking after all.

Get a grip, Sophie, I warned myself, feeling lightheaded. Instinctively touching mine and Luke's wedding rings, under my shirt, I tried to steady myself on the side of the sink.

'Hey, are you ok? You don't look so good,' Grayson's voice sounded so far away, and I knew what was coming. 'Sophie,' I thought I heard him yell before the world went black and I waited for the thud that would inevitably follow as I hit the floor.

A thud that never came.

Or perhaps I passed out before I hit the floor. Either way, I would feel that later.

'Sophie, it's ok, you're going to be ok,' a gentle voice assured me.

I wasn't sure why the voice was so tainted with concern. I knew I was fine.

I was more than fine, I was being held by strong arms.

My head resting against a warm, solid shoulder.

I was perfectly happy here, content even, there was no need for concern, I wanted to say, but couldn't find my voice. How odd.

And then it started to come back to me; the kitchen, Grayson, watching the floor getting closer and then....

It should have hurt. I should have felt pain shooting through me as I hit the floor, but arms had embraced me instead, and hadn't let me go. The same arms that were still wrapped around me now.

I tried to open my eyes and focus, blinking rapidly, until I saw his face above mine. Felt his warm breath wash over my face.

'Welcome back,' he eventually breathed as though he had been holding his breath all this time.

'Sophie, thank goodness, are you ok?' I heard Rosie's voice, but I couldn't see her.

Grayson's face and broad shoulders took up my whole world.

I struggled to move, needing some space, but he seemed reluctant to let go. A small crease developing between his brows.

'Let her up, Grayson, before you smother the poor girl,' I heard Rosie instruct.

Thankfully he listened to his mother.

'I'm so sorry, I came in to get Sam and I more water and I just...' I trailed off, embarrassed by what had happened.

'Fainted,' Grayson finished.

'I guess I did. It's my own fault, I was at the beach yesterday and clearly didn't drink enough water, and it's been so hot today. I need to get back to Sam, we need to finish the fence,' I started to get up, but Grayson's arms shot out before I could get too far, steadying me.

'Don't worry about Sam, Caleb's out there helping him. You just rest a minute,' Rosie placed a wet towel over my forehead. 'You're staying here tonight and I'm not taking no for an answer. I'm not letting you behind the wheel in your state,' Rosie stated.

In my state? I'd only fainted.

'Thank you, Rosie, I really do appreciate that, but I don't have a change of clothes or even a toothbrush,' I protested.

'Don't you worry about any of that, we always keep spares in case we have visitors. I'll wash and tumble dry your clothes, so they'll be ready for you tomorrow. Grayson will take you out to the cottage, his house is the closest to the cottage, and you can lie down. We'll come and get you for dinner. Until then, you just get some rest and don't worry about a thing.' Rosie's tone was final, and I knew there was no point arguing.

'Would you mind if I called my parents to let them know?' I couldn't remember where I'd left my cell phone.

'Of course, honey, there's a phone in the cottage you can use,' Rosie assured.

With that and the (unnecessary) help of Grayson, we made our way over to the cottage, which wasn't far from the main house.

It was nestled against the edge of the woodland that surrounded the north side of the farm and it was beautiful.

All wooden beams and pastel colours, so light and airy.

The décor was minimalistic, but warm and rustic, giving

the cottage a cosy, homely feel, which struck me as soon as we walked inside. It felt like home.

I put the odd sensation down to my recent fainting spell. I wasn't thinking clearly.

'The fridge is stocked with water and a few soft drinks. You should probably have a Coke to get your sugar levels up, and make sure you drink lots of water,' Grayson instructed.

Yes Mom, I thought, almost laughing out loud at this brooding man, busying himself around the kitchen, treating me like a child.

The living room and kitchen were open plan, separated only by a breakfast counter.

'Thank you,' I replied awkwardly, suddenly uncomfortable being in a more intimate surrounding, alone with him.

'My mom gave me these for you,' he placed a pile of clothes on the love seat nearest the kitchen. 'If you need anything else, just call the house, the number's next to the phone.'

'Grayson,' I called after him as he went to leave, 'Thank you for your apology earlier too,' I walked over to him and extended my hand, 'Hi, I'm Sophie.'

He looked at me with fresh concern, as if I had in fact hit my head earlier. Either that, or I'd grown a third eye.

'Fresh start?' I offered and he smiled.

I think it was the first time I'd actually seen him smile. It lit up his whole face, making his piercing blue eyes shine brighter.

It suited him.

'Hi, Sophie, it's nice to meet you. I'm Grayson,' he took my small hand in his much larger, stronger one and gave it a squeeze.

It felt so strange. I hadn't had any physical contact with another man (besides my dad and brother of course), since Luke.

I had the sudden, irrational feeling that I was cheating on him.

My hand started to tremble, and I felt the same cold sweat start to bead over my skin, my heart rate increased, and I drew in shallow breaths.

'I'm feeling a little lightheaded again, would you excuse me please,' I tried to keep my voice even while I pulled my hand back, needing to be on my own.

I didn't want him, or anyone else for that matter, witnessing me fall apart, looking like a crazy person.

'Would you like me to stay?' He asked, but I was already walking away.

'I'm ok, I'm just going to lie down for a minute,' I called back, heading towards the bedroom, not caring if I'd just destroyed any chance of us starting over.

My pills! I didn't have my pills on me, I suddenly realised, my heart hammering harder in my chest.

I sunk down to the floor, my back pressed against the bedroom door and put my head between my knees, trying to slow my erratic breathing.

I felt like a complete and utter mess!

That's when the tears started and didn't stop until I must have fallen asleep, right there on the bedroom floor.

When I woke, it felt like someone was using a jack hammer in my brain.

I opened my eyes, looking around the room in confusion, taking a moment to remember where I was.

There it was again. Only, it wasn't hammering, I realised. It was knocking.

Standing slowly, steadying myself on the door frame, I made my way to the front door on slightly wobbly legs.

'Rosie, hi,' I breathed a sigh of relief, half expecting to see Grayson or Caleb, before stepping aside for Rosie to come in.

'How are you feeling?' She asked tentatively.

'I'm ok, just a little tired.'

Rosie carried a plate of something that smelled amazing into the kitchen and my stomach let me know it fully agreed, with a soft rumble.

'And hungry,' Rosie placed the plate on the breakfast counter, grabbed a fork from one of the drawers and ordered me to eat while she made us a cup of camomile tea.

She didn't have to ask me twice, I started devouring the pasta dish.

'This is delicious, thank you,' I said between mouthfuls.

'You're very welcome,' she replied, placed the tea down beside me and sipped her own. 'The boys are all asking after you. Sam feels terrible, he thinks he worked you too hard.'

'It's completely my own fault, I feel so embarrassed for making a fuss,' I touched the spot on my chest once again, feeling our wedding rings safely in place.

'No one thinks that, so don't you worry yourself, you

just focus on resting and getting better. Nothing heals quite like the country air.'

I got the distinct feeling we were no longer talking about my little fainting spell earlier and I couldn't help wondering if Rosie knew about Luke.

'It's funny how fast your life can go from a bustling city that never sleeps, to the quiet country life overnight,' I said, reflecting on the polar shift my life had taken in such a short space of time.

'I think we find what we need at just the right time in our lives. I'm glad you found your way to us, Sophie.'

I was touched by her kind words.

'Thank you, Rosie. So am I.'

With the exception of earlier, I could feel glimmers of my old self returning in the short space of time I'd been here.

Whether that was simply because it was such a drastic change from New York, it was keeping my mind off things, or something more, I wasn't sure, but I was going to make the most of it while it lasted because I feared it wouldn't last forever.

'Why don't you get showered and I'll come back in a little while to get your clothes,' Rosie suggested, after I'd finished dinner, feeling full and satisfied, curled up on the couch.

It was so easy talking to Rosie, about anything and nothing in particular. I could see how our families had gotten close.

This time I was the one to pull Rosie in for a tight hug before she left.

'Thank you for everything, it means more to me than you know,' I told her honestly.

'You're welcome Sophie, you come to me if you need anything, you hear?'

'Yes ma'am,' I replied, having picked up the way the boys usually called her that.

I found it so endearing, it was respectful and old school, just how it should be.

Stepping out of the shower I felt like a new person.

Having stood under the warm water until I started to look like a prune, just letting the water wash away the events of today.

After Rosie left, I called my parents to let them know I'd be spending the night.

After being drilled with questions by my mom, who instinctively knew something was wrong, I told her what had happened earlier, reassuring her for the hundredth time I was fine.

Wrapping myself in the soft towel that was clearly made for a giant, I padded into the bedroom to get changed.

The clothes Rosie had lent me were a little big, but I didn't mind, I was just grateful for clean clothes. About to pull the sweater on, I heard a knock at the front door.

'Come on in, Rosie, I'll only be a minute,' I called from the bedroom, quickly scraping my damp hair into a messy bun on top of my head.

'Oh, Caleb!' I said in surprise. 'I thought you were your mom.'

'Well that's a first,' he laughed. 'I volunteered to come

and get your clothes, I wanted to check in and see how you were doing.'

'I'm fine, honestly,' I'd gotten so good at saying that after Luke's funeral that it apparently still came naturally to me to lie about how I really was.

Kaitlyn was one of the only people who ever really knew, and I missed her so much.

I had relied on her far too much these past few years, I knew that, and I needed to learn to stand on my own two feet again, it was just difficult.

Even more so after a day like today.

'I felt terrible when I heard what happened, I should have made sure we had enough water yesterday at the beach. It was so hot out,' Caleb went on.

'It's not your fault. I was trying so hard to make sure we got the fence done in time today, and I guess I hadn't really been keeping hydrated. I guess you're right, I really am just a city girl,' I laughed.

'Trust me, you're not just a city girl, Soph. I'm just glad you're feeling better. I brought some dessert by the way. My mom makes the best banana cream pie around, you have to try a piece.'

I wasn't particularly in the mood for pie, but I found it difficult to turn Caleb down.

He was like an excited puppy waiting for you to play fetch and when you didn't, he would certainly win anyone over with those big puppy dog eyes.

I often forgot that he was a few years older than me, he seemed so young at heart all the time, so carefree.

'I'd love some,' I took the pie, while Caleb got two forks

from the kitchen and we made ourselves comfortable on the couch.

I didn't regret the pie. It really was the best I'd ever had.

If Caleb hadn't been there, I probably would have licked the plate too.

'That was incredible. Your mom sure is a good cook. I need to learn some of her tricks.'

I'd always been an ok cook, but nothing quite like my mom or Rosie.

'How did it go today by the way? Are the animals ok?'

'They are, for now, but we need to get back there tomorrow morning to pick them up, the sooner we get them here the better.'

'Oh no! The enclosure, is it ready?' I asked, panicked, feeling like I had let them down.

'Relax Soph, I helped Dad finish it off when we got back earlier, it's all ready for them,' Caleb replied with an easy smile.

That was a relief.

'I'm really sorry I couldn't finish it and I'm sorry you had to step in,' I said, guilt rising again.

'You can make it up to me, don't worry,' Caleb winked.

He was so full of it, but it did make me think, for a split second (and in another life) how easy it would be to fall for someone like Caleb.

Not that I had any interest, especially after earlier, if that's what can happen, simply from shaking another man's hand, it just proved how far I was from being ready to even consider dating, despite my dad's best efforts.

Still, I was grateful for Caleb's company.

He reminded me so much of Rosie, so easy-going and kind-hearted.

Grayson was more like their dad, quietly thoughtful, occasionally brooding, some might say. Grayson certainly seemed older than his thirty-three years.

Caleb and I stayed there a while longer, talking about the animals that would be arriving tomorrow and about Caleb's work with the wild horses.

It got me thinking about what I could do to help more. There was one thing I was good at, something they didn't seem to have much of out here.

Marketing.

I had enough experience from past novels and book tours. I was well aware of how to drum up interest in something.

A plan started forming in my head and I made a mental note to pack my camera when I got home, to get some shots of the sanctuary.

A short while later, we said our goodnights and I went to bed that night with a lighter heart, feeling grateful to know the Danvers.

Chapter 5

I really needed to stop bed hopping.

Ok, that sounded bad, but going from New York, to my parents' house and now the cottage on the Danvers' farm was throwing me out of whack.

Add that to the fact that I was so not a morning person (it usually took me a few minutes to actually wake up and start functioning like a normal human being), had me looking around in confusion, yet again, wondering where on earth I was, yet again.

When it all came back to me and I rolled out of bed, headed straight for the kitchen and a cup of coffee, I noticed that it was seven o'clock.

At least I hadn't overslept.

After a quick shower and thanks to Rosie, having my own, now clean, clothes to change back into, I made my way over to the main house, not wanting to miss another day and make Rosie and Sam regret taking me on.

'Sophie, what are you doing up so early, you should be resting,' Rosie scolded when I walked into the kitchen.

'I feel a lot better today and I don't want to let anyone down again today. I want to make sure everything's ready for when the animals arrive.'

'Honey, you didn't let anyone down, don't ever think that. But there is something I was hoping you could help me with today. There's a bake sale in town tomorrow and I could really use an extra pair of hands, I've taken on a bit more than I usually do,' Rosie explained.

I eyed her suspiciously, wondering if this was just a ruse to keep me indoors, but her honest smile had me rolling up my sleeves, telling her to put me to work.

And that's exactly what she did.

We spent the rest of the morning in the kitchen, baking, rolling, kneading, icing. My mom even came over to help, while my dad went out to the barn to see Sam.

Caleb and Grayson would be arriving back in a few hours with the animals.

After the initial fussing from my parents, worrying about how I was, it was shaping up to be a good day.

I loved learning new tricks and techniques from my mom and Rosie, both of which were so skilled in the kitchen, they could easily start their own cooking show.

'Why don't the three of you stay for dinner? To say thank you for your help today. Besides, I feel like we haven't seen you in ages,' Rosie said to my mom and I could see how fond they were of one another, like old childhood friends.

'We'd love to. Oh, that reminds me, I brought you a change of clothes, Sophie, in case you wanted to stay another night,' my mom gestured to the overnight bag in the corner.

'Thanks mom, but I should probably come home, I don't want to impose.'

'Nonsense, it's no imposition at all, we'd love to have you

stay. The offer still stands to stay on, you know,' Rosie smiled encouragingly.

'It makes perfect sense honey. Your dad and I are fine and we're not far. I hate the thought of you driving back and forth every day,' my mom added.

I thought about it for a moment and remembered how welcoming and homely the cottage was.

'Ok, but only if you're sure you don't mind?' I asked Rosie.

'Are you kidding, nothing would make me happier. Besides, it's about time I had some female company around here,' Rosie laughed.

'I'm not sure how you've survived this long with those three,' my mom chuckled along with her and I had that strange sense of calm again, that feeling of coming home, belonging.

I watched these two strong, independent, woman in front of me, so much wisdom and kindness and love between them and thought again how truly blessed I was.

Once the baking was done, I went out to the barn to check on Beast, who seemed more restless today, so I decided to take him out to the paddock and let him have a run around to let off some steam.

I'd swiped a few apples on my way out of the kitchen, which he seemed very grateful for, gobbling one down, then another.

'Ok, ok, save some for later,' I laughed and stroked his face.

He was still a little skittish, even around me, but he'd come such a long way in a short space of time.

I'd always admired and loved that about animals, even if they were ill-treated by hideous scum of the earth humans (I felt very strongly about animals being mistreated), so many of them could trust again, if you had the patience to earn their trust.

After quite literally running rings around me for a few minutes, Beast slowed and eventually walked back over towards me, sniffing greedily.

Giving him the rest of the apples, I smiled at myself; how easily I'd given in to him.

The sky was looking ominous, big grey clouds had started rolling in and I didn't want to get caught in the rain with Beast, so we made our way back to the stables.

Once there, I brushed him down, as much as he'd let me anyway, and closed the stable door, giving him one last stroke along his soft nose.

'Goodnight beautiful boy,' I whispered to him.

'You really do have a way with him, don't you,' Grayson's voice came from behind me, making me jump.

'Could you start wearing a bell or something, so I know when you're around,' I placed my hand over my heart for dramatic effect.

'Sorry,' Grayson chuckled. 'Seriously though, it's impressive,' he nodded towards Beast.

'Would you like to try?' I asked, stepping back to let Grayson closer to Beast, but as soon as Grayson took a step forward, Beast let him know he wasn't happy about it.

'Wait, I have an idea,' I stepped between them for a moment, whispering soothing words to Beast, stroking his nose.

'Give me your hand,' I reached back and felt Grayson's warm hand in mine.

I gently pulled him forward, feeling the entire length of my back heating as he moved in closer.

Maybe this hadn't been the brightest idea.

Ignoring my inner voice, I continued stroking Beast and then gently placed Grayson's hand on Beast. Keeping my own on top of his, almost using Grayson's hand as a brush, to continue stroking down Beast's face.

It was working, he hadn't freaked out… Yet.

After a few moments, I slowly backed away, all the while continuing to stroke Beast's face, gently talking to him, letting him know everything was ok and he had nothing to worry about or be afraid of, and when I was a few feet away and Grayson's was the only hand left on the stallion, he remained calm.

Sort of.

His ears went back, and he huffed unhappily, but he didn't move.

Until he gave a stern shake of his head and Grayson backed off, but it had worked, for a moment he'd let someone else close, let someone else touch him.

I was so happy I wanted to burst.

'Oh my gosh! I can't believe that worked, it actually worked, that was amazing! He's such an incredible creature, he's starting to trust,' I was rambling, I knew it, but I was buzzing, it was progress. Small, but still progress, nonetheless.

'You really are a horse whisperer,' I thought Grayson was teasing me, but when I turned to face him, his eyes were serious. 'It's like you've healed him overnight.'

Those piercing blue eyes burned into mine and I felt my cheeks heating with the intensity.

'He's the one who's healing me,' I suddenly realised and then something dawned on me. 'Apollo!'

'Um, Marco?'

I laughed, 'Not Polo! Apollo. Your dad said I could name Beast, or re-name him, whatever, and I want to call him Apollo.' Grayson looked blank. 'In Greek mythology Apollo is the God of healing and that's what Beast, I mean Apollo, embodies. Look how far he's come in such a short space of time. He's healing and I think he has the potential to be a healer in return.'

'Apollo huh, what do you think Apollo?' Grayson asked the stallion who gave us a firm nod and stomp of his hoof.

'I think we can take that as a yes. Apollo it is then,' I beamed.

'How did it go today by the way?' I'd completely forgotten to ask in my excitement.

'Would you like to meet the new recruits?' Grayson asked with a breath-taking smile.

'Can I?' I asked, feeling a fresh wave of excitement wash over me.

Another emotion that had returned recently, I noted.

Grayson laughed and I wasn't sure if it was at me or with me, either way, I didn't care, I was enjoying this high I was riding and if I'd learnt anything at all in my twenty seven years, it was that you had to enjoy the good moments while they lasted because sometimes those moments are what get you through the hard times.

'Some of the nearby farms took on the larger animals, like the cows and horses. Another farm took most of the pigs, so that left us with the goats, a few pigs and the chickens,' Grayson explained as we walked towards their shelter, which had been designed with different sections so that the pigs could be kept together, the goats together and so on.

What was more impressive was that Grayson had designed the whole thing, Sam had told me proudly when I was helping with the fence.

This was going to replace the old enclosures, which were a little dated and needed an uplift. So while that was being done, the animals would be housed here.

Grayson opened the main gate and stepped back, letting me enter first.

I was greeted by three adorable goats, looking a little skittish, which was to be expected after they'd been uprooted and moved somewhere unfamiliar.

'Hi there, babies. It's ok, you're going to be just fine now, you hear. We're going to take good care of you. That's it, come on,' I encouraged and then wished I hadn't.

Suddenly I was bombarded by, well, I had no idea how many, precious goats, all trying to get my attention.

I ended up landing on my butt, in the dirt, laughing hysterically, while one of the goats tried to eat my hair, another my shirt and I could have sworn I felt one trying to chew on my boot.

'Grayson. A. Hand,' I spluttered between bouts of laughter.

'Are you sure? You look quite comfortable down there, I wouldn't want to interrupt,' I could hear the smile in his voice, which made me laugh even harder.

'Grayson!' I reached out, trying to be serious for a second, and failing miserably.

'Ok, ok,' he finally gave in and took my hand, holding on a little longer than necessary.

The sky rumbled and the first few raindrops splattered the ground around us.

'We should get going before it really starts to come down,' Grayson warned, holding the gate open for me.

With a final look over my shoulder, to make sure the animals had gone into the shelter, out of the rain, we made a dash for the main house, only getting caught in the downpour as we neared the house. Even so, we were soaked through within seconds.

Out of breath from our mad dash to the house and laughing harder, I held my arms out wide on either side of my body and spun around in the rain, just like Paul and I used to do as kids, lifting our heads up to the sky, letting the rain wash away our troubles.

Of course, when you were ten years old, your only troubles were things like homework, or wanting ice-cream for dinner.

When I stopped spinning and turned towards the house, I saw Grayson watching me, only briefly before he turned to open the front door for me, but there was something deep and intense in the flash of his blue eyes.

Suddenly feeling a chill run down my spine (and not from the rain), I jogged inside the house, out of the rain and away from the unnerving look in Grayson's eyes.

‘What on earth happened to you?’ My dad asked, taking in our soaked, and I guessed my filthy, appearances.

‘Your daughter was rolling around in the dirt with the goats,’ Grayson laughed and shrugged.

‘Don’t ask,’ I grinned at my dad who eyed me suspiciously.

‘Rosie, would you mind if I showered before dinner?’ I asked, wanting to get cleaned up and into dry, clean clothes.

‘Of course, you can use the spare bathroom down the hall.’

Grabbing the overnight bag my mom had brought, I secretly thanked her for always thinking ahead, and headed for the bathroom.

It didn’t take me long to get cleaned up, and when I made my way out, I found everyone sitting on the porch.

My parents were laughing, along with Rosie and Sam and I simply stood there watching them all, just taking it all in. Feeling happier than I had in such a long time.

Another emotion returned, tick, the little voice inside my head whispered.

‘Penny for your thoughts?’ I didn’t need to turn to see it was Grayson.

‘Just enjoying the view,’ I replied, a small smile on my lips. ‘That reminds me.’

My mom knew me so well. I dug in the overnight bag and pulled out my camera and snapped a few candid shots of everyone before turning the camera on Grayson.

Taking one of him smiling, watching everyone else and then another as he turned to me.

'No way, I'm not photogenic at all,' he tried to cover his face, but he wasn't fast enough.

'Oh please, you and Caleb could be models,' I lowered my camera, as Caleb approached.

'That's a given. Just check out these boyish good looks,' Caleb put his arm around his brother and squished their faces together. 'Well, I'm not sure what happened to yours bro.'

'I'll show you what happened to them,' Grayson pretended to sucker punch his brother, while I snapped a few more candid shots of them goofing around.

'Caleb, Grayson, stop that and come get your dinner,' Rosie scolded and the two of them straightened up before heading outside.

They reminded me so much of Paul and I growing up.

It was nice to see them messing around, I hadn't seen much of that since arriving here.

In fact, come to think of it, I'd hardly seen them spend more than a few minutes together, and even that was fleeting, simply discussing the farm, before going their separate ways.

Odd, given how close the family seemed.

'This looks amazing, Mom,' I heard Grayson thank his mom as I walked outside to join them, seeing him plant a kiss on Rosie's forehead.

Everyone said grace before we tucked in.

'We have an announcement to make,' Grayson said looking across the table at me.

'We do?' I nearly chocked on my breadstick, feeling my cheeks burn at everyone's glances between Grayson and I.

I had no idea what he was talking about.

'Sophie's come up with a new name for Beast.'

Oh, whew! That was all.

'I was thinking we could call him Apollo,' I said, looking around apprehensively.

'Apollo. I like it,' Sam was the first to comment. 'Here's to Apollo and to Sophie, who have both been wonderful additions to the family.'

I was touched and smiled warmly at Sam and Rosie.

'Oh, we have more news,' Rosie chimed in. 'Sophie will be staying with us on the farm to save her driving back and forth every day. Not that you need it, Sophie, you've always been welcome, but officially, welcome to the farm.'

'Thank you, I'm so grateful to be here and to have met all of you.'

'That's enough gooey talk. Let's toast and drink,' you could always rely on Caleb to ruin a meaningful moment, but I laughed despite myself.

I found Rosie bustling around the kitchen the following morning, getting ready for the bake sale.

We packed up the car and met my mom in town, along with a few of their friends who'd offered to help.

As much as I wanted to be on the farm with the animals today, I knew this was important to Rosie, and the sanctuary too, and I wanted to help as much as I could, so once again armed with my camera, I took a few shots of Rosie selling baked goods and a few of my mom just for fun.

My mom was a beautiful woman, with flawless olive skin

and the warmest, deep blue green eyes.

Unlike me, mom had short brown hair, framing her delicate face perfectly. She was also shorter than me – petite she preferred being called.

She was the strongest, kindest, most loving, caring woman I knew, and I had always aspired to be even half the woman she was.

When God was handing out parents, I certainly had hit the jackpot with mine.

I'd somehow forgotten how much I missed and needed my family while I was in New York. A mistake I wouldn't make again.

That's not to say that we weren't close while I was away, we spoke all the time and saw each other as often as we could, but I guess sometimes you just get wrapped up in your own life, and after Luke, I don't know.

I guess I stopped making an effort with a lot of things in my life, including keeping in touch with my parents.

But being out here, back in my hometown, with my family, and now on the farm, was the first time in a long time I'd felt alive again, rather than simply existing.

I still had a huge hole in my heart, that I was sure could never be filled, or fixed, but at least I was starting to remember the things that mattered in life; family, friends, doing something worthy, something that made a difference, like working at the sanctuary.

I loved writing. I always had, from a young age I was a complete book worm, but I doubted my books impacted anyone's life, not in the way the Danvers hard work did, or my parents work.

It made me take a step back and want to re-evaluate my life.

Baby steps, I thought. Let's just take things one day at a time.

By the end of the day we had completely sold out of all baked goods. There wasn't a single cookie or chocolate brownie left.

'Thank you both for your help, I couldn't have done it without you,' Rosie thanked Mom and I while packing up.

I was hoping my plan would help a whole lot more.

Speaking of which, I needed to pick up a few things while we were in town, so I told Rosie and my mom I'd catch up with them in a little while and headed towards the printers we'd walked passed earlier.

I was going to need a little help and thankfully I wasn't disappointed, leaving the store with a much heavier bag and a much bigger smile on my face.

'What's got you grinning like a happy house cat?' Mom asked when I found them loading up the car with the last of the containers.

'Can't a girl just be happy?' I winked, hoping our mother daughter bond was strong enough that she would realise not to push for answers.

I wanted this to be a surprise for Rosie and Sam.

Our bond must be rock solid because she simply smiled knowingly and let it drop.

Rosie thanked my mom again and we said our goodbyes. I was heading back to the farm with Rosie, but I planned to spend the weekend with my parents.

'That was quite a day. How often do you do things like this for the sanctuary?' I asked Rosie on the drive back.

'As often as we can. It can be difficult trying to raise money for the sanctuary, but this is a strong community and we all pull together when we need to,' Rosie said proudly.

'I can tell. It's the kind of place Luke and I imagined raising a family.' The words were out before my brain even registered what my mouth was saying. I froze.

It had been a long time since I'd spoken about Luke with anyone new.

'Luke was your husband,' Rosie said gently.

'Yes, do you know what happened?'

'I do, but only because your parents were devastated when they got the news. We helped them get ready to fly to New York for the funeral,' Rosie replied. 'Do you want to talk about it?'

'There isn't much to say really, we were in love, we got married and two years ago he died so unexpectedly I don't think I've ever gotten over it.' My voice sounded hollow.

'Sophie, I'm so sorry, I can't imagine how difficult it must have been for you,' Rosie reached over and squeezed my hand.

'Thank you, it was. Difficult.' That was the understatement of the century.

'Do you know what I think you need?'

'I have no idea,' I said hesitantly.

'You need a night out on the town.'

I couldn't help but laugh, firstly at her description and secondly at the thought of it.

'I'm serious, I'm sure Grayson and Caleb would love to show you the hot spots,' she continued earnestly.

Ok, now I was definitely out.

The thought of going out with those two, or more to the point, the thought of the trouble I'd land myself in, going out with those two. No, thank you!

'I'm not sure that would be such a good idea,' I replied.

Although I had to admit the thought was kind of amusing. I'm sure Caleb would be a laugh to hit the town with.

Grayson on the other hand. I wasn't so sure of.

'At least think about it. They've got a great group of friends. It would be healthy for you to get out with kids your own age and let your hair down.'

She may have a point, and if it was a group of people it might not be so bad.

'Ok, I'll think about it.'

In the weeks that followed, I fell into a comfortable routine at the sanctuary; mornings and late afternoons were usually spent with Apollo, while the rest of the time mostly consisted of helping Sam, Grayson or Caleb.

There seemed to be a constant flow of jobs; fences needed fixing, the animals needed feeding, poop needed shovelling.

Hey, no one said it was glamorous work, but it felt amazing doing something so worthwhile and meaningful.

It gave my life a new sense of much needed purpose.

The days spent with Sam were great, he was a fountain of knowledge, not just about the sanctuary or the animals.

His brain was like a vault of random and fantastic pieces of information. He was a kind and gentle soul and I loved working with him.

His sons on the other hand…

Working with Caleb was never dull.

He kept me on my toes, and he was nothing if not entertaining. I was guaranteed a day filled with laugher when it came to Caleb.

Grayson, I couldn't quite figure out.

After our first, not very good introduction, things had done a full three-sixty. He was like a different person.

He wasn't quite the clown that his younger brother liked to be, but he certainly wasn't the grouch I'd pegged him for after our first run in.

I found myself laughing far more than I thought I ever would again.

Even my mom had commented on how much happier and lighter I seemed, and it was clear it delighted my parents to see me gradually becoming more like my old self.

That in itself made me happier and I found myself smiling as I hammered another post into the ground.

Grayson and I were working on extending the new shelter, now that we had a little more time to focus on it, since the new recruits had arrived.

'Penny for your thoughts?' Grayson asked, handing me a bottle of water.

Since my fainting spell, it was like having three fathers, not to mention Rosie, fussing, making sure I was fed and hydrated all the time.

I'd be worried about gaining weight if it wasn't for the physical demands of the job. I think I'd actually lost weight since starting.

All those years of running and going to the gym and doing yoga and all I needed to do was work on a farm.

If only the women of New York weren't scared of ruining their perfectly manicured fingers, we'd be onto something huge.

'If you keep giving me pennies, you're going to end up a broke man,' I teased. 'I was just thinking about my parents. My dad seems more relaxed since I first arrived.'

'They've both changed, for the better, since you came home. They both seem a lot happier with you here. I think they worried about you more than they let on after-' Grayson stopped, his eyes widening.

'It's ok, I assumed you knew,' I tried to lighten my tone. Not entirely succeeding.

'I'm sorry, I didn't mean to bring it up. We can talk about something else,' he scrambled.

'Honestly, it's ok. I think I'm ready to talk about what happened, to talk about Luke. I want to remember him, and I want people to know who he was. He would have loved it here and he would have really liked you and Caleb. He was such a goof, always making me laugh. In some ways Caleb reminds me a little of him, they're both the entertainers, the comedians. But he was also kind and had a huge heart,' I took a drink of water before continuing.

'We met in college and I had the biggest crush on him for the longest time, but he was two years ahead of me and I didn't think for a second he'd be interested in a freshman.

Turns out I was wrong and after a few months he asked me out. Kaitlyn, my best friend, said she knew the minute she saw us together that it was the real deal and that she'd be a bridesmaid at our wedding one day – which she was by the way. Luke proposed a year later, much to a lot of people's silent objection. I guess a lot of people thought we were crazy and far too young, but we just knew and told everyone to either get on board with it or they could gladly exclude themselves from our big day, but after my family met him and I met his, I think everyone realised that we truly were in love. We got married the year I graduated college and were happily married for four wonderful years, before Luke collapsed on the floor of our apartment and never made it home again. That was two years ago, but I can still remember it like it was yesterday. It was so sudden, there were no warning signs, he was fine one minute and the next…' I trailed off, the lump in my throat preventing me from finishing.

I wiped away the single tear that rolled down my cheek and automatically touched our rings, tucked under my t-shirt.

As hard as it still was to talk about, it also felt good talking about Luke and I meant what I said, I wanted to honour his memory, not brush him under the carpet and forget he ever existed.

'Sophie, I don't know what to say other than how truly sorry I am that you had to go through that. I think you're an incredibly strong, brave woman and I know I didn't know Luke, but I think he would be proud of you, how far you've come.' Grayson's eyes briefly filled with emotion, almost understanding, but he quickly blinked it away.

'Thank you, Grayson, that means a lot,' I managed to smile up at him.

He held out his hand, 'Come on, I want to show you something.'

'What is it?' I asked curiously, taking his hand, letting him help me up as though I weighted nothing.

'You'll see,' he replied, a glint of mischief in his baby blues.

'Grayson, this is beautiful,' I breathed, taking in the lake that lay before me.

Nestled amongst tall trees, which surrounded the entire lake, making it feel closed off from the rest of the world.

It was small, as far as lakes went, but beautiful, nonetheless.

Wildflowers grew amongst the trees and the tall grass surrounding the lake, but what completed the picture-perfect scenery was the delicate waterfall that trickled over the rocks at the far end. The sun glistened on the water like a mirror. It was incredibly inviting.

Clearly Grayson had the same idea, he'd already started unbuttoning his shift.

'Oh, um,' I turned around, not knowing what to do with myself.

I heard Grayson laugh behind me, a deep rumbling laugh that came from his belly and then not long after a loud splash.

I was almost too scared to look. Almost.

'Come on in, the water's great,' he called, dipping under the water.

‘I don’t have a bathing suit,’ I replied when he reappeared.

‘Neither do I. Come on Sophie, live a little. I’ll even turn around.’

Oh my! What was I thinking?

I was living, that’s what, I thought, pulling my boots off and stripping down to my underwear before running into the cool water and diving beneath the surface.

‘Great, isn’t it?’ Grayson swam towards me.

‘It’s heavenly.’ The water felt silky against my warm skin. ‘Is this part of the farm?’ I wondered aloud.

‘Not exactly.’

‘Are we trespassing?’ I squeaked, shooting up out of the water.

It took Grayson a minute to answer and it took me a minute longer to realise why.

I was standing, waist deep in the water, my upper half (my half naked upper half) completely on show.

Yikes! I ducked back under the water again, cheeks burning.

‘No, we’re not trespassing, but this technically isn’t our land. It belongs to the next farm over, but they’re an elderly couple who never come out here, so don’t worry, it’s just the two of us. This is where I like to come when I want to get away from things, you know?’

Did I ever! I’d left my home, my life.

That kind of took getting away from things to the next level.

‘I can see why,’ I replied.

It was so peaceful. I could have stayed there forever.

We floated around a while longer, talking about everything from our first crushes, to our favourite music and movies, before we heard a deep ominous rumble from above.

How had we not noticed that the sun had disappeared, and grey clouds had taken its place?

We didn't even have time to get out of the water before the rain started hammering down so we did the only thing we could; we laughed our asses off, splashing one another, which, given the pouring rain, seemed pointless, but we did it anyway until a bolt of lightning shot across the sky.

'Time to go. I don't want to have to tell your parents that you were electrocuted while we were swimming in the rain,' Grayson laughed, helping me out of the water.

I felt naked (which wasn't far off), but Grayson was the perfect gentlemen, turning away while I got dressed, leaving me with a good view of his long, lean legs and back.

He was all long lines and muscle. Not like the body builder types with muscles so big they looked like they were walking around with watermelons under their arms.

No, Grayson was just the right amount of muscle, as I could see quite well from this angle when he bent down to pick up his clothes and the muscles along his back flexed.

I noticed a tattoo on his upper left arm, but another crack from the heavens brought me back to earth before I could figure out what it was.

Quickly, we finished getting dressed before making another dash back to the sanctuary.

What was the deal with us and getting caught out in the rain!

Chapter 6

Most evenings were now spent putting together the Willow Farm Sanctuary website. My mini project.

It's what I had spent the past few weeks snapping pictures for, and it was coming together perfectly.

I only hoped Rosie and Sam didn't think I was overstepping by just taking charge and running with it, without getting their input first. Not that I was planning on going live without their ok first.

It just seemed like the perfect way to promote the sanctuary, and hopefully gain a lot more funding than we had from bake sales.

Speaking of which, I took another look at the flyers I'd ordered the day of the bake sale, which were ready surprisingly quickly and I had to admit they looked great.

Apollo took centre stage, naturally, but there were a few shots of Rosie and Sam and of course Grayson and Caleb.

I wondered if they'd do a topless shoot.

Hey, don't judge, it would be a guaranteed selling point with the ladies. We could make a killing!

For now, I'd settle for the flyers and the website, but I had bigger plans.

We could start social media pages too and perhaps open

the sanctuary to volunteers or working holidays. The opportunities were there, they just needed to be snapped up.

Stifling a yawn, I took my tea out onto the back porch of the cottage and snuggled into the love seat I'd recently purchased.

I loved spending my evenings under the stars, so I'd bought a small table, love seat and two matching chairs for the small back porch, but it was perfect, it was all I needed, I thought, sighing happily.

I liked to think that Luke was watching over me, looking down from above and I often found myself looking up at the sky talking to him – not out loud for fear of being caught and locked in the looney bin, but I would look up and imagine him smiling down on me.

Some nights were better than others, sometimes it hurt too much to think about (those nights I would usually stay indoors and busy myself with the website), but tonight I felt ok, not quite whole again, but not shattering into a thousand tiny pieces either.

I'd always thought romance films were so overdramatised, when the girl falls to pieces after a breakup, feeling like she was going to break in two because missing her love hurt so much.

Well, I can tell you from personal experience, that's no overdramatization. At least not in real life.

There were so many nights I thought I was physically going to snap in half from my breaking heart, from the pain of missing Luke so much.

Time helped in some ways, but it didn't get any easier,

you simply got better at dealing with it.

Just then my phone buzzed, pulling me back to the present, and I smiled when I saw the name.

'I thought you'd forgotten me,' I teased.

'I'm so sorry, Soph, things have been so insane here, it's the height of the season – summer fashion shows. Long photo shoots and crazed models. It's exhausting!' Kaitlyn sounded utterly spent.

'I wish I was there. Better yet, I wish you were here. You would love it out here Kay, it's so peaceful and a far slower, simpler way of life and the scenery is amazing. You would constantly be snappy happy,' I laughed, imagining the camera glued to my best friends face.

'You sound happy, Soph.' I could hear the smile in Kaitlyn's voice.

'I'm a work in progress. But tell me about you, how are you, really?'

'Tired. You may be on to something, maybe it's time for a change for me too. The city was never the end goal anyway.'

Kaitlyn and I were so similar, we really could have been sisters.

Both having grown up in Beaufort and ending up in The Big Apple, we always imagined getting married and starting families in our hometown or at the very least in a much smaller city.

I guess I'd had a head start with at least one of those.

'You could always join me at the sanctuary, we could use the extra help, that's for sure.'

'Ha-ha very funny. Can you imagine me shovelling cow poop?'

The thought made me laugh out loud, 'I can actually, and it's a hilarious picture.'

'Laugh it up, at least I'm not the one who's traded her Prada's for cowboy boots,' Kaitlyn shot back.

I did, in fact, own a pair of Prada's; a gift from Luke for our first wedding anniversary, but I was just as happy in my cowboy boots, thank you very much.

As much as I enjoyed dressing up and sporting a stylish pair of high heels, I was equally happy in a pair of jeans and boots or flats.

Kaitlyn, on the other hand, was far more girly and preferred dresses over jeans any day of the week.

'Why don't you take a break and come out here for a few days?' I offered, wanting her to have a break, but selfishly, I wanted to see her.

I couldn't believe I had been here for almost a month. It was the longest we'd been apart.

'I would love to, but it'll have to wait another few week's I'm afraid. Roger freaked when I asked him for the Fourth of July weekend off.'

Roger was Kaitlyn's slavedriver of a boss, who didn't believe in spending the holidays with family and friends.

'I'm sorry, that sounds miserable.' I really wished there was something I could do to help.

'It's ok, I'll spit in his coffee next time he sends me to Starbucks,' Kaitlyn giggled, knowing full well she would never do anything that gross.

We spoke for another hour before both of us were trying (and failing) to yawn inconspicuously, so we said our goodbyes and I made my way back inside, falling into bed –

one of the perks of working on the farm; a sound night's sleep, thanks to spending most days working my entire body.

I would take any and all of life's small mercies, I thought just before drifting off.

The Fourth of July weekend came around faster than I could have anticipated, but thankfully I had my surprise ready for the Danvers and I was like a kid in a candy store all day.

'What's up with you today? You're all... Hyper,' Caleb eyeballed me suspiciously.

I was on the farm helping, despite the fact that it was seven o'clock on a Saturday morning, but I wanted to make sure all the work was done so that we could all enjoy this weekend.

'Can't a girl just be excited about the celebrations?' I asked innocently.

'Mmhmm,' Caleb muttered, clearly not buying it.

Our families were going to watch the parade in Beaufort this afternoon and I had somehow let Caleb talk me into going out with him and Grayson and their friends afterwards.

I was far more apprehensive about that, but I wasn't going to let it ruin my mood. I was so excited to show the Danvers the website and flyers.

Not much longer to wait, I thought, noticing the time.

Rosie called us all in for breakfast a short while later and as soon as the table had been cleared and the dishes washed, I asked if everyone could join me in the living room.

They all followed me in with concerned expressions.

'Good grief, don't look so worried,' I couldn't help but laugh at their nervous glances. 'I have something to show you. Something I'm hoping you'll like.'

I really, really hoped they liked it, I thought, connecting my laptop to the TV.

I was all for dramatic effect, but I figured it would also be easier to show them all at once, rather than cramming around my laptop.

'I've put something together for you and I fully understand if you want to change things, or if you think I've overstepped, we can pull the plug on the whole thing,' I was rambling, suddenly feeling like a teenager, about to give a speech in front of the whole school.

'Well, come on, the suspense is killing me, what is it?' Caleb encouraged.

I pulled the website up on the screen and it popped up on the TV.

'I've put together a website for the sanctuary. I thought it might be a great way to promote the sanctuary and hopefully raise more funds, maybe even get some volunteers signed up. Rosie, Sam, I know it might seem daunting, but these days everything is done via social media. I would be happy to handle anything online,' I offered, before continuing. 'The website shows the hard work you do here, and it would give people a bit of a background story too,' I showed them the different sections, a small piece about the sanctuary and the family.

I'd put together a gallery of all the pictures I'd taken; we briefly flipped through those. There was a section on how to donate or other ways people could help.

I then showed them the flyers and waited with bated breath while they took everything in.

'Sophie, I don't know what to say. You did all of this for us?' Rosie was the first to speak and I could see from the gleam in her eye that she was touched.

'This is great, Sophie, it's exactly what we've been needing,' Caleb was next, he truly looked blown away.

'Really? You like it?' I asked hesitantly.

'Sophie, we love it. I don't know how we can ever thank you,' Sam offered, looking as awestruck as his son.

'She can take a few shots of me with my shirt off, that's how,' Caleb joked.

At least I hoped he was joking.

I risked a fleeting glance in Grayson's direction and felt my cheeks heating at the look on his face; gratitude was the first thing that came to mind, followed by a mix of admiration and something else I couldn't quite put my finger on.

I didn't have time to try figure it out, as we continued throwing more ideas around, I was so thrilled that they, not only liked the website and flyers, but were happy with the layout and design and didn't want to change a thing.

We spent the next hour looking everything over and I answered their questions about how the website worked – Rosie and Sam were so much like my mom and dad – they didn't mix well with technology.

But that was ok, that's what I was here for.

They thanked me again and as I left them to go get ready for the parade, Grayson gently caught my arm just before

I left the house.

'Hey, I wanted to thank you. No one's ever done anything like that for us before, for the sanctuary, and I want you to know how much it means, to all of us.'

It was the most earnest I think I'd ever seen him, and I didn't know what to say.

'It was nothing, really.' Was all I could come up with, feeling flustered under his scrutiny.

'It wasn't nothing, it was huge. Thank you, Sophie,' he gave my arm a little squeeze and I realised he hadn't let it go.

'You're welcome,' I replied awkwardly. 'I better go get ready. I'll see you soon.'

I just needed space to breath and to get out from under his intense crystal blue eyes.

It was at times like this I missed Kaitlyn more than ever.

The cottage looked like a bomb had gone off, clothes and shoes were everywhere.

I must have tried on every piece of clothing I owned and ended up back at the start. While looking at my reflection in the full-length mirror in the corner of my bedroom I sighed, thinking *this is as good as it's gonna get*.

I'd opted for a teal lace spaghetti strap dress that pulled in at the waist and sat just above my knees, with a jagged lace hem.

It wasn't too flashy for the parade, but it would (hopefully) be dressy enough for tonight.

I'd paired it with matching wedges that criss-crossed around my ankles, which were comfortable enough for the parade and would just have to do for the evening.

I wore my hair loose, in long waves tumbling down my back, with a delicate braid along my hairline, keeping it off my face.

I hadn't gone overboard with my makeup; just the faintest hint of smoky eyes, bronze blush and my favourite cherry lip balm. Simple, but elegant.

Taking a shaky breath in I wondered why I suddenly felt so nervous. I'd been to this parade so many times I'd lost count.

Ok, if I was being honest with myself, which I clearly wasn't, it had nothing to do with the parade and everything to do with what was to come after.

Only that was the problem, I didn't know what to expect.

It's just dinner and a few drinks, maybe some dancing with a group of friends.

Even though I would only know two people, that still wasn't what bothered me.

Ok fine, what bothered me was Caleb's comment about saving him a dance and Grayson's intense stare, between the two of them they would be my undoing.

Well, I could either stand around fretting, or put my big girl panties on and get on with it. I chose the latter.

'Wow, you look great,' Caleb was never one to be discreet, or subdued for that matter.

If he saw something he liked, everyone knew about it and this was no exception.

He eyed me hungrily in front of his parents, making my

cheeks burn.

Inappropriate much? I thought, embarrassed.

'You look lovely Sophie,' Rosie kissed my cheek.

'Thank you, so do you. You scrub up well too, Sam,' I grinned, and he fussed with his shirt, clearly not happy with his attire.

'Come on, lets load into the car, Grayson will be over in just a minute,' Rosie instructed.

Right on cue, Grayson appeared, looking like a model, instead of a farm boy.

He wore dark blue jeans that hugged his long muscular legs with a pale blue button up shirt, rolled at the sleeves which didn't surprise me given the heat.

His normally unruly mop of dark locks was styled to perfection tonight, making him look like he'd just walked off a Calvin Klein shoot.

When my eyes met his I got the distinct sensation that he had just been thinking the same thing, as he took me in, looking me up and down.

Thankfully he was far more discreet than his brother, but Rosie didn't miss a beat, I caught her smiling and wondered what was going through that head of hers.

No good comes of those mischievous looks from a mother, that was for sure.

'Come on you two, let's get going,' she shooed us towards the car where Sam and Caleb were waiting, already buckled in.

Sam was driving us all into town and apparently Grayson had booked us a taxi home later, even though I offered to drive, but I had to admit, I was grateful for not having to be the responsible one.

I was taking Rosie's advice, letting my hair down and enjoying myself.

Even though it wasn't a long drive to Beaufort, it felt like a mini road trip, the excitable buzz in the air was infections and I found myself genuinely looking forward to the day ahead.

'So, where are you all going after the parade?' Rosie asked no one in particular, while Sam hummed along to a country song on the radio.

My parents always had music playing when I was younger, whether it was classical or rock or a bit of pop, there was always music playing in our house and it suddenly hit me how little I played music these days.

In fact, other than the occasionally having the radio on in the car (and even that was rare), I couldn't remember the last time I'd had music playing.

I'd have to dig out my old CD's.

'We'll hit Deluca's for dinner and then check out the new beach bar, I hear they've got a Cocktail kind of vibe going,' Caleb replied, pulling me from my reverie.

'As in the movie, with Tom Cruise?' I asked with a giggle when Caleb nodded.

I could totally picture Caleb doing that, tossing cocktail shakers around, giving the ladies a show.

'Just make sure you two look after Sophie, you hear,' Rosie told her sons sternly, and although I was perfectly capable of taking care of myself, I liked the way it sounded, making me feel like I was part of their family.

Shortly after arriving in Beaufort, we found my parents, along with Paul and Sarah, and headed towards the parade.

It brought back so many childhood memories.

Paul and I loved the parade growing up, we always ate far too much ice cream and cotton candy, but it was like our annual pass to go wild and bounce around on a sugar high.

It was a beautiful day out and the waterfront look fantastic, all decked out with red, white and blue decorations and flags.

I hadn't been to the parade in years and was impressed at how far along the floats had come.

It felt great being back and being a part of it all again.

Soon I'd have a niece or nephew to bring to the parade and spoil with far too many sugary treats.

I watched my brother and Sarah with a happy heart and smile on my face. They were so in love.

'You look happy, honey,' my mom linked arms with me.

'Hey mama,' I squeezed her hand. 'I am. It's been good for me, I think, being home. I was so worried that leaving New York was a mistake and that it would make me forget Luke. Instead, I think it's helping, healing, somehow. I can talk about him without feeling like I'm going to shatter into a million pieces. It still hurts, of course, and I still miss him, every single day, but it's somehow better out here.'

'Home is where the heart is and when you find your way home, that's when you can truly start to heal.' My mom always knew just want to say.

I wrapped my arm around her and pulled her close into my side as we walked along, lagging behind the others.

'I've missed you and our hour-long talks. No one gives advice like a mom can.'

'Oh honey, we've missed you too. It's so wonderful having you home and seeing you happier, we were so worried about you.'

'I know,' I felt a pang of guilt remembering Grayson's words about how worried my parents had been these past few years.

'You do?' My mom tilted her head questioningly.

Shoot!

'Oh, um, it's just that Grayson mentioned that you and Dad seem happier, more at ease, with me home, is all.'

'Have you been spending much time with Grayson then?' She tried to ask casually and failed horribly.

I tried to stifle a laugh.

'Don't go getting any funny ideas, Mom,' I recognised the exact same look from Rosie's eyes earlier.

Meddling mothers!

'I don't know what you mean honey,' she replied, feigning innocence.

'Mmhmm,' I wasn't buying it.

The day passed us by far too quickly, and I tried to soak it all in, not wanting to miss a thing.

Snapping photos along the way (using my phone this time, I didn't think it wise to bring my camera on a night out).

Seated at a table under the shade of an oak tree, I watched my parents dancing to the live band.

Rosie and Sam soon joined in, as did Paul and Sarah,

leaving me with Grayson and Caleb.

'Come on Soph, let's show 'em how it's done,' Caleb stood, extending his hand.

I didn't want to leave Grayson sitting there on his own. Looking over at him, he must have sensed my hesitation.

'Go ahead, I'll keep our table,' he smiled easily, but I thought I noticed, just for a fleeting moment, disappointment flash in his eyes.

'Ok, sure,' I took Caleb's hand as he led the way to the dancefloor.

I was twirled and spun around and dipped before I could even catch my breath.

'I'm impressed,' I said between laughter. I had to admit, I was having fun. 'Where did you learn to dance?' I finally managed to ask when the band opted for a somewhat slower number and Caleb made no move to leave, so we continued swaying together.

'My mom thought it would be a good idea to send Grayson and I for dance lessons. She clearly wanted daughters, but I have to admit, as embarrassing as it was at the time, it's been a hit with the ladies in recent years,' he gave me his easy lopsided grin with a wink.

'I'm sure it is. Have there been many ladies then?' I suddenly wondered aloud.

'There have been a few,' Caleb's usually bubbly personality sobered momentarily.

'I get the sense there's more to the story?' I raised an eyebrow.

'Isn't there always?' Caleb laughed, but this time it didn't touch his eyes, and I hoped I hadn't overstepped.

'So, tell me more about this beach bar we're going to?' I asked, wanting to change the subject, not wanting to ruin the fun we'd been having.

And with that the animated expression I'd come to know so well lit up Caleb's face and he went into a full run down of the bar.

'Mind if I cut in?' My dad asked Caleb a short while later.

'Not at all,' Caleb replied courteously, leaving me with my dad.

'How are you feeling, old man?' I joked.

'Could an old man do this?' My dad spun me around, whirled me back in and dipped me backwards.

Was everyone a dancer around here? I thought, giggling like I was suddenly five years old, dancing around our living room on my dad's feet.

'No, he certainly couldn't,' I replied with a grin. 'But seriously, how have you been feeling?'

'A lot better now that my baby girl is home. I never liked you living in such a big city. It's been great having both my children living in the same town again.'

'Dad, I'm sorry if I worried you, while I was away. I'd hate to think I could have had anything to do with your heart-attack.'

'Is that what you think? Sophie, you could never cause me that amount, or that kind of stress. Of course your mother and I worried, that's just what parents do. It doesn't matter how old your kids get, you'll always worry about them, but we always knew you were safe with Luke. It's only been these last few years that we've been more concerned with how you were coping. We felt you needed your family around you after what happened,' Dad explained.

'I know, I was just scared to leave, scared of leaving our memories behind,' I told him, having a sense of déjà vu from the conversation I'd had only a few hours ago with my mom.

'Honey, the people we love are with us everywhere we go. You'll never leave him behind, or the memories you shared, he's with you always.' My dad was starting to sound just like Kaitlyn. 'We all love and miss Luke, but his memory will live on through all of us, we'll never forget him, and we'll never let you forget him.' I could feel myself tearing up.

'Thank you, Daddy,' I gave my dad a squeeze before my mom came over and asked for another round on the dancefloor with Dad.

As I turned to leave, I almost walked straight into Grayson.

'Care to dance?' He simply smiled and offered me his hand.

I sensed my mom's craftiness hard at work as I took Grayson's hand and recognised the slow song that was playing; it was one of my parents' favourites and seemed like far too much of a coincidence to be playing just as I ran into Grayson.

'Are you having a good time?' Grayson asked as we swayed close together on the dancefloor, under a grand old oak tree which was covered in fairly lights, making it look like we were dancing under the milky way.

'I really am.'

I was close enough that I could smell his heavenly scent and a hint of aftershave, which only added to the intoxicating allure.

He smelled of a summer rainstorm, when the rain cuts through the hot summer air and hits the earth, making you think of all things summer; freshly cut grass and salty sea air, sunshine and long grass growing on sand dunes.

It was extremely distracting, and I had to concentrate hard to focus on what he was saying.

'You sound surprised?' His smooth voice whispered against my ear and I shivered despite the July heat.

'I guess it's been such a long time since I felt happy and let myself have fun. I think I forgot how for a while,' I replied, feeling giddy, despite only having water to drink so far.

But Grayson's strong arms held me tightly.

'You deserve it Sophie, you deserve to be happy and have everything you want from this life,' were the words Grayson spoke, but his eyes said so much more.

The implications in those beautiful blue eyes frightened and exhilarated me, but I wasn't ready for any of it.

I started to pull away just as Grayson opened his mouth to say something, but the song ended and he closed his mouth again, instead, asking if I wanted something to drink.

'A soda would be great, thank you,' I replied, following him back to our table.

Shortly after that last dance with Grayson, Caleb suggested we get going, and I was grateful for the distraction.

I said goodnight to our parents, and we met up with Grayson and Caleb's friends at Deluca's for dinner.

Deluca's had been around longer than I had. They served everything from seafood to pasta to pizza and the most mouth-watering desserts.

Once I was introduced to everyone, we took our seats and conversation flowed easily.

Turns out they had all known each other since school.

April and James had dated since then and were still going strong and although Paige and Tyler were a relatively new couple, Tyler said he'd always known they'd end up together.

I couldn't help smiling. They reminded me so much of Luke and I.

'So, Sophie, tell us about New York, what did you do? I bet the nightlife was amazing,' Paige quizzed me, eyes sparkling with interest.

'The nightlife is definitely something else. I'd often be heading out for an early morning meeting while couples, or groups of friends, were only just stumbling home. There's no other city in the world like New York, it's so diverse and exciting and full of culture, but in all honesty, I've missed the slower paced lifestyle of Beaufort.'

'You don't get much slower than Beaufort,' Tyler joked.

'You love this sleepy little town,' April shot back.

'Sure I do, I just wish it wasn't quite so sleepy sometimes,' Tyler replied.

'Well don't worry about that, tonight is going to be

anything but sleepy,' Caleb interjected, arriving with a tray full of cocktails and shot glasses containing something green – I didn't even want to know what they were.

Chapter 7

Two hours, and I'm not sure how many cocktails later, we arrived at the beach bar, simply named Joe's Beach Bar.

It was safe to say that, by this point, I was pretty buzzed, but I had enough sense (and experience) to keep drinking water in-between cocktails.

I'd made that mistake too many times before and paid the price the next day. I was grateful when Grayson handed me another bottle of water, after Caleb ordered yet another round of drinks.

'Thanks,' I smiled gratefully.

'You're welcome,' he replied casually.

It seemed the intensity that had appeared behind Grayson's eyes earlier had fizzled out. Or maybe I'd simply imagined it.

No, no, I knew what I saw, but what I couldn't figure out was why I suddenly felt disappointed. It had been what I'd wanted after all. Hadn't it?

Well, no point in dwelling on things, especially when I was in a less than logical state of mind after another shot – this one clear, tasing of sweet summer fruit, but it still burned all the way down.

It was still relatively early, but the bar was already heaving with bodies.

We shimmied our way to the outdoor seating area (luckily Caleb had the sense to reserve a table for us).

The decking area was large and filled with cosy seating, along with festoon lighting all around.

Not that we needed it tonight. The full moon and stars provided enough light to cast silvery shadows across the sand and the water.

The dancefloor was off to the side of the seating. Done in a similar way, with festoon lighting and a wooden dancefloor laid out on the sand.

Good thing I had opted for wedges, I thought dubiously. That looked like an accident waiting to happen in high heels.

'Ok, it's time to get this party started people!' Caleb announced, jumping up, 'Who's joining me on the dancefloor?'

April and Paige squealed in unison and were by his side in a flash.

'No way, it's going to take another few beers before I brave that,' Grayson gestured towards the already crowded dancefloor.

'I'm with you there, bro,' James said, clinking his beer bottle with Grayson's.

'Party poopers,' Tyler joined the pro-dancefloor goers.

'Come on Sophie, you don't want to stay here with these two grandpas, do you?' Caleb raised an eyebrow and extended his hand out to me.

With a fleeting glance at Grayson, who was back to

intense brooding looks, I took Caleb's hand, deciding the dancefloor was probably the safer option.

I certainly didn't regret my decision, giggling at Caleb, who was apparently in his element on the dancefloor, spinning April and Paige around and then April and I. He really was like Tom Cruise in Cocktail.

'What's so funny?' Caleb whipped me up into the air and spun me around before placing me back down.

'Whoa, easy there,' he steadied me as I wobbled, no thanks to his spinning.

'I was just thinking you should do this,' I gestured around us.

'Party? I thought that's what we were doing?' He took my hand and spun me out before pulling me back in again and I noticed how many envious looks I was getting.

This didn't really come as much of a surprise, given his rugged good looks.

'You know what I mean – open your own beach bar.'

'You know I can't do that,' Caleb twirled me again, this time keeping my back to him as he moved his hands to my waist, moving us in unison to the music.

More daggers came my way. Great! I certainly wasn't going to make any more girl friends tonight.

'We're going to the ladies' room, be back in a few,' April called over the music.

I nodded in response, watching the three of them walk towards our table, catching Grayson's eye only for a moment but what I saw in those baby blues looked an awful lot like the daggers I'd been getting from the other woman on the dancefloor.

Strange, I thought, turning back to Caleb.

'You can do whatever you want, it's your life, you need to live it for you,' I continued, not letting him off that easy.

'You're great, you know that?' Caleb suddenly said, pulling me in a little too close.

'You're not too bad yourself,' I laughed, trying to lighten the mood. 'You know, I need the little girl's room too,' I tried to take a step back, putting some distance between us.

Maybe I should have taken my chances with Grayson.

'What is it with women going to the bathroom together? What do you really do in there?' Caleb smiled a wicked smile and I couldn't help laughing.

Swatting him away, I told him I'd be back in a minute.

After fighting my way through the packed bar, I finally made it to the bathroom, but couldn't see April or Paige, so I went into one of the stalls, realising I did in fact need to use the bathroom, which was no wonder after all those drinks.

I stood in the bathroom stall a moment longer – that last cocktail had gone to my head and I really didn't want to end up falling on my butt, making an idiot of myself tonight in front of Grayson, Caleb and their friends.

I hadn't been paying much attention to anything or anyone, until I heard Grayson's name and recognized April's voice.

I was about to join them when something stopped me.

'I mean it's like history is repeating itself. Have you seen the way they've been looking at her? I totally get it, she seems great and gorgeous, of course, and the fact that she's a New Yorker gives her an air of sophistication, but didn't they learn their lesson the first time around? I don't want to see either of them go through that again, it would destroy them, for good this time.'

'I know, but they're big boys, they know what they're getting themselves into,' that was Paige.

'Do they though? They both seem oblivious of the other's intentions,' April again.

'She's nothing like Catherine though, do you remember how self-centred she was? That was half the problem, she wanted the attention from both of them. Sophie doesn't seem like that at all,' Paige sounded sincere. What on earth was going on, and who was Catherine?

'You're right, she seems the complete opposite of Catherine. Poor girl, I just hope she knows what she's getting herself into,' April said sounding almost sad.

After waiting another few moments, until I was certain the coast was clear, I exited the stall, taking my time washing my hands.

Looking up at my reflection in the mirror, I replayed the conversation I'd just overheard in my head. I needed to get some air.

Instead of going back the way I came, I headed out one of the side entrances, which led directly onto the sand, the water not much further.

Taking my shoes off, I walked along the sand, away from the sounds and lights of the bar, into the darkness, where I could be alone with my thoughts.

Who was Catherine and what had happened to make April and Paige worry that history was repeating itself?

And what had they meant about Grayson and Caleb's intentions?

I wasn't full of myself, by any means, but I wasn't blind either. I'd noticed the way Grayson sometimes watched me when he thought I wasn't looking, that deeply intense look in his eyes.

As for Caleb, he wasn't exactly discreet. I'd caught him blatantly checking me out more than once, but that didn't necessarily mean anything, Caleb was a flirt, end of story.

He checked most women out, I was certain of that.

Dipping my toes in the cool water, my mind drifted to Luke and I wished more than anything I could talk to him.

Ask him what was going on and what I was doing, because it suddenly felt like I was heading down a very rocky road. One I couldn't return from.

He would have known exactly what to say to set the world to rights. At least to set my world to rights, he always did.

He was the one who would talk me through my writers' block, telling me to step away from whichever book I was working on, to quiet my mind and lo and behold, it always worked.

He was the one who would calm me down if I was ranting about something that, looking back now, was probably meaningless in the grand scheme of things.

He was my rock and I needed him.

I wanted to scream into the darkness, give him back to me!

A strong, warm hand grasped my shoulder and I almost did scream.

'Grayson! Oh my God, you nearly gave me a heart-attack!'

'Likewise, we didn't know where you were.' I could see his face under the moonlight and hear the concern in his voice.

'I'm sorry, I didn't mean to worry anyone, I just needed some air.'

'Are you ok?' Grayson wiped my cheek and it felt wet.

Had I been crying? I hadn't even realised.

'Yeah, I'm fine, just thinking of Luke. I could really use his advice right about now and he gave the best advice, you know? He never judged or took sides, he would simply sit and listen, and then give an unbiased opinion, which would usually be exactly what I needed to hear.'

'You must really miss him,' Grayson said quietly, looking out across the water. 'I know it's not the same, but I'm here for you Sophie. Any time you need to talk, day or night, I'm always here.'

I let Grayson's words sink in for a moment, before reaching out and squeezing his hand.

'Thank you, that means a lot to me, Grayson.' I was truly touched by his words.

We stood there in silence, still hand in hand for what felt like an eternity, until Grayson gently drew his hand back.

'We should get back before Caleb sends out a search party,' Grayson's voice was thick with emotion.

I didn't say anything, simply let him lead the way back to the others, who were now all on the dancefloor, calling us over.

'If you can't beat 'em?' Grayson smiled, taking my hand, leading me to the dancefloor, where we spent the rest of the night, getting lost in the music.

I don't think any of us really took much notice when the music died down, we were having far too much fun, but as the crowd dispersed, we realised it was time to go.

After saying goodbye to everyone, Grayson, Caleb and I hopped in the taxi and a short while later we were being dropped off at the entrance to the farm.

The three of us walked the suddenly exceptionally long winding road towards my cottage, despite me insisting I could make it there just fine, but of course Grayson and Caleb wouldn't have it. So I let them walk me to my door, one brother on either side, like my own personal bodyguards.

'Your friends are really great,' I told them both.

'They're your friends now too, you passed their test,' Caleb joked but I couldn't help wondering just how much truth was in that statement, especially after what I'd overheard.

We eventually made it to the cottage, thank goodness. All I wanted was a hot shower and to climb into bed. I couldn't believe it was two o'clock in the morning! I hadn't stayed out this late in, well, I couldn't even remember the last time.

Unlocked my front door, I stepped inside before turning to say goodnight to Grayson and Caleb.

Both brothers looked at me expectantly and I felt like it

was prom night and my date was waiting patiently for his goodnight kiss.

Except there were two of them – both looking at me with different levels of intensity.

I wasn't sure if I was too tipsy for this, or not drunk enough. Either way, it was time to call it a night.

'Thank you both for a great night, I had a lot of fun,' I told them both.

'We should definitely do it again soon,' Grayson replied first.

'Definitely, soon,' then Caleb.

Still watching me expectantly.

'Well, goodnight. And thank you for walking me home,' I said, taking a step further inside, hoping they got the hint.

'Goodnight, Sophie,' Grayson.

'Goodnight,' Caleb.

Closing the door softly behind me, I leaned my back against the cool wood as April's words sounded in my head.

What was I getting myself into, indeed?

As much as I wanted to know who Catherine was, I never found the right moment to ask either of the brothers.

In the weeks that followed and the more time went on, the less I thought about what I'd overheard and the whole night simply became a wonderful, fun memory.

Perhaps being tipsy had me blowing the whole thing out of proportion. In the cold light of day, it hadn't seemed quite that bad.

Or was I just burying it, not wanting to know the truth?

That annoying voice in the back of my mind chimed in.

Oh, be quiet, I shushed, focusing on Apollo. We were in the paddock and I was astounded, as always, at his progress, now happy to let the others near him, although he wasn't always thrilled about it, but at least it was a start.

It meant Grayson or Caleb or even Sam could take him out if I was busy elsewhere on the farm.

I had fallen head over heels in love with all the animals and I loved working here, more than I would have ever thought possible a month and a half ago.

It was so strange to think I'd been here such a short time when it felt like this was already my home, the place I belonged.

Days like today were my favourite kind; I'd stopped to check on the three new calves and their adoptive mom, Buttercup, who was the sanctuary's foster mom to most of the animals. Even other species.

Buttercup was the most affectionate and loving cow, so it was a no brainer to pair her with Violet, Daisy and Snowdrop – who was currently trying to sit in my lap.

I laughed and fell back on the soft grass, Snowdrop flopped down beside me, resting her head on my arm.

'Hi, little one,' I cooed and stroked her face.

I loved them all and couldn't imagine my life without any of them in it.

Kaitlyn teased me whenever I sent her photos with the animals, saying I was becoming a country bumpkin, but I think deep down she wished she were here too. Or at least not in New York.

I was going to make it my mission to try get her out here

and fall in love with this place, so she would move here too.

Until then, I enjoyed the days like today, when I got to lay in the grass, under a blue sky, watching white puffy clouds drift by, with Snowdrop by my side.

Things didn't stand still for very long though.

'I got a call today,' Sam told Grayson at dinner, one exceptionally hot July evening.

The five of us were sitting around the table on the porch (it was too hot to eat inside), having just finished a meal I'd made. Under the supervision of Rosie, of course.

I was actually becoming a fairly good cook, thanks to Rosie and my mom's amazing cooking skills.

'From a ranch in Norton, Virginia. They found us online, thanks to Sophie's web-thingy, and they need our help with some of their horses and smaller animals. They're on the verge of going under and they don't want anything bad to happen to the animals, so they've asked if we could take some of them in. I think we can do it now that the old barn is back to its former glory and we have the new shelter too,' Sam continued.

The website had been a huge success. We'd already started receiving donations and had a handful of volunteers, with a few more possible recruits to see next week.

Some of them helped out during the week, others at weekends, which made me feel less guilty for going home at weekends.

But thanks to the extra pairs of hands, we were able to repair the old barn, which meant we had more stables.

'The thing is, your brother is signed up for the agricultural fair in Charleston, so I'm going to need you to go to Norton. I was thinking, Sophie could go with you. It'll be great experience for her. If that would be ok with you, Sophie?' Sam asked, turning towards me.

'Of course, I'd love to go,' I hope I sounded convincing because the thought of a road trip, alone, with Grayson, terrified me.

'Good, then it's settled,' Sam said, resting back in his chair.

'When do we leave?' Grayson asked casually.

Was I the only one feeling nervous about this?

'Day after tomorrow would be ideal. It's about a six-hour drive there, so you're best off staying overnight and collecting the animals the following morning. I'll call ahead and make sure they're ready to go.'

Overnight? As in spending the night with Grayson!

Ok, not literally spending the night together, not like that, but where would we stay? I only hoped we'd get a motel or something and have separate rooms. I had no desire to live out that particular chick flick cliché.

You know the ones; two people go on a road trip, get stuck in some small town with only one room available, end up sharing a room – sharing a bed!

That wasn't going to be my story and I couldn't imagine Grayson wanting to share a room. But I did wonder if he would want to sleep in his truck instead.

That might be worse!

To say the following day was a mad rush to make sure everything was done before our trip, was an understatement.

Getting up at the crack of dawn, I took Apollo out for a few hours, even treating him with a trip to our clearing – which is what I'd started referring to it as, since that's where we made our first connection.

He was such a good-natured boy. I didn't want to leave him.

I knew it was silly, we were only going to be away for two days, tops, but I was going to miss him, given that once we got back, I'd be leaving again, to go to my parents for the weekend.

'I'll be back before you know it, ok?' I promised him and he nuzzled my neck.

'I'll miss you too boy,' I stroked his long beautiful face.

I knew he would be in good hands with Sam and Rosie (he wasn't quite ready to let any of the newbie volunteers near him just yet).

'How about we make a little detour on the way home?'

He neighed and I took that as a yes.

I got back in the saddle (this was something apparently only I had the privilege of doing and I didn't take it lightly) and steered him in the direction of the lake. We had time for a quick dip and a drink for Apollo, before heading back to the barn.

As we neared the lake, I could already feel the cool water on my skin, and couldn't wait to dive in.

It turned out I wasn't the only one who thought that.

'Grayson, hi,' I stuttered, not sure if I should stay or go.

'Hey, Sophie, great minds, huh,' he smiled easily and I figured that meant it was ok to stay.

'I hope I'm not intruding,' I said, dismounting Apollo with a lot more ease and grace than I had a few weeks ago. Cringing at how clumsy I'd been at the beginning.

'Not at all, come on in, the waters great,' he turned around once again so I could strip down to my underwear and dive in the deliciously cool water.

'I think this is fast becoming my favourite place too,' I sighed when I surfaced from beneath the water.

'It's our very own little piece of paradise,' Grayson replied, floating on his back.

'Is it ok that I'm coming with you tomorrow?' I asked, unsure if it was something he preferred to do with a family member, instead of an inexperienced city girl.

'Of course. Dad was right, it'll be great experience for you, and I could use the help,' he replied in the same casual tone. Not giving anything away.

'Ok good, I didn't want to feel like an annoying little sister tagging along,' I replied, relieved.

'Good thing you aren't my sister then,' Grayson gave me a devilish grin and suddenly the nerves were right back again, fluttering around in my belly like giant butterflies trying to break free.

We floated around a while longer, making small talk about the trip and how we could take turns driving until I reluctantly got out of the water to get dressed and head back to the sanctuary. I still had work to do after all.

'I need to get some supplies from town later, so I won't see you at dinner, but I'll see you tomorrow morning, six sharp,' Grayson called from the water, once I was dressed and he'd turned around to face me.

'I'll be ready,' I replied, feeling like I was about to go on my first date, which of course was utterly ridiculous.

This was a business trip. A rescue mission, if you will.

That was all it was, I thought, trying to convince myself. Not doing a great job, I might add.

I was exhausted!

The kind of tired that makes your feet feel like lead and the simple act of placing one foot in front of the other require intense concentration, or you'll end up face down in the dirt.

So, when I saw Caleb waiting for me outside my cottage when I got back later that day, I couldn't pretend to be happy to see him – or anyone.

I'd just left the main house, after practically inhaling dinner, with Sam and Rosie, and all I wanted to do was shower and crawl into my soft, comfy, cosy bed and drift away into a blissful sleep.

I wasn't really up for entertaining at the moment.

'Sophie, hi. Rough day?' Caleb asked as I got closer.

'You could say that. Just trying to get everything ready before we leave tomorrow,' I replied, stifling a yawn.

'Well I won't keep you long, you look exhausted. I've been getting ready to leave for Charleston tomorrow too,' he was rambling, why was he rambling? He never rambled. He seemed nervous too, which was extremely unlike Caleb. 'Anyway, I just wanted to see you before we leave. I hope you have a good trip. Don't let my brother get on your nerves too much,' he half laughed. He was acting so weird!

'Thanks, Caleb, you too. I hope everything goes well at the fair.'

'Hey, Sophie,' Caleb called back, just as he started to leave.

'Yeah?' I turned around, the front door still half open.

'Maybe we could grab dinner sometime, you know, once we get back?'

'Sure Caleb, that would be nice,' I replied, trying not to yawn in his face.

And it was only when he brightened and gave me a whopping smile that I suddenly wondered what I'd just agreed to.

Dinner with a co-worker, or a date with the boss's son?

Perhaps I'd just stay in Norton, it seemed far less complicated than life here on the farm with the Danvers brothers!

Chapter 8

My alarm sounded at five o'clock the following morning and all I wanted to do was lob it against the wall, crawl back under the blanket and go back to sleep.

Unfortunately, things didn't work that way, not out here anyway. So I got up, grudgingly, showered, had a cup of coffee and grabbed my overnight bag which I'd placed by the front door the night before.

Taking one last look around, to make sure everything was turned off, or unplugged, I locked up and walked the short distance to the main house, where Grayson was securing the horse trailer to his truck.

'Good morning,' he said, far too brightly for this hour.

'Morning,' I grumbled.

'Not much of a morning person, huh?' Grayson chuckled.

'This isn't morning, this is pre-morning. No one should be awake this early.'

'You should be used to it by now, city girl,' Grayson retorted.

'We can't all be rays of sunshine like you, country boy,' I threw back.

'How many cups of coffee will you need before you can

function?' Grayson tried to ask with a straight face but burst into laughter at the unimpressed look on my face.

'A few,' I mumbled, getting into his truck.

In my defence, I wasn't usually this grouchy in the morning and I wasn't up much later than this during the week when I was working, but I hadn't had the best night's sleep last night thanks to my brain working overtime and giving me absurd dreams which involved a half-naked Grayson who then morphed into Caleb who morphed back into Grayson.

Damn these brothers, playing havoc with my brain, my sleep pattern, my life, it would seem.

After an hour on the road (and another coffee) I was starting to feel somewhat with it.

With the radio turned right up, I found myself humming along to songs that were fast becoming familiar to me.

Feeling my phone buzz in my pocket, I felt a pang of guilt when I saw Kaitlyn's name. I'd been so busy these last few days that I hadn't had a chance to call her.

'Kaitlyn, hi,' I answered, as Grayson turned the radio down.

'Sophie, I was beginning to think you'd been abducted by aliens, or worse, children of the corn.'

I snorted, thinking, for a brief second, I wish I had been.

'I'm sorry, things have been a little crazy. I've been getting ready for a last-minute trip to Virginia, to collect a few horses than need rehoming, so it's been non-stop at the sanctuary. We're on the road now actually. How are things with you?'

'Never mind that, who's we?' Kaitlyn asked, missing nothing.

'Huh?' I pretended not to know what she meant.

'You said we're on the road, so who's we?'

'Grayson and I. Sam thought it would be a good idea for me to come along and get some experience,' I explained, feeling conscious that Grayson was right next to me and could hear every word, even though he graciously kept his eyes fixed on the road, pretending not to listen.

'Experience in what exactly?' Kaitlyn laughed. 'So, a road trip with the brooding Grayson Danvers huh? Sounds juicy.'

Naturally I'd told Kaitlyn about Grayson and his occasional intensity, she was my best friend after all, we had no secrets from each other.

'Yep, that's right,' I replied casually, hoping she would get the hint.

'Don't worry, I know you can't talk now, but I expect all the gory details as soon as possible.'

'Sure, ok,' there wasn't much else I could say.

We caught up for a while longer, Kaitlyn was having a rough time at work and was planning a trip to Beaufort in the next few weeks. I couldn't wait to see her.

'I have to go, but I'll call you again soon. Take care of yourself and enjoy your mini getaway. And Soph? Have fun. You deserve it and you deserve to be happy. Love you, always,' Kaitlyn said, and I felt my eyes water.

Gees, I was turning into such a sap.

'Love you always,' I replied, and we hung up.

'Sorry, that was Kaitlyn,' I told Grayson.

I'd already told them all about her and couldn't wait for them to meet her.

'That's ok. Are things any better for her at work?' Grayson asked and I was surprised he remembered.

I was pretty sure I'd only mentioned her work problems to him once before. He clearly had a good memory.

'Not really, but she's planning on coming to Beaufort soon, so that'll be good for her I think, to get away and get some clarity. I can't wait to see her, and I can't wait for you to meet her, you'll love her. She's the best.'

'If she's anything like you, she'll fit right in,' Grayson's compliment had my cheeks burning and I was grateful he couldn't see me.

Large grey thunder clouds had started rolling in up ahead.

We were only about two hours outside of Norton when the rain started to pour. Splattering the windscreen faster than the wipers could clear it.

'Maybe we should pull over,' I suggested, worried about driving in these conditions.

Storms out here could get real ugly, real fast, and I didn't want to be stuck on the road if that happened.

'Yeah, I think you're right, it doesn't look like it's going to ease off anytime soon. I'll pull over at the next exit,' Grayson replied, slowing down even more.

'The closest town is Abingdon and that's another twenty minutes away,' I told Grayson after checking the GPS and re-programming it.

I didn't like the idea of being out in this for another

twenty minutes, but we were due to travel through Abingdon anyway, so it would only mean stopping until the rain eased off, which would hopefully be soon.

Then again, maybe not, I thought nervously, another ten minutes later when it only seemed to get worse.

As if the hammering rain wasn't bad enough, it was now thundering, and we'd seen a few flashes of lightning as well.

'It's ok, we're almost there,' Grayson soothed, as anther flash of lightening cracked through the sky, making me jump.

We drove past a sign for Abingdon and I breathed a sigh of relief. He was right, we were almost there.

I couldn't even take in the surroundings, for keeping my eyes glued on the road ahead. Two sets of eyes were better than one, as my dad always used to say, if we were ever caught in a Carolina storm, as he called them, and he was right.

As we approached a rather rickety looking wooden bridge, crossing over a gushing river below, I noticed something up ahead.

'Is that...' I trailed off trying to get a better look, hoping it wasn't what I thought. 'Oh my God Grayson, that car is losing control!'

Almost at the far end of the bridge, a car was suddenly veering towards the railing.

I went to open my door, but Grayson grabbed my other hand.

'What are you doing?' He asked, eyes wide.

'We have to help them,' I replied, trying (and failing) to

break his iron grasp.

'And we will, but we'll do it safely,' Grayson looked back to the car, which, thank heavens had now stopped moving. Albeit too close to the side of the bridge. 'Stay put, I'll drive us across. The only way we can help them and keep the trailer, is by making it across and unhooking the trailer on the other side. I'll then back up and tow them out.'

Grayson started to inch his truck onto the bridge, which creaked and groaned under the weight of it.

It didn't look like it was going to hold, but I trusted him. I knew him well enough to know that he wouldn't put us at risk.

At least he was being calm (or appeared calm, on the outside) and rational. We couldn't risk losing the trailer, for the sake of getting the animals back to the sanctuary.

As we drew closer, I could see movement and my heart sunk when I realised there were five people in the car.

Two in the front, I assumed the parents, and three scared children in the back. The all looked shellshocked.

Rolling my window down I yelled out to get their attention.

'We're coming back to help you, hold on,' I yelled through the pouring rain, meeting the drivers frantic gaze.

Continuing past them, another bolt of lightning struck, this time much, much closer and we heard the bridge groaning in protest.

This could not be happening! My heart raced and my hands trembled.

We needed to get them out, now!

Grayson's truck had just reached the road on the other

side of the bridge, when the bridge shifted, moving the trailer along with it.

And although it only moved a few inches, it was enough to stop us in our tracks. I gripped onto Grayson's arm.

'It's ok Sophie, we're going to be fine. I need to check if the hitch is broken before I try again. Don't move!' Grayson ordered before stepping out into the rain.

Yeah sure, like I could just sit here and wait. I got out and followed him around to the back of his truck.

'Of course you couldn't stay put,' he simply shook his head while checking the hitch.

I didn't know much about these kinds of things, but it didn't look good.

I was about to offer him a hand when an awful sound, like the blood curdling sound of nails down a chalkboard, came from the bridge.

I looked up instantly, fearing the worst. The car was starting to move again.

'Grayson, we need to help them. You get this sorted out, I'm going to see if I can help them out of the car.'

'Sophie, no, just give me a minute,' Grayson pleaded.

'We don't have time, this isn't up for debate Grayson, I'm going to help them. You get this off the bridge before it drags us all down with it,' I gestured to the suddenly dauntingly large trailer, perched ominously on the unstable bridge. 'Trust me,' my eyes pleaded with his.

He knew I was right. I didn't wait for his response, I took off back in the direction we'd just come from, towards the car.

As I got closer, I realised that they must have hit the railing, which was, in part, the reason the front of the car was now teetering on the edge of the bridge and which was also partially what was keeping the car from going over completely.

Part of the railing was wedged against the side of the car, as though it was holding onto the car, trying to prevent it going over.

Since the front of the car was the nearest point to the edge, I went with my instincts, get the parents out first.

The driver's side window was open, and I peered in at the frightened family.

'It's going to be ok. We're going to help you out. I need you both to slowly get out of the car.'

'Please, help our children first,' the mother cried out, tears streaming down her pretty face.

'I will, I promise, but we need to get more weight in the back of the car, so it doesn't go over, ok?' I tried to calmly explain my logic. 'Trust me, as soon as you're out I'll help your children. Now give me your hand,' I reached over for the wife first, since she was closest to the edge, and the angry river below, I noted, trying not to focus too much on that.

Don't look down, don't look down, I repeated over and over, not wanting to imagine what would happen if the car went over.

The river below was flowing faster, and it looked about to burst its banks. Come on, Sophie, you can do this, I told myself sternly.

The woman was small and didn't weigh much – I was

grateful for small mercies at this point, so she was easy enough to help out of the car.

It was only when the car creaked that I held my breath for a split second, before helping her husband out of the car.

Now to get the kids out.

'Hey there, it's going to be ok, just give me your hand.'

One down, straight into mom's arms.

Next one out, into dad's arms.

One more to go. A little girl, who must have only been about two or three, younger than her siblings and the most afraid.

She looked at me from the far side of the car, eyes wide with fear.

'It's ok, I won't let anything happen to you, but I need you to reach out and give me your hand,' I tried to stretch as far as I could without leaning against the car for fear of any extra weight pushing it over. 'Come on, you can do it,' I tried to smile comfortingly, but I must have failed miserably.

The poor little thing scrambled down onto the floor of the car.

When would this nightmare end! It felt all too familiar, like the events from that faithful night in my New York apartment were playing over.

Only this time I vowed I wasn't going to lose anyone. I wouldn't let anything happen to this family.

As carefully as I could, I leaned into the car, resting my hand precariously on the seat, stretching out for the little girl who had big crocodile tears in her eyes, but didn't make a move in any direction.

'It's going to be ok, we're getting you out of here,' I tried to put on my best calm, comforting voice, but I wasn't kidding anyone, I was terrified.

Suddenly the car started to twist, and I braced myself, ending up completely inside the car. I could hear her parents cries behind me, but I kept my eyes fixed on the little girl.

It's now or never, I thought, reaching out I grabbed her, holding her only for a second before placing her safely on the bridge, trying not to handle her too roughly.

And that was all it took for my whole world to shift.

I heard the screeching of metal on metal and somewhere in the distance I heard Grayson call out my name, but it was too late, the car was going over and it was taking me down with it.

I wasn't going down without a fight, I thought vehemently, but I guess the universe had other ideas for me.

I tried to push off, to jump out of the car before it went over the bridge, but as the car careened and twisted, the door slammed shut, sending me flying backwards, hitting my head hard against the opposite window before being thrown around once again when the car dove nose first into the rushing water below.

Water started pouring in so fast, too fast! I couldn't think straight, but instinct kicked in and I knew I needed to get out, now!

Trying the back door, it didn't budge. Kiddie lock, damn it!

Plan B; climb into the front seat and out the window. Yes, that was it, the driver's window had been open.

My limbs moved slowly through the gushing water, which was already almost to the roof of the car. I didn't have much time.

Finally making it into the driver's seat and although the water level was just under my chin, in that moment, I thought I was going to make it. I was getting out of this death trap!

But as I reached for the door frame, to pull myself through the window, something jarred the car, lurching me forward, my head hitting the steering wheel and that's when it happened. That's when everything went black and I lost the fight.

Chapter 9

When I opened my eyes, I felt different, lighter somehow. Looking around, I felt confused and disorientated.

A beautiful garden surrounded me; neatly trimmed umbrella trees lined the edges, while flowers of every colour grew in neat rows in front of them. In the middle of the garden stood a beautiful fountain with a little angel perched on the top, spouting water from its mouth.

The air was sweet with the scent of the flowers and a gentle breeze rustled the leaves.

I had the strangest sense that I should know where I was, but it wasn't coming to me. Until it hit me like a wrecking ball – the bridge, the river.

My heart pounded in my chest. Breath, Sophie, breath, but it was no use. I stumbled backwards, landing on a little wooden bench.

I think deep down I knew where I was, but my mind refused to believe, or accept it.

'Why so glum, chum?' A voice said behind me.

It was a voice I would have known anywhere.

Luke

My heart did somersaults. My head spun around so fast I probably looked like something from the exorcist.

'Luke,' I breathed out, unable to move for just a few seconds, before launching myself into his arms.

He laughed. I cried.

'This really must be heaven,' I finally said, my sobs subsiding, as I pulled back and looked at the face I thought I'd never see again.

'This isn't heaven, my love,' he replied, stroking my face.

'Am I dreaming?' I wondered aloud, relishing in the feel of his touch.

'You're somewhere in between,' Luke said calmly, and I opened my eyes to look at him again.

'I don't understand.'

We sat on the bench and he took my hands in his, 'You were in a terrible accident, Sophie. You were under the water for a long time, but Grayson got to you and pulled you out.'

I didn't remember that.

'Your body is in the hospital, but your soul, well, your soul, my love, is somewhere between life and death.'

'How can I see you?' I asked, certain this was all just a dream.

'Let's just say I got a hall pass to come and see you,' Luke chuckled. 'And to send you back,' he continued, more sombrely.

'Send me back? I don't want to go back, I want to stay here, with you. We belong together Luke, you were taken away from me too soon!' I tumbled over the words, feeling my heart racing.

I'd only just got him back. I couldn't bear the thought of losing him once again.

'It's ok, Sophie,' he soothed.

'It's not ok,' I got up angrily, 'None of this is ok. I can't lose you again, I won't survive it a second time, Luke.'

'Don't you see Sophie? I'm always with you, always watching over you. You never lost me. I've been with you all along. I was with you when you left New York and I've been with you all the while you've been in Beaufort. I live forever in your heart,' Luke placed his hand over my heart, and I felt an odd tingling sensation.

'I'm not letting you go this time, I'm staying with you,' I said sternly.

'Soph, you know what happened to me wasn't your fault. There was no way either of us could have known,' Luke said to my unspoken thoughts.

'I should have seen the warning signs. I should have known!' I argued.

'There were no signs, my love. It was simply my time,' Luke said gently.

'How can you say that? We had our whole lives ahead of us. It was not your time!' More sobs raked through my body.

'I can't explain why it happened, or why it was my time, but I've come to terms with it and I've realised that He has a plan for each of us. We just need to trust in Him and let Him guide us through life and Soph, this isn't your time. You've still got so much good to do at the sanctuary and further afield. You have to go back, my love. I know it's hard, but trust in me, trust that I know it's the right thing to do.'

I didn't know what to say to that, but I let his words sink in, thinking about my parents, Paul and Sarah, my niece or nephew, and as badly as I wanted to stay with him, I knew he was right, I couldn't stay here.

'Can we sit a while longer?' I asked quietly, resigned.

'Of course we can.'

For the longest time we simply sat on the bench, Luke's arm wrapped around me, my head on his shoulder, holding on to him for as long as I could.

I had no idea how much time had passed when Luke broke the silence.

'It's time, my love.'

I could feel it, as though a tether was pulling me back, pulling me away from Luke and my eyes blurred with fresh tears.

'Before you go, I want you to promise me something,' Luke took my face in his hands, eyes serious.

I couldn't speak so I simply nodded.

'Promise me you'll forgive yourself. You couldn't have prevented what happened, no one could have. Know that I've come to terms with it and I'm at peace now. But above all else, promise me that you'll move forward with your life. You have the biggest heart, Soph, let people in, let them see that. Open your heart again, love again, be young and reckless and live, not just for you, but for the both of us, let me live on through you.'

Tears poured down my face and I could only nod again, knowing full well I couldn't find my voice.

'That's my girl. That's all I wish for,' Luke said, pulling

me in for one final embrace. ‘I love you Sophie, forever,’ he whispered.

‘I’ll love you forever,’ I whispered back, chocking back the sobs.

Luke kissed me tenderly then for the second time, my whole world went black.

‘Welcome back,’ a gentle voice said. ‘You’re ok.’ I felt a soft hand touching my arm and I blinked rapidly, trying to bring the world back into view.

Slowly shapes started to form and a figure standing next to me came moved. I tried to rub my eyes, but something pulled on my wrist.

I tried to ask where I was, but my voice was raspy, and my throat felt like I’d swallowed a sea urchin.

‘You might want to refrain from talking for a while, you took in a lot of water, but you got lucky. Your friend over there saved your life.’

After blinking several times before the room became clearer and the elderly nurse next to me smiled. Resting her hand gently on my arm, reassuringly, she nodded her head to the far side of the room.

I followed her gaze and saw Grayson curled up in what was possibly the smallest chair ever, looking extremely uncomfortable, but passed out cold and I couldn’t help but smile too.

I couldn’t remember everything, just flashes of water, a car, a family.

I felt too exhausted to try and remember so I slumped back onto the pillows that the nurse had been propping under my head.

'You rest dear, you're going to feel tired for a little while, but you're going to be just fine, you just need to rest now,' the nurse squeezed my hand and left the room.

I must have fallen asleep because when I woke the light was different, dimmer.

Turning my head to the window, to see nothing but darkness outside, I also noticed there was no Grayson.

I couldn't understand why, but that awful icy prickling sensation that I'd become far too accustomed to, started creeping up my spine and I tried to sit up, needing to find him.

'Whoa, easy, tiger,' Grayson burst through the door and looked as relieved to see me awake as I was to see him at all.

I relaxed back down.

'How are you feeling?' He pulled the chair closer to my hospital bed and I noticed how tired he looked.

'Ok, I think,' I croaked.

'The doctors said it might take a few days for your voice to go back to normal,' Grayson explained.

'How long have I been here?'

I tried to remember what Grayson had been wearing, had he changed or were those the same clothes? But my mind just wasn't playing ball. Instead, it felt as though it was moving through a thick fog, holding my memories back, weighing them down.

'Two days,' his voice was tainted with concern.

Two days! I'd lost two days!

'The family!' I almost shrieked and then winced, that hurt.

'They're ok. Thanks to you they were all fine.' He stood and started pacing. 'What were you thinking Sophie!' Grayson leaned against the window ledge, looking exasperated. 'You could have gotten yourself killed.'

He raked his hands through his dishevelled hair before sitting back down again.

'I'm sorry, I've just been so worried about you,' he continued after a moments silence.

'I'm sorry,' I eventually whispered, not knowing what else to say.

'You have nothing to apologise for, you did a wonderful thing for that family. I just can't remember the last time I was so scared, seeing you go over…' He trailed off, resting his head in his hands.

I reached out and took one of his hands in my own.

'I'm ok.'

I was starting to realise that Grayson's angry bear impressions came from a place of concern for me and it was truly touching.

He gave my hand a gentle squeeze before the nurse returned to check on me.

After a lot of arguing, mainly done by me, the hospital agreed to release me the following day, only on the condition that I stay in town for another few days, close to the hospital, and don't travel or do anything to exert myself.

With Grayson playing the loyal bodyguard, that would be nigh on impossible, even if I had the energy to, which I didn't.

Near death experiences were immensely draining.

So eventually, around midday, I was released. While being wheeled to the car, yes, wheeled – in a wheelchair, in case that wasn't obvious enough – the little voice inside my head whispered, be careful what you wish for.

I folded my arms, knowing full well that I probably looked like a petulant child, but seriously, this was ridiculous. I was perfectly capable of walking, thank you very much. It was humiliating and completely unnecessary.

'The only place that had a room available is an inn, on the outskirts of town. Apparently, this is a busy time for Abingdon,' Grayson explained as he pulled away from the hospital.

I didn't care, I just wanted a hot shower, to be able to wash my hair, and a clean change of clothes.

'Problem is,' he continued hesitantly, 'there was only one room available.'

'Oh,'

You have to be kidding!

'I mean, it's a twin room, but we can try find somewhere else if it would make you feel more comfortable,' the words rushed out and I smiled.

'It's fine Grayson, we can be roomies for a few nights.'

Watching the town go by on the short drive to the inn, I was able to take in its picturesque tree lined streets, with pretty flowers on every corner.

I had been slightly preoccupied, what with trying not to die and all, when we'd arrived, but taking the town in now, I noticed how green it was and I had the strangest sensation of déjà vu.

How odd, I knew I'd never been here before. Perhaps it reminded me of Beaufort. That had to be it.

I didn't have much time to dwell on the feeling. We arrived at the inn a few minutes later and it fitted the pretty little town perfectly. It was picture postcard perfection.

Complete with white picket fence and a pristine lawn, the inn oozed southern charm.

A wooden plaque hung just above the stairs leading onto the front porch, with deep blue curly writing that read: Dragonfly Inn

It mustered thoughts balmy summer nights. Sitting on the porch swing chair, sipping iced tea, listening to the crickets serenading you while you star gazed.

Grayson held the door open for me and we entered the reception area.

The décor inside matched the exterior perfectly. It was all pale yellows and whites with little warm touches here and there, giving it a warm, inviting feel.

Grayson went over and spoke to the young woman at the front desk, while I waited.

I couldn't help noticing the way she shyly looked at him from under long lashes, her cheeks tinted with the faintest hint of a blush.

I watched in fascination as she tried to keep her head down and be professional but failed miserably, glancing up at him when he wasn't looking.

'Here's your spare room key, Mr. Danvers. If there's anything else you need, please don't hesitate to ask,' she stuttered, handing him the key and it was all I could do not to burst out laughing right there.

'What's so funny?' Grayson asked, as we headed up the stairs to our room.

'I've never quite noticed the affect you have on people,' I told him, thinking about the nurse at the hospital and the girls from the beach bar, from the fourth weekend, who hadn't only been drooling over Caleb.

'And what affect would that be exactly?'

'You…' I thought a moment, trying to find the right word. 'You dazzle them with your rugged good looks and charm,' I giggled, thinking of the poor girl downstairs.

'My rugged good looks, huh?' Grayson raised an eyebrow.

'I mean, you're not bad – for a country boy,' I teased, nudging him with my elbow.

'You're too kind,' he replied dryly, but I saw his smile. 'This is us,' he opened our bedroom door and it didn't fail to impress.

It was a far larger room than I'd imagined, with two double beds against the far wall and a small seating area, consisting of a couch and coffee table.

Paintings of pretty woodland landscapes and invitingly warm sunsets dotted the walls around the room, while a large wooden framed mirror stood in the far corner, near the bathroom.

Our room was on the top floor and I couldn't resist walking out onto the balcony to take in the breath-taking view.

'Nice, isn't it?' Grayson asked, stepping out behind me.

'It's beautiful,' I replied, looking out across the pristine grounds.

Another perfectly kept garden spread out beneath us, the lawn extending as far as the eye could see.

A few benches had been placed under the trees that ran the length of the garden, while tables and chairs were neatly positioned on the deck area below, overlooking the garden.

Beyond the lawn, a woodland, which seemed to stretch out forever, engulfed the property in a protective embrace, keeping the rest of the world out.

No wonder there hadn't been many rooms left, it was beautiful inn.

I breathed in deeply, letting the smell of jasmine and oak wash through me, revitalising me.

There was something so calming and therapeutic about being in nature (or at least near it, in this case).

'Would you like to take a shower and maybe go for a walk around the grounds before dinner?' Grayson asked from the balcony chair.

'That sounds perfect,' I smiled, before heading back inside, noticing my overnight bag on the bed near the bathroom.

Thank goodness I always packed extra clothes.

Grabbing my bag, I disappeared into the bathroom and stripped out of my clothes, noting the faint sterile smell that always accompanied hospitals.

Turning the shower on as hot as I could handle it, I stepped under the streamy spray, relishing in the feeling, letting the water wash away the events of the last few days, and all the tension that I had unknowingly been holding onto.

When I emerged from the shower, I felt like a new person.

Never underestimate the healing powers of a hot shower.

Towelling my hair off, I noticed something on my chest, directly over my heart.

Odd, I'd never had any birth marks there. Perhaps it was from the accident.

Grabbing a pair of dark blue skinny jeans and pale blue spaghetti strap top with delicate white flowers, I quickly got dressed, before walking back into our room to inspect the mark on my chest in the full-length mirror, since I'd completely steamed up the bathroom mirror and could no longer see a thing.

Moving the strap of my top to get a closer look, a little gasp escaped my lips when I realised it looked like a handprint.

And then, just like that, it all came flooding back.

Every glorious, painful, heart-breaking memory of my dream. Only the handprint on my chest told me it hadn't been a dream.

Somewhere behind me I heard movement and I thought I heard my name, but I couldn't move. I was rooted to the spot, staring at the handprint over my heart, knowing exactly who's hand would fit that mould.

'Sophie, what is, what's wrong?' Grayson gently shook my shoulders, finally bringing me back from my trance.

I looked up at him, eyes wide, mouth slightly agape.

'Sophie?' Grayson's eyes mirrored mine, only, the look in his eyes was concern for me.

It was a look I was becoming all too familiar with.

I couldn't blame him, he probably thought I'd

completely lost my mind. Heck, I thought I'd completely lost my mind.

'It was real. It was all real,' I murmured. 'I saw him.'

'Saw who? Sophie I'm worried, I'm going to call the hospital.' Grayson reached for his phone.

That snapped me back to reality.

'No!'

I grabbed his hand, knowing full well where I'd end up if I told the doctors what was truly wrong – somewhere with padded walls and straitjackets came to mind.

'I saw Luke. I saw my husband.' I could see confusion in the depths of Grayson's blue eyes. 'I think we should take that walk now.'

Chapter 10

As we walked through the grounds, I barely noticed our surroundings, I was on autopilot, stepping one foot in front of the other but paying no particular attention to where we were going.

We reached a bubbling brook, curving its way through the trees, etching itself into the land and I sat down on a large rock next to the water, suddenly feeling exhausted.

'Do you believe in miracles, Grayson?' I asked him, not meeting his gaze.

'Sure, I do,' he replied cautiously, and I got the feeling he was waiting for the crazy to begin.

Well, you asked for it.

'Do you see this?' I stood and showed Grayson the handprint on my chest, hoping more than anything that I hadn't, in fact, lost my mind completely.

When he nodded, I let out a sigh of relief. Well, that's something I guess, I wasn't imagining it.

'What happened? Is it from the accident?'

'No, it was Luke. I saw him just before I woke up in the hospital. I hadn't even remembered it until just now, when I noticed the handprint. I thought it had been a dream. My subconscious seeing what it wanted to.' I touched the handprint and felt a tingle. 'I know how this sounds, Grayson, please believe me, but I'm not making this up, or going crazy. After the accident I remember waking up in a beautiful garden and I thought for sure I was dead. That's when Luke appeared. He said he'd been sent to send me back, that it wasn't my time yet.' My throat constricted and my heart stuttered. I turned to face the brook before continuing.

'I didn't want to go. I didn't want to lose him again. I didn't think I could survive it a second time, but as he always did, he talked me down off the ledge. He told me that I had more to do here and that I had to come back. He told me that he would always be in my heart. That was when he laid his hand over my heart and I guess that's when the imprint appeared somehow. He told me that I needed to forgive myself, that his death hadn't been my fault and that I needed to make peace with it and move on. I promised him that I would live my life again, truly live, for the both of us, but I'm not sure I can keep that promise…' I trailed off. I wasn't sure when I'd started crying, but tears poured down my face and my shoulders shook with silent sobs.

Before I could catch my breath, Grayson engulfed me, holding me together while I let it all out one final time.

Yes, I'd had closure and I'd been able to say my goodbye's to Luke, but I needed to grieve him again, grieve for the man I'd loved for almost a decade. Grieve for the man I'd just lost, for the second time.

The tears streamed, the sobs racked through me, threating to rip me apart, but Grayson's embrace held firm, keeping me intact.

I had no idea how long we stayed like that, but eventually the sobs started to ease and there were no more tears left to cry.

I realised that my arms were wrapped around Grayson, holding on to him for dear life, and I released my grip on him. He loosened his grip but kept his hands on my arms.

'I believe you, Sophie. I believe that you saw Luke,' Grayson barely whispered.

'You do? You don't think I'm crazy?' I wiped my tear stained cheeks.

'I think if a love is strong enough it can overcome anything. Luke obviously loved you as much as you loved him. Enough to find a way back to you. Call it a miracle or call it the power of love, but whichever way you look at it, you're far from crazy, Sophie. You're one of the lucky ones. Not many people get a second chance to say goodbye, to get closure,' Grayson's tone had changed, and I wondered if we were talking about me, or him.

'Thank you, for believing me,' was all I could say.

I knew it wasn't enough to express my gratitude to Grayson, but it was all I could give him in that moment.

'Come on, we should get back before it gets too dark,' Grayson wrapped an arm around my shoulders, pulling me in close, my arm around his waist, and we walked back to the inn, leaning on one another for support, in ways I didn't even know about yet.

Looking at my reflection in the large bathroom mirror, once we were back in our room, I noticed small dark circles under my eyes and how sallow my skin looked.

After splashing cold water on my face and dabbing it dry, I picked up my make-up bag and hoped I had enough in there to make myself look presentable.

Luckily, by the time I was done with my make-up, I no longer looked like something from Dawn of the Dead.

I took a deep, slow breathe in and let it out just as slowly, feeling the tension in my shoulders ease and the weight on my heart lift.

I noticed my anxiety pills in my make-up bag. Taking them out, turning them over in my hands, I opened the cap and poured them down the drain when the realisation hit me that I had been the cause of the attacks all along.

The guilt and pain I'd been carrying around with me had to manifest into something. To go somewhere. And I guess the anxiety attacks were my body's coping mechanism.

Not the best way of dealing, obviously, but Luke had been right. There was nothing anyone could have done.

We couldn't have predicted what was coming. And although I knew I would never stop missing Luke, I was able to admit, after all this time, that it wasn't my fault.

Feeling like the weight of the world had been lifted off my shoulders, I was able to breathe again. No longer stuck in limbo, no longer weighed down by pain and guilt of it all.

I looked up at my reflection once again, touching my chest where Luke's handprint showed, and said a silent vow to him, wherever he was.

I would keep my promise to him, I would start living again.

I would embrace life with all I had. Not just for me, but also for Luke.

'I'm really sorry about earlier, I didn't mean to have a complete meltdown,' I apologised again to Grayson over dinner.

We were seated on the decking area, in the far corner, overlooking the garden. There weren't many other people out on the deck, so we had the entire section to ourselves.

'Would you stop apologising already. You have nothing to apologise for. You've been through a lot, Sophie. More than most people your age should have to go through. No one expects you to keep it together all the time.'

'Well, if I haven't said it already, thank you, Grayson. You saved my life. I'm not sure how I'll ever be able to repay you for that. Or for believing in me, or simply being a shoulder to cry on, quite literally. I guess I could start by buying you a new shirt.'

'Yeah, you did kinda ruin my favourite shirt,' Grayson laughed, ducking when I playfully tried to smack him.

He picked up his wine glass, lifting it towards mine.

'A toast to,' he thought a moment. 'To Luke. To life. And to living it to the full.'

I felt my heart tug, but this time it wasn't out of sadness. It was out of joy.

I clinked glasses with Grayson, and we sipped our wine, just as our dinner arrived.

We ate and drank and exchanged desserts. Ok, I helped myself to Grayson's dessert.

'What?' I asked innocently as I popped a piece of his pie

into my mouth. 'This is the best part about ordering different desserts, we get to sample both,' I grinned and pushed my chocolate fudge cake towards him.

'Mmhmm, you're right, two desserts are far better than one,' he helped himself to another piece of mine, and I couldn't help but smile.

Sitting back, feeling full and content, my mind drifted to the fact that this day had done a full three-sixty, but it was certainly ending on a good note.

'Would you look at that view,' I sighed, gazing up at the breath-taking night sky.

The stars shone so brightly, the moon hung low in the sky, casting silvery light across the grounds, making it feel magical.

'It sure is beautiful,' Grayson's voice was weighed down with something, but before I could ask him if everything was ok, a yawn escaped my lips.

'We should turn in. You must be exhausted.'

Another yawn was the only reply I needed to give him.

After thanking the wait staff, we made our way upstairs to our room, where I changed into my pyjamas – wondering why on earth I'd opted for short shorts and a strappy top that showed a little too much skin, then remembering that I hadn't planned on sharing a room with anyone.

Oh well, not much I could do about it now, so after giving my shorts one final tug, trying to cover more of my legs, until I gave up entirely, I finally left the safety of the bathroom.

Grayson clearly didn't have any problem with being half

naked, since I found him sprawled out across his bed, wearing only his boxer shorts. Looking like he was on his father's yacht, utterly at ease in his own skin.

I tried to avert my gaze, feeling my cheeks burn. This was most definitely not how I'd imagined spending our trip.

Then again, there were a number of things I could never have imagined happening, or even being possible.

'I hope that bed's ok. We can swap if you'd prefer?' Grayson asked. I could hear the smile in his voice.

'No, no, this one's fine,' I stuttered like an idiot before climbing under the covers and pulling them up as high as they'd go.

I heard a low chuckle from Grayson, but still, I refused to look at him.

I had enough emotional baggage to try sort through right now, without Grayson's good looks and charm interfering. Sending me into a complete tailspin.

He turned the light off, and I felt myself relax, safe in the darkness.

'Goodnight, Grayson,' I whispered a few moments later, feeling my eyelids getting heavier by the second.

'Goodnight, Sophie, sweet dreams,' he replied, his voice sounding husky in the darkness.

'Hey, Grayson,' I said through a yawn.

'Yeah?'

'I'm really glad I met you,' I tried to stifle another yawn, darkness quickly pulling me under, but not before I heard him whisper back.

'Me too, Sophie. Me too.'

Birds chirped merrily, a breeze rustled the curtains, swaying them gently to natures melody, while the smell of coffee ignited my senses.

Stretching out across the bed, sending my fingers and toes in opposite directions like a starfish, I couldn't remember the last time I'd slept so well.

I wondered what the time was, as I swung my legs out of bed, grabbing the robe that lay at the foot of the bed. Cursing myself for not noticing it last night. Grayson must have left it there for me.

Where was he? I wondered, noticing his bed was empty.

Padding over to the balcony, I found him sipping a cup of coffee, just watching the world go by.

'Good morning,' I smiled shyly.

'Good morning, sleeping beauty,' he smiled back.

'What time is it?' I asked, helping myself to a cup of coffee.

'Nine o'clock.'

I looked up in surprise.

'Wow, I guess I needed that more than I thought,' I replied, taking a sip of coffee, relishing the warm, velvety liquid.

'I didn't want to wake you, you looked so peaceful.'

'I honestly can't remember the last time I had such a good night's sleep. I feel wonderful.'

'Bad dreams?' Grayson guessed.

'Something like that.'

More like one recurring nightmare, but maybe, just maybe, I was finally free of my nightmares and sleepless nights.

Grayson didn't push the subject. He didn't need to, he simply gave me a knowing smile and continued to look out over the grounds, watching the couples, old and young, some with children, some on their own, having their breakfast or going for a morning walk.

I watched an elderly couple walking hand in hand down the length of the garden.

The man stopped, picked a rose and handed it to the woman, who smiled, leaned over and kissed the man on the cheek before smelling the rose. I wished I had my camera.

'Let's do something today, let's go exploring, see what this little town has to offer,' I smiled excitedly at Grayson.

'Ok, but I need sustenance first, I can't survive a day on just coffee.'

'Give me five minutes and I'll be ready,' I sprang to my feet and dashed into the bathroom to get changed and freshen up.

Today was going to be a good day, I could feel it in my bones.

Turns out this little town had more to offer than I would have guessed.

After having breakfast at the town's quaint café, we discovered that Abingdon was gearing up for its annual summer festival, which included live music, a wide variety of food stalls, picnics, arts and crafts, you name it, they seemed to have it.

It sounded like a pretty big deal, something the locals were extremely proud of.

'Well, how could we say no?' I laughed, as Grayson and I left the café.

A few of the locals we'd met were rather persuasive.

'The trailer won't be ready for another few days, and the hospital did say you shouldn't travel just yet, so another few nights won't hurt,' Grayson replied and although he feigned reluctance, I could see he was just as excited to stay as I was.

It turned out the trailer had been damaged during the storm and was currently being repaired, so it's not like we could leave yet anyway.

Grayson had contacted the farm, where we were due to collect the animals, to let them know what had happened, and thankfully they were able to keep them until we could make it there.

After another quick call, to his parents, reassuring them (just as I'd done with my parents when I'd spoken to them) that we were both fine and the situation was far worse than it sounded, we were able to relax and make the most of our time here.

The festival wasn't starting until tomorrow, giving us the whole day today to explore and thanks to café owner recommending we check out the Virginia Creeper Trail, that's exactly where we were headed.

Well, first to the bicycle hire store, then on to the trail.

We walked along Main Street, in the direction she'd said, while I snapped photos of the old buildings and children playing in the fountain.

Managing to get a few of Grayson in the process because, well, why not?

'Please, no more photos, there are more than enough on the sanctuary's website, don't you think?' Grayson grumbled playfully.

'I'm pretty sure most of those photos are the reason it's been so successful,' I winked, before continuing to snap away.

'Have you always been into photography?' He asked, patiently waiting for me to get a few shots of a young couple wrapped in each other's arms.

'For as long as I can remember. My mom took so many pictures of Paul and I growing up, I guess that's how it started, but now I prefer being behind the camera. Unfortunately, my mom still has loads of pictures of me as a chubby, curly haired child.'

I snapped another candid of Grayson, proving my point.

'Now those I'd like to see,' Grayson laughed.

Ignoring that – I sincerely hoped he never saw my baby photo's – I went on, 'Kaitlyn is a far better photographer. I'm hoping she'll take some shots for the website when she visits.'

'I'm looking forward to meeting her, and getting all the embarrassing dirt on you, of course.'

I laughed, enjoying this side of Grayson, and thinking about how much Kaitlyn was looking forward to meeting him. For all the wrong reasons!

Kaitlyn had wanted all the gossip about the Danvers brothers, but she was usually disappointed, given that there wasn't much to tell.

I knew I'd have a hard time convincing her of that when she visited. My best friend missed nothing. And I really missed her.

'There's the bike shop,' Grayson called up ahead, pulling me from my thoughts.

An hour later, we were well on our way, immersed in the natural beauty surrounding us.

Engulfed by the forest, forgetting the world outside existed and finding peace in the cool, calm shade of the trees.

Stumbling across a clearing, alongside the river, we decided to stop for a break.

'It's beautiful isn't it,' I said, taking in the tall trees and wildflowers. Listening to the birds high above.

Grayson nodded, taking off his shoes, and I followed suit, wanting to dip my toes in the enticing water.

'What are you doing?' I stuttered when I realised Grayson wasn't stopping with his shoes, he had taken his shirt off and was currently removing his pants.

'Taking a dip, I bet the waters great,' he gave me a kilowatt smile and I just stared at him.

He was a fine specimen of a man, there was no denying that.

Dragging my eyes away, I walked over to the water's edge. Damn, he was right, the water felt amazing, not too cold. The perfect temperature for a dip.

'Coming?' Grayson's breath tickled the side of my neck and I jumped, I hadn't even heard him approaching.

'What if someone sees us?' I looked around, waiting for someone to appear and tell us off.

'When was the last time we saw anyone?' He had a point.

I heard a splash a moment later and looked up to see his head breaking the surface of the water. He shook his hair out, sending water droplets flying in every direction.

Kaitlyn would have a field day taking pictures of him, I thought with a smile.

'You don't know what you're missing, this feels incredible,' Grayson called, before diving under the water again.

I readied my camera this time, and when he came up again, I snapped a few photos. They were going in my private collection.

Ok, this sucked. Why was I standing on the side-lines watching someone else have all the fun? I thought, watching Grayson floating in the inviting water.

Live your life, Sophie. I reminded myself before stripping down to my underwear and diving in.

'About time,' Grayson flicked water in my direction when I surfaced, that mischievous glint appearing once again in his eyes.

'Well I couldn't let you have all the fun,' I flicked water back at him and regretted it instantly.

A wicked grin crossed his face before he disappeared under the water and before I could even attempt to get away, firm hands gripped my waist, lifting me out of the water, before dunking me right back under.

I came up laughing and spluttering, but mostly laughing.

'Oh, you asked for it.'

Hoisting myself onto Grayson's shoulders, I pushed him under the water. Although I'm pretty sure he let me, feeling his strong shoulders flex under my fingertips.

We came up, tangled together, my hair fanning out around us as I wiped the water from my eyes, still laughing. But Grayson was quiet.

My eyes met his and the laughter left my lips instantly.

The depths of his blue eyes – no longer icy blue, but warm, inviting – bore into mine and my heart pounded in my chest.

We were so close I could feel his warm breath wash over my face, his hands still gently holding my waist, while my hands rested on his strong arms and I knew I should remove them and put some distance between us, but his eyes held onto mine, trapping me like a moth drawn to a flame.

He slowly moved one hand up to the side of my face, tucking a wayward strand of hair behind my ear. His hand lingering there before running down the side of my arm, sending delicious shivers through my entire body.

I was completely and utterly frozen, with pleasure, with fear, with uncertainty.

Was he going to kiss me? Did I want him to kiss me? Was I ready for this? So many questions, so few answers.

I could almost see my inner turmoil mirrored in his eyes and I opened my mouth to say something, anything, I just needed to break this spell I was under, but no words came out.

Suddenly Grayson ducked under the water again, hands still on my waist and once again lifted me out of the water before dunking me under.

And just like that I was free, able to move, able to breathe again.

Only, I wasn't sure that's what I wanted.

I wasn't sure of anything anymore, only the feeling that Grayson's touch had awakened something in me, something that had been buried for a long time.

'Hey, look, there's a vineyard up ahead. What do you say?' Grayson smiled casually at me, as if everything was back to normal, and the moment we'd clearly shared had never happened.

Heck, maybe it hadn't, maybe I'd imagined the whole thing. Maybe I truly was losing my mind.

'Sure, let's do it,' I smiled back, trying to shake off these feelings of doubt, of second guessing, and get back to our carefree day.

Riding through our beautiful surroundings did just the trick. It was hard not to lose yourself in the beauty of it all, and I felt the tension slowly ebb away.

Deciding to treat ourselves to a tour of the vineyard, and of course a wine tasting – it would just be rude not to – we found ourselves having a picnic next to a trickling stream, under the cool shade of the trees.

'I could stay here forever,' I sighed happily, popping another strawberry into my mouth, savouring the soft, sweet flesh.

'Me too,' Grayson was sprawled across the blanket we'd borrowed from the vineyard shop.

'You'd miss the sanctuary too much.' I thought about Apollo and all the other brave, wonderful animals.

Rosie and Sam had been taking good care of Apollo, giving us regular updates, but I still missed him.

'So, would you,' Grayson propped himself up on his elbows, giving me a thoughtful glance, before turning his gaze back to the stream. 'You've taken to farm life far better than I could have imagined, Sophie. I may not say it, but I'm grateful for all your hard work and getting the website up and running.'

I didn't know what to say.

My time on the farm had changed me, made me feel whole again, mending my shattered soul. The farm (and the people on it) had done far more for me than I could ever do for it, or any of them.

'I've loved every minute of it. I finally feel like I'm doing something worthwhile, you know. I love writing and taking pictures, of course, but working at the sanctuary is different, more meaningful. Hey, does that mean I'm no longer city girl?' I asked with a grin.

'You'll always be my city girl,' Grayson replied.

I liked the way that sounded a little too much – the way he'd called me his city girl.

'Have you written anything lately?' Grayson asked absentmindedly.

'No, not in a while,' I replied quietly, watching the water trickle over the rocks, in search of the river that lay beyond.

'You should give it another go, you never know when inspiration might strike,' Grayson said simply, understanding my unspoken words.

I hadn't written since Luke.

'Maybe.' A small smile touched my lips and I tilted my head back.

Brilliant bursts of sunlight filtered down through the

trees above, and my mind drifted to what I would write about, where I would even start.

It's not that I had given up completely. I'd attempted writing a year after I lost Luke, but I'd spent more time staring at a blank screen than writing anything.

I hated the thought of repeating that, but maybe Grayson was right. Maybe it was time I tried again.

Remembering the promise I'd made to Luke, I vowed that I would give it another go once we got home.

Not wanting to think that far ahead just yet, I spent the afternoon learning about Grayson instead.

Who his best friend in school was, what foods he liked, what books he liked to read, or films he liked to watch. What kind of music he liked, where he'd travelled.

Some answers surprised me – like the fact that his taste in music varied from reggae to indie to rock and a wide variety in between.

'What can I say, I'm like an onion,' he laughed, and I gave him a quizzical look.

'I have many layers.' It was so corny that I couldn't help but laugh.

'Ok, moving on. Where have you travelled?'

'I've been to a few places in the States – New Orleans, California and of course more local states for work, but further afield, I've been to Morocco, India, Bali, Africa – mostly on volunteer work, but some places I've gone back on holiday.'

I was envious, my passport held far less stamps that Grayson's clearly did.

'Which was your favourite?' I asked, enthralled by his tales of the places he'd visited, exotic foods he'd tried, and different cultures he'd immersed himself in.

'Probably Africa. It's one of the most vast, beautiful, wild places I've experienced. Once you pass through the city limits and leave behind the hustle and bustle of the larger towns and cities, it's just nature at its very best and for as far as the eye can see. Oh, and you've never seen a night sky quite like an African one. The stars look so big and bright you feel as though you could just reach out and pluck one right out of the sky. I lost myself in one of the small villages on the outskirts of a game reserve. We were out there helping build new houses and a school and the children were truly inspiring, they had so little, yet they were so happy and grateful for what they did have. It was one of the most humbling experiences of my life and I'll never forget it. It's part of my tattoo.' Grayson lifted his shirt, showing me all the different meanings and symbols on his arm.

The tattoo consisted of a combination of places he'd visited and animals who had held a significant amount of meaning to him, all laced together in an intricate tale of his travels and his life.

I traced my finger lightly over each image, in awe of the artistic design.

I didn't have any tattoos myself, but I'd always wanted to get one, I just couldn't decide on what to get or where to get one and the moment eventually passed.

I had to admit that I was admiring more than just the ink on Grayson's arm, as I let my hand linger longer than necessary, enjoying the feel of Grayson's warm, muscular arm underneath my fingers.

Needing a distraction, I continued drilling him with more questions. Anything I could think of, from his favourite memories as a child to first and last love.

'I thought I was in love once. I even proposed. It was a few years ago. We met at a conference, exchanged details, went on a few dates and within the year I had proposed. She said yes, but needless to say, things didn't work out, and we went our separate ways.'

'Grayson, I'm so sorry, I had no idea.'

'It's ok, it wasn't meant to be, but it messed with my head for a long time. I've only recently made peace with what happened and have been able to move on. It was just hard I guess, planning your life with someone, only to find out they weren't the person you thought they were. But I have no regrets, everything I did and everything that has happened in my life has brought me to this point. I'm in a good place now and I'm happy with my life.'

Grayson left it there and I didn't push further, knowing that when he was ready, he would share the rest of the story.

Chapter 11

The following day Grayson had to make a few work calls, so I ventured into town, where he planned to meet me later for the festival.

The small town had come alive with stalls being set up and food trucks gearing up for the crowds.

A band had just arrived and were busy unloading their equipment, creating an excited buzz in the air.

I was camera ready, always, and couldn't resist snapping a few shots as everyone prepared for the event.

My camera landed on a little girl sitting on her own near a tent.

As I snapped a shot of her she looked up and beamed up at me, showing a missing front tooth.

She was as cute as a button, with curly blonde hair that most women paid far too much for, to try replicate, and large green eyes, and when she smiled two dimples appeared, making her just about the cutest little thing I'd ever seen.

'Hi,' she continued grinning up at me.

'Well, hello there.' I took a few steps forward and bent down to see what she had been so engrossed in. 'That's a beautiful drawing,' I complimented her picture of, what looked like a family, standing next to a house, complete with trees and a smiling yellow sun.

'Thank you. I'm drawing it for my momma because she's sad today,' the little girl looked down at her picture, her smile disappearing.

'Why is she sad?' I couldn't help asking.

'My daddy left, and we don't have enough money for all the bills,' she recited as though she'd heard it a million times before.

It broke my heart.

'Where's your mom now?'

'Inside,' the little girl gestured towards the tent, 'She's getting ready for the festival. Momma's the bestest fortune teller around, you know. She could read your fortune,' the little girl squealed with excitement.

A plan started forming in my head.

'What's your name, sweetheart?'

'Abigail,' she replied with another toothy grin.

'Well, Abigail, my name's Sophie. Can you tell your mom to keep a space free for me tonight and I promise I'll be back later to see her, and she can tell me my fortune then, how does that sound?'

'Oh yes, I'll tell her to keep a space for the pretty lady, Sophie,' Abigail clapped her hands happily.

She made me promise I'd be back later and after crossing my heart and hoping to die (which was a little too close to the mark after recent events), I left her to continue with her drawing, heading back in the direction I'd just come from, certain I'd seen a jewellers in town and hoping they would be able to help me.

'Fancy meeting you here.' A familiar voice whispered into my ear, sending a shiver down my spine.

'You made it,' I turned to see Grayson looking extremely handsome in a blue t-shirt and faded blue jeans.

How could he make something so casual look so incredibly sexy!

I secretly thanked myself for always packing a few extra items, just in case, as I always said because you just never knew when you'd need a little black dress, or a pair of high heels.

Otherwise, I would have been wearing tatty jeans and an old shirt, instead of my white lace summer dress and favourite pair of wedges.

At least I looked somewhat respectable next to Grayson, the Greek God.

'Sorry it took so long, work stuff,' he dragged a hand through his tousled hair.

'Everything ok?'

'Yeah, just sorting out food deliveries and a few maintenance issues. It's just frustrating not being there to make sure everything's running smoothly.'

'Sometimes you need to put faith in other people. Your family wouldn't let anything go wrong, so relax, and enjoy tonight,' I gave my best stern look.

'Yes ma'am,' Grayson grabbed my hand and pulled me along.

'Where are we going?' I laughed, trying to keep up with his long strides.

'Following your instructions of course. We're going to grab a bite to eat and then we're dancing,' he replied matter-of-factly.

Little did I know that Grayson's idea of grabbing a bite to eat was trying one of everything, from almost every food truck, and then getting cotton candy too.

'Where do you put it all?' I laughed, feeling so full after only a quarter of what Grayson had consumed, but picking a sticky ball of his cotton candy anyway.

You couldn't come to a festival and not have cotton candy, after all.

Grayson patted his belly – as if he had one, yeah right!

All I could see was muscle underneath the thin layer of his t-shirt and I was momentarily distracted, imagining what his abs would feel like.

Shaking my head, I looked up to see the same tent from earlier, only this time there was no adorable little girl sitting next to it.

I wondered where she was.

'Fancy joining me over there?' I gestured towards the tent.

'Seriously? You want to go to a fortune teller?' Grayson raised an eyebrow.

'Sure, it'll be fun, come on,' I pulled on his arm, not sharing my ulterior motive.

'You first,' I told Grayson, but before he could argue, I shoved him into the tent and waited patiently, keeping an eye out for Abigail.

It seemed to take forever, but eventually Grayson emerged looking sombre.

'Are you ok? What happened?' I asked, ignoring the prickly sensation creeping up my spine.

Grayson looked up and met my worried gaze before smiling and telling me everything was just fine and that it was my turn, but everything didn't look fine.

Still, he held the curtain open for me and I stepped through to find an attractive woman sitting on the other side of a round table.

A miniature version of the fortune teller appeared by my side, her eyes lighting up when she saw me. Grabbing my hand, she marched me over to the table.

'Momma, this is the pretty Sophie lady,' Abigail ushered me into the chair opposite her mother.

'It's nice to meet you, Sophie, my daughter couldn't stop talking about the nice lady who kept her company earlier. Thank you for that,' Abigail's mother whispered the last part so her daughter wouldn't hear.

'She's a sweetheart,' I replied honestly.

'My name's Lexi,' Abigail's mother introduced herself before picking up her tarot cards, 'Shall we begin?'

I nodded, suddenly nervous, as Lexi took my hand in her own and began looking at my palm.

Emerging from the tent, I blinked, as though trying to clear the fog in my brain.

I'd never believed much in fortune tellers and the like, but that was something.

'I know, right?' Grayson appeared, smiling at the expression on my face, which I guessed looked a lot like his had, after he'd emerged from the tent.

'That was…'

'Intense?' Grayson finished when I couldn't think of the

right word.

'Intense is definitely one word for it,' I replied, wondering how Lexi had done it.

How could she know so much about a person she'd never met before?

Sure, there were the usual cliché's like your life will come to a crossroads, but how could she know the specific details?

'Beer?' Grayson asked and I nodded, lost in my own thoughts, wondering when and where I would reach my own crossroad and which path I would take.

As the afternoon turned to evening and the music drifted through the balmy air, our moods lightened, and after a second beer, we both let ourselves go to the night.

All thoughts of the fortune teller pushed to the back of my mind. At least for now.

We walked around the festival grounds a while longer, looking at the different stalls and I couldn't help stopping at a jewellery stall – I was such a magpie, as my mom always called me, always drawn to shiny objects.

A dainty turquoise necklace, hanging on a thin silver chain, caught my eye, so delicate and pretty. It also happened to match the colour of my eyes almost identically.

'That one's sea glass, it would look lovely with your eyes,' the elderly lady behind the counter commented.

'Sophie, have a look over here,' Grayson pulled me over to look at the hats for Sam.

I smiled apologetically at the woman before helping

Grayson choose the perfect cowboy hat for Sam.

'He'll love it, thanks. Care to dance?'

'I'd love to.' The music had been calling to me all evening.

The makeshift dance floor was surprisingly busy, but once we found a spot, we danced for what felt like hours.

Simply losing ourselves to the melody, to the night, to this pretty little town we happened upon, where I'd felt so many changes within me.

'Penny for your thoughts?' Grayson eyed me with piercing interest, as though he was trying to read my mind.

'Do you believe in fate? Destiny?' I asked suddenly.

Grayson swayed to the music, pulling me closer, as the band switched to a slower melody.

With my wedges, I was a little taller and I found myself leaning into him, resting my head in the nook of his neck, where I could smell his unique scent. I breathed it in deeply.

'I think I believe everything happens for a reason and sometimes the universe throws us a curveball that we either dodge or it ends up hitting us smack in the face, but I think it's up to us to find our way back to the right path again,' Grayson replied after a moments deliberation.

'I do. For me personally, I believe that coming home, working at the sanctuary, all of it, is my destiny, it's my path. As awful as some parts have been in my life, I believe everything has happened to get me to this point right now, right here.'

With you, Grayson, the voice inside my head whispered. I shushed her.

'Well, whatever the reason, call it fate, or destiny, or witchy juju, I'm glad you found your way to us, Sophie,' Grayson whispered my name, his warm breath tickling my ear, making me shiver in his arms.

I wasn't sure if it was the beer, or the music, or the fortune teller, or all of it, but I found myself leaning into Grayson a little more.

Suddenly curious about the feelings bubbling under the surface. About how he made me feel and wondering if there was any truth in what the fortune teller had said.

'Miss Sophie, Miss Sophie,' a little voice yelled out and I turned to see Abigail running towards us.

Grayson had just returned from the restroom and we were about to head back to the inn when I heard her little voice calling my name.

'Hi, sweetheart. This is my friend, Grayson. Grayson, this is Lexi's daughter, Abigail.'

'Well hello there, Miss Abigail, how do you do?' Grayson greeted the little girl and I recognised all too well the dazed look in her young eyes. I stifled a laugh.

'Momma said you paid our bills. Thank you, Miss Sophie, you made my momma so happy,' Abigail reached up to hug me.

Kneeling down, I squeezed Abigail tightly, before replying, 'You are very welcome, sweetheart. Now you take care of your momma, you hear?'

'I will, I promise.' And with that she ran back to the tent, with one last look back and a wave before disappearing behind the curtain.

'What was that about?' Grayson asked.

'It's a long story,' I replied, not wanting to tell him what I'd done.

'We have time,' he persisted.

Looking at Grayson, reading the curiosity in his eyes and knowing full well he wasn't going to drop it I told him how I'd met Abigail earlier and what she'd told me about her father leaving, their money problems and that I'd managed to sell mine and Luke's wedding rings for a really good price – after not settling for anything less than what I knew they were worth – to give the money to Lexi.

I'd handed Lexi the envelope at the end of my reading earlier and asked her not to open it until I was gone, not thinking that we'd bump into either of them again.

Grayson just stared at me blankly.

'What?' I asked, unable to read his expression.

'You sold your wedding rings?'

'It was time,' I replied simply, truthfully.

Not only was it time, but it was for a good cause. Luke would have approved, I knew that deep in my heart.

'Sophie Hamilton, you are truly unlike anyone I've ever met,' Grayson replied, a small smile on his face.

And with that we left the festival behind us and I gladly accepted another wonderful memory.

I was starting to feel like the Grinch, near the end of the film, when his heart grows bigger.

All these little happy memories were filling my heart, not only piecing it back together, but making it grow twice its size.

'Fancy taking a dip in the stream before turning in?' Grayson asked, a lopsided smile on his beautiful face.

'Has a woman ever said no to you?' I wondered aloud.

A dark expression flashed across Grayson's face, turning his cocky smile into a scowl, so fast that I thought I'd imagined it, before he turned on a kilowatt smile and leaned towards me in his truck. I stopped breathing.

'Not usually,' he all but whispered, reaching across me to open my door before getting out.

I sat there for a moment, trying to calm my racing heart.

'So?' He held my door open for me, while waiting for my answer.

'No,' I replied and then burst out laughing at the dejected puppy dog look on his face. 'I just wanted to see how you handled rejection. Not well, I might add. Of course I'm coming, you're not having all the fun,' I jumped out and raced him to the brook.

Although it wasn't quite deep enough for a swim, the cool water still felt heavenly as it swept over my feet and legs.

'Aren't you coming in?' Grayson leaned back on his elbows, almost completely submerged.

'This is enough for me tonight,' I replied, flicking water at him.

Moments later, Grayson stepped out of the water, shaking off before getting dressed, while I perched myself on a rock next to the water's edge, trying not to ogle him.

Something that was becoming more and more difficult. Especially since he kept stripping in front of me.

'I had a really nice time tonight, Grayson. Thank you,' I

said, turning back to the water, to stop myself from watching him.

Ok, to stop myself from getting caught watching him as he finished getting dressed and joined me on the rock.

Moonlight washed over us, illuminating our little piece of heaven.

'Sophie,' Grayson whispered, while pulling something from his pocket.

I looked up, intrigued.

'I know this can never replace what you lost tonight, but I wanted to give you this, as a keepsake of our trip, at least the good parts of it,' he handed me a small box.

'Go on, open it,' Grayson coaxed.

I did as he said, discovering a turquoise necklace inside. The same turquoise necklace I'd been looking at earlier, at the festival.

I looked up at Grayson, moonlight caressed his face, making him look even more handsome, emphasising his chiselled cheekbones and full lips and those eyes!

'Grayson, thank you, it's beautiful,' I whispered, touched by his kind gesture.

'Shall I?' He extended his hand.

Handing him the necklace, I bundled my hair up so he could fasten the little clasp at the back of my neck.

I felt his hands brush my neck, sending involuntary shivers through me and once the necklace was securely in place, he let his hands linger for a moment, smoothing out the delicate chain before removing his hands.

I turned back to face him and looked down at the pretty pendant that sat in the middle of my chest.

'I love it, thank you.' I leaned over to hug him and felt him stiffen momentarily before relaxing and hugging me back.

I could have stayed like that forever, safe in Grayson's arms, under the moon and stars, beside the water's edge. But Grayson pulled back too soon.

He stood, offering me his hand, 'We should get back, we've got a busy day tomorrow.'

We were going home the following day.

That was a good thing, I missed my parents and the sanctuary and the Danvers and Apollo.

Then why did I feel so sad?

The following morning, we were up early and after enjoying our final breakfast out on the deck, we packed up the car and drove the short distance to pick up the trailer before heading to the farm to collect the animals. Soon to be leaving Abingdon behind us.

How strange to think how much had changed in just a few short days.

Not only between Grayson and I, but inside myself. I finally felt as though I was able to forgive myself for what had happened to Luke and begin to move forward – not in forgetting Luke, but move forward with my life, rather than being stuck in limbo, unable to go back and impossible to move forward.

I couldn't help wondering how different my life would be had I stayed in New York.

I would probably still be taking the anxiety pills, still having anxiety attacks, still beating myself up over something that I had no control of in the first place.

I still vividly remembered my brief time with Luke, real or not, it didn't matter, what mattered was that I could remember him with happiness in my heart and no longer crippled by the pain of losing him.

He was in a better place, watching over me, and knowing that he was always with me gave me a sense of peace.

'We're nearly there,' Grayson said, pulling me from my thoughts.

I was eager to get to the animals, I hated the thought of them waiting longer than necessary because of me, but on arrival we found them in good condition.

We collected four horses, six goats, a donkey and the cutest little piglets I'd ever seen.

'We can't leave them! Who knows what'll happen to them,' I pleaded with Grayson, holding on to the wriggling bundles of pink fuzz.

Apparently, we'd only agreed on the horses, donkey and goats.

The farm owners didn't look too pleased at my holding the piglets they intended to sell.

I didn't care! We'd gone into the barn to round up the goats and the piglets had come squealing over to me and that was it, I was a goner the second their little squishy pink snouts nuzzled into me.

'Give me a minute,' Grayson replied, walking over to the owners.

'Don't you worry, I won't let anything happen to you two, you hear,' I whispered to them, causing them to nuzzle further into my arms.

Grayson returned a few moments later and told me to get in the car.

Without needing to be told twice, I dashed around to the passenger side, securing the piglets on my lap as soon as we were in the car.

'How did you get them to agree?' I asked, as we pulled away from the farm.

'Let's just say that's the most expensive bacon I've ever bought.'

'Don't you listen to him, you'll never become bacon.' I stroked the little piglets who were almost asleep in my lap. 'Thank you, Grayson,' I smiled at him and hoped he knew that I wasn't only thanking him for the piglets, but for everything these past few days.

He had been so calm and supportive throughout, never losing patience with me or looked at me like I was crazy – which I'm sure I sounded on more than one occasion.

His returning smile said that he understood, and I settled in with the piglets, still on my lap.

Chapter 12

The drive home didn't seem to take long, something I was exceptionally grateful for. The closer we got, the more excited I was to get home.

It was Friday afternoon, so I'd be spending the night on the farm, which would give me time to check on Apollo and the other animals, before driving to my parents for the weekend.

I couldn't wait to see them, and the Danvers. It suddenly felt like we had been away for months.

Soon enough I could see the farm in the distance, and I was practically bouncing in my seat, much to the piglet's annoyance, since they'd been sound asleep.

'Just wait until you see your new home, you're going to love it!' I squeaked happily. Grayson chuckled.

'It will be good to be home,' he said quietly. 'You do realise that you're going to have to look after those two, don't you? Seeing as they've got no mom, you're going to have to be the substitute, which will require feeding them every few hours, day and night.'

Oh. I hadn't even considered that.

'That's just fine, I'll manage.' I wasn't sure who I was reassuring the piglets or myself.

Hmmm, I wonder how my parents would feel about grand-piglets, I thought, grinning to myself, already knowing full well what my dad's reaction would be.

Pulling up to the main house a few minutes later, Grayson got out and stretched, before helping me and the piglets out of the car just as Rosie and Sam appeared in the doorway.

'Welcome home you two, we're so happy you made it back ok. Sophie, how are you feeling?' Rosie called, as they both made their way over to us.

'I'm fine, Rosie, thank you. It really wasn't as bad as it sounded,' I replied, realising this was the first time I didn't have to lie about being ok.

'Welcome home son, it's good to have you back.' Sam patted Grayson on the shoulder.

Men were so macho all the time, why couldn't they just hug it out like Rosie and I were currently doing.

'You look well honey,' Rosie cupped my cheeks and eyed me, looking for signs of the accident I assumed.

'Thanks to Grayson, I'm fine,' I smiled, sneaking a look at Grayson who flashed me a breath-taking grin.

'I can see that.' Something in Rosie's voice made me turn back to look at her.

She had that knowing look in her eyes, like she knew something had changed between Grayson and I, and I suddenly felt embarrassed, which was ridiculous, nothing had actually happened. Yes, we'd had a few incredibly intimate, special moments, but that was it, nothing had developed between us. We'd simply grown closer, like you would with any new friend.

‘And who are these two cutties?’ Rosie lifted one of the piglets from my arms.

‘That’s Maggie.’ I had decided on the name shortly after leaving the farm, given her attraction for my necklace, the seatbelt clip, basically anything that sparkled. ‘What? She’s like a little magpie, attracted to shiny things,’ I nodded as she tried to eat Rosie’s bracelet.

‘And this is Patch.’ Needing no explanation, given the few darker patches on her wriggly little bottom.

‘Welcome to your new home, little ones,’ Rosie cuddled Maggie and I smiled, thinking how wonderful it was to be home.

‘I can’t believe you named them without me,’ Grayson shook his head, feigning disappointment.

‘Only because I’m so much better at it than you,’ I laughed, taking the piglets inside with Rosie, while Sam and Grayson began offloading the other animals from the trailer.

‘Welcome home, beautiful,’ before I could fully turn around Caleb had embraced me in a death grip, lifting me off the ground and spinning me around, making me giggle like a silly teenager.

I’d missed his youthfulness, and the way it rubbed off on me.

‘On a scale of one to ten, how much did you miss me?’ He asked once he’d set me back down on the ground.

‘Hmmm, maybe like a two,’ I gave him a cheeky grin.

‘Oh, that’s just mean. And I know it’s not true,’ he winked and knelt down to take a closer look at the piglets.

'Hey cutties, I hope Sophie fattens you up real good. I do love bacon.'

I smacked him on the shoulder, 'Don't say the B word around them – they will not become the B word, ever! Understand?' I folded my arms sternly.

'Yes ma'am,' Caleb saluted and then laughed. Always the joker. 'Seriously though, it's good to have you back, and in one piece,' he added quietly.

Ok, maybe not always the joker.

'It's good to be back,' I smiled, relishing in how much their home, the farm, felt like my own.

'Why don't you go help your dad and Grayson with the new load of animals, while Sophie and I catch up.' Rosie shooed him out of the house before returning to the kitchen.

'Now, let's get these two something to eat, shall we?' The piglets squealed in response.

While Rosie busied herself in the kitchen, making up some formula for the piglets, we caught up about the trip, the accident, most of what came after – I wasn't going to tell her about the little moments Grayson and I had shared, getting the distinct feeling she'd have a field day with that information.

When I couldn't wait any longer, I asked Rosie if she could keep an eye on the piglets while I checked on Apollo.

'Sure, honey, take your time.'

'Thank you.' I leaned over to kiss her cheek, 'It's good to be home.'

'It's good to have you home, sweetheart,' Rosie beamed back and I found myself thinking, once again, how fortunate I was to have them in my life, they were fast becoming a second family to me and I'd missed them almost as much as I'd missed my own family.

It appeared Apollo had missed me too, huffing and stomping his hoof as soon as I entered the barn, as though he could sense I was back.

'Hi, boy, it's good to see you too. I've missed you so much,' I whispered, stroking his face and soft neck.

'Do you want to go for a ride?' I got the gear ready and he stood patiently while I placed the saddle on his back.

Before long we were riding to our spot in the clearing, the wind whipping through my hair, the sunlight dancing over my skin.

I felt so free, so alive.

As we entered the clearing, I pulled the reigns gently and Apollo slowed, eventually coming to a stop. Almost immediately putting his head down to make the most of the long grass.

Well, it's nice to see you too, I thought to myself with a smile.

Grabbing a water bottle from the saddle bag, first pouring some water in my hand for Apollo and then taking a long drink myself, I sat back in the long grass, leaning on my elbows, letting the sun wash over my skin, warming me through.

Growing up, summer had always been my favourite season.

A time for building sandcastles and swimming in the sea. Searching for fairies in the woods and trying to devour ice cream before it started to melt, dripping down your hand.

Not much had changed, I still loved everything about summer, I thought, breathing in deeply, loving the way the air smelled like sunshine and freshly cut grass.

I found myself wondering if I would ever be lucky enough to have children one day, wishing that if I did, they could experience life, especially their childhood, as I had, the way all children should – simply being children and losing themselves in long summer days and fairy tales.

Apollo huffed, his ears standing to attention as he looked up.

Following his gaze, I noticed someone approaching in the distance. Squinting into the sun, I realised it was Caleb.

'Hey there, mind if I join you?' He asked once he was closer.

'Sure, come on in, the grass is great,' he chuckled, dismounting his horse, sitting next to me among the tall grass.

'Are the new arrivals all settled in?' I asked.

'Yeah, they're fine and they'll be even better now that they're here.' Caleb removed his hat and lay back in the grass, closing his eyes. 'You gave us quite a scare, you know,' he said quietly, eyes still closed against the sunlight.

'I'm sorry, I didn't mean to worry anyone. I just couldn't sit back and do nothing. That family on the bridge could have gone over if we hadn't done something.'

'I know. You did the right thing. I just hate the thought of anything happening to you, Soph.'

'I'm ok,' I smiled, squeezing his arm reassuringly.

His eyes fluttered open and he looked up at me with so many emotions brewing behind those blue eyes, so similar to Grayson's, but so very different.

'I wish I'd been there. I hated being stuck here, not knowing how you really were,' he propped himself up on his elbows.

'Well, we're back now, and we're both ok.'

'Apollo really missed you too. He's been such a grump since you left.'

Apollo huffed in response, took one look at us and then continued munching the grass.

'I missed him too. I really missed this place and all of you too. It feels like home to me.'

'That's good because I think my parents actually missed you more than they ever miss Grayson, or me,' Caleb laughed. 'They're going out for dinner tonight with friends and I was wondering if, maybe, you wanted to come over to my place for dinner?' Caleb averted his gaze. Was he embarrassed?

'Sure, that sounds great. You can bring me up to speed on what's been happening while we've been away.'

'It's a date,' Caleb beamed and got to his feet, 'I better get back, my dad will probably be wondering where I've disappeared to. I'll see you tonight, say seven?'

'Seven it is,' I replied, feeling uncertain suddenly.

I didn't like the sound of our dinner being a date. Not when I'd assumed it would just be a casual dinner between friends.

I only hoped I was wrong.

I knocked on Caleb's door a few minutes after seven (having piglets to look after was becoming a full-time job and had made me late, but once they were fed and tucked in for the night, they eventually fell asleep).

I heard Caleb's voice from inside, telling me to come on in.

Opening the front door, I was hit with the most wonderful smell.

'Something smells heavenly.' My stomach agreed, rumbling in response.

'I hope it tastes as good,' Caleb smiled easily.

He looked different, more relaxed and at ease, finding his way around the kitchen effortlessly, like he was in his element.

'Can I do anything?' I suddenly wished I'd brought something with.

'Yeah, you can pour the wine, glasses are in the top cupboard.' Caleb indicated to the cupboard above the sink.

I poured us each a glass just as he was dishing up.

'Let's sit outside, it's a perfect evening for it.' He grabbed the plates and walked through the back door, into his garden.

I'd never been to his house before and I was pleasantly surprised, he clearly took a lot of pride in his home and I could tell a lot of work had gone into it.

Following him, I emerged into his back yard, consisting of a small table and four chairs on the decking.

The garden beyond that was neat and tidy, mainly consisting of shrubs and bushes, no flowers – which I suppose you couldn't expect from a guy, but it all worked so well together.

'This is beautiful,' I gestured to the garden.

'Thank you,' Caleb replied with a smile. 'Well, don't let it get cold. Bon Appetit.' Caleb lifted his wine glass and I did the same, clinking them together.

He didn't have to ask me twice. The delicious aromas were making my mouth water.

'Caleb, this is amazing! I didn't know you could cook like this,' I said between mouthfuls.

I wasn't even entirely sure what I was eating, I knew it was a chicken dish in the most mouth-watering sauce, garnished with all kinds of delicate and wonderfully tasting vegetables.

'Thanks, it's something I've always been interested in,' he replied casually, sipping his wine.

'This isn't just some past time, this is restaurant worthy food.'

'Funny you should mention that. You remember I told you about wanting to open a beach bar?' I nodded, popping another piece of chicken into my mouth. 'That was only part of the dream. I want to be the chef too. To cook great meals, but in a relaxed atmosphere. People shouldn't have to get all dressed up and go to stuffy restaurants just to experience fine dining.'

'You would do amazingly well, truly, this is the best meal I've had in forever. Do not tell your mom I said that,' I added quickly. Caleb laughed. 'Seriously, you should pursue all of it, the beach bar, cooking, if that's your dream, you need to grab it with everything you've got. Life is too short. We need to live it like every day may be our last.'

‘That’s kind of heavy for a Friday night, Soph,’ Caleb joked.

‘I’m serious Caleb. Do you want to wake up one day and look back on your life and wonder about all the missed opportunities, or the what ifs? I can’t imagine living like that. Your family will understand. I’ll help. We can talk to them together.’

‘You would do that?’

‘Of course I would, that’s what friends do, they help each other and stand by one another.’

Before Caleb could respond, we heard a knock at his front door.

‘Come on in, it’s open,’ he called and a few seconds later Grayson appeared.

‘Hey, bro,’ Caleb leaned back in his chair, taking another sip of wine.

‘Sorry, I didn’t realise you were having dinner, I should have called.’ Grayson took us in with the strangest expression on his face.

‘Don’t be silly, join us,’ I offered, pulling out a chair. ‘We were just catching up.’

‘That’s ok, I can’t stay. I only came to get the spare key for the office in the stables. I can’t find mine. Some of the new horses aren’t settling, so I’m going to make up some of the special horse feed, with the calming herbs. It usually helps sooth and settle them,’ Grayson explained.

‘Maybe we should go too, we could help?’ I looked from Caleb to Grayson, neither responded.

‘That would actually be great, I could use the help,’ Grayson finally said.

Reluctantly, Caleb nodded, finished his wine, we followed Grayson to the barn.

'I'm sorry dinner was cut short, but maybe we can pick up where we left off another time?' Caleb asked, leaning in a little too close to whisper in my ear.

'Sure,' I replied, just as we reached the barn, where I could already hear movement from inside. They certainly didn't sound happy, but we would fix that.

Two hours later, another shower, another feed for the piglets, I finally flopped into bed, exhausted.

It had taken longer than we'd hoped, but eventually, with the help of the oils and having all hands-on deck, the horses had settled.

Grayson had taken my hand in his, placing my fingers gently on one of the horse's heads, on the spot just between their eyes, and had told me to gently massage that spot, in circular motions, while him and Caleb mixed up the horse feed and herbs.

'It'll take a little time, but they'll get used to the place and they'll realise that they're safe here. We just have to be patient. Remember what it was like with Apollo?' Grayson asked as we were packing up, once the horses were docile.

I remembered all too well.

'He's come a long way,' I smiled warmly, remembering those first few days with Apollo.

'I think we all have,' Grayson replied, and I looked up at him to find a small smile curling up at the corners of his mouth.

I guessed we were no longer just talking about the horses.

A flood of sweet memories washed over me, from our time in Abingdon, and I smiled back at Grayson, who's eyes were suddenly clouded, troubled.

I wanted to reach up and smooth away the frown lines that marked his beautiful face.

'Ready to go?' Caleb called from across the barn.

Grayson blinked, but the troubled look remained on his face.

I wanted nothing more than to talk to him, ask him what was wrong, or if there was anything I could do to help, the way he'd been there for me.

He didn't suit this suddenly troubled expression that seemed to etch its way into his eyes, and I longed for the carefree, open book Grayson I'd spent the past few days getting to know.

Caleb insisted on walking me back to my cottage, although I was perfectly capable of finding my way back, even though it was pitch black by the time we left the barn.

'Sorry again about dinner, but I'll make it up to you,' Caleb said, leaning against my doorway, a lopsided grin on his face.

'There's nothing to make up for, dinner was delicious, thank you. I really hope you think about what I said too.'

'I will. Thanks for always being there, Soph,' Caleb leaned in to hug me, his strong arms wrapping tightly around me and as much as it caught me off guard, what was more surprising was how good it felt.

Caleb was a flirt, that was just a simple fact and I'd gotten used to his flirtatious ways and inappropriate comments but that didn't mean I didn't shy away from an intimate touch, or when he leaned in to whisper something in my ear, so I had fully expected my body to automatically recoil from this invasion of my personal space.

Instead, my body had responded the polar opposite.

I'd welcomed his warm embrace, leaning into him so I could return the hug, feeling his toned back through the thin fabric of his t-shirt.

I couldn't help comparing it to Grayson's embrace.

The only thing I wasn't sure of was who's embrace I wanted more.

Chapter 13

'It's good to have you home honey, you look tired,' my mom took my hand, concern furrowing her brow.

I felt tired. Having hardly slept at all the night before, eventually, around five o'clock in the morning, I'd given up and driven back to my parents' house, where I would be staying until Monday night, at the strict instruction of Rosie, who said that after the accident I needed to rest.

As much as I'd tried to get out of, I should have known better. Rosie had been the clear winner.

Rosie had also insisted that she look after the piglets, even though I wanted to bring them with me, but I understood her reasoning, not wanting to unsettle them further.

Sitting on my parent's porch now, hot cup of coffee in hand, I was happy that Rosie had won. I felt like I needed some time away to clear my head.

'How are you really doing, honey?' Mom asked.

'I'm really doing a lot better. I know it may sound crazy, but I think the accident was exactly what I needed. It's given me time to accept the things that I couldn't change and move on.'

'I'm so happy to hear that Sophie. We were all so worried

about you.' My mom squeezed my hand and I felt horrible for making them worry, especially in my dad's condition.

'How is Dad doing?'

'Oh, he's just fine, don't you worry about your old dad.' Mom smiled, and it still amazed me how much they loved each other.

It was the kind of love that lasted a lifetime, that could get them over any hurdle life threw at them.

I wondered if I would find that again. Could someone be that lucky to find that kind of love twice in one lifetime?

I wasn't sure, but I knew I would be ok if I didn't.

No matter what happened to me, I would be ok knowing that Luke was at peace and knowing that I had been lucky enough to know a great love at least once in my life.

I would always be one of the lucky ones.

The following day Paul and Sarah came over to the house for lunch.

Mom and I were busy setting the table in the garden, with the help of Sarah, while Dad and Paul talked shop.

'Hey sis, how are you feeling?' Paul appeared in the kitchen.

Mom had sent me in to get the iced tea.

'I'm good, honestly,' I repeated for what felt like the hundredth time.

'You gave us quite a scare!' Paul scolded in a typical older brother fashion.

'I know, I'm sorry, I didn't mean to worry anyone, not you guys with the baby on the way and certainly not Dad.

Is he really ok?'

'He's getting better day by day. Don't worry sis. They were initially worried when we heard about your accident, but somehow they knew you were going to be ok. Don't ask me how, they just knew. So Dad's been fine, it hasn't set him back, if that's what you're worried about,' Paul explained, knowing me all too well.

'I've missed you guys. Even you, you dork,' I lobbed a cherry tomato at him, but he was quicker, ducking as it rolled across the floor, stopping at my mom's feet.

'Now what did that tomato ever do to you,' Mom tutted, picking it up.

Paul and I burst into laughter, and in a flash, we were kids again, running around barefoot, giving my mom grey hairs.

'It's good to have you home sis,' Paul gave me a squeeze on our way out to the garden, where we spent the rest of the afternoon telling old stories and new ones.

Talking about baby names and whether it would be a girl or boy.

It was another perfect day and I wished every weekend could be just like this one – surrounded by family and happy memories being shared. The promise of new ones on the horizon.

Later that night I called Kaitlyn. I was in serious need of some girl talk.

'How are you feeling?' Kaitlyn asked.

I repressed a sigh at being asked this question yet again and reminded myself that it came from a place of love.

'I'm fine, it was just one little accident.'

'Sophie, you could have died,' Kaitlyn's voice was grave.

'I'm sorry, I'm just tired, I guess. I didn't take what happened lightly, but I promise I'm fine. I'm better than fine. I haven't needed my pills. Actually, I threw them out while Grayson and I were in Abingdon.'

'You what? Soph, I'm all for moving forward, but do you think that was wise? Shouldn't you have held onto them, just in case?' Kaitlyn couldn't hide the alarm in her tone.

'I don't know how to explain this right, but something happened out there, Kay, after the accident. It gave me clarity and a sense of peace. I was able to forgive myself for everything that happened with Luke. All I knew for sure was that I wouldn't be needing those pills anymore.'

'Well, as long as you're sure,' Kaitlyn replied hesitantly.

'I am. Now, tell me what's been going on with you, and please tell me you're coming out here soon?' I hated that I sounded like so whiny, but I missed my best friend terribly.

She was also working too hard and needed a break.

'I was going to surprise you, but I'm far too excited. I'm coming out in two weeks.'

I couldn't contain my squeal of delight and we spent the rest of the call planning Kaitlyn's trip.

She would be here for a week, which wasn't long enough, but I wouldn't take what I could get.

When I heard her yawning, I told her we could catch up again in a few days and that I couldn't wait to see her before hanging up the phone.

I went to sleep that night with a small smile on my face, feeling like a kid on Christmas morning.

I couldn't wait to see her and introduce her to everyone on the farm.

It was strange having a Monday off, I wasn't quite sure what to do with myself, so after a morning run and breakfast with my parents, I decided to grab my notebook and pen and head to the Shackleford Banks, feeling inspired to write for the first time in a very long time.

I'd chosen the perfect day for it, the sun was shining, the sky was a brilliant blue for as far as the eye could see.

The only downside being, that same blue sky reminded me a little too much of a pair of eyes I'd grown accustomed to getting lost in quite frequently of late.

Walking along the sandy shoreline, I opened my mind and let it wonder across all the events that had come to pass since arriving here.

My imagination started to run wild, and as soon as I found a quiet spot on the beach, near some of the wild horses, I started writing.

It was the first time I was attempting to write something that stemmed from real life, from my own experiences, rather than something I'd made up in my head.

It was the first time I'd wanted to write something true, something meaningful, something real, and it flowed from me, onto the pages.

I wrote page after page, lost in the story, lost in the words and emotions that came with it and when I surfaced, almost an entire notebook later (yes, notebook – occasionally I liked to go old school and actually write, instead of typing a book out on my laptop), the sun was dipping low in the sky.

Flexing my fingers, I stretched my arms up above my head, having gone stiff from sitting in one position too long.

It felt good to be writing again, but it felt even better to have such a clear vision of where I wanted this story to go.

Although I had a clear vision in my head for the story, it was the ending that I couldn't quite envision and that had me vexed.

Was it because I wanted to see how the story unfolded, or because I didn't in fact know for certain how I wanted it to end yet?

This was the difficulty with writing a story that was so close to home. It blurred reality with fiction.

Either way, I would continue with it all the while it flowed from me like a river making her way to the ocean, enjoying the ride while it lasted.

I leaned back in the soft sand, soaking up the glorious warmth from the sun, hating that summer was coming to an end – not that winters here were as cold as New York.

Then again, perhaps it was the memories of this summer that I wanted to last more than summer itself.

My mind drifted back to Grayson and his reaction at finding Caleb and I having dinner together.

What had troubled him? Was he jealous? If so, why? It's not like we were together.

Surely he knew how much he meant to me, just as Caleb did. They were both important parts of my life now.

Or maybe he didn't. Maybe he needed to see how important he was to me.

And just like that, I knew what I needed to do.

Gathering up my things, I made my way back to the ferry, making a mental checklist of what I needed to pick up in town before going back to the farm tonight.

Something I'd learned early on in life was that occasionally, making plans didn't work, sometimes you had to just wing it and hope for the best.

I was reminded of this on my return to the farm.

'Morning, Rosie, have you seen Grayson?'

I found Rosie in the kitchen on Tuesday morning when I stopped in to check on the piglets (who were currently sound asleep after a feeding) and grab a cup of coffee.

'He's not here, honey, he had to leave yesterday for Greenville. We received an urgent call on Sunday night for a rescue, someone found twin calves in a field, no sign of their mother or owner,' Rosie shook her head in disgust and I wholeheartedly shared her sentiment.

I wondered if I would ever get used to how horrid some human beings could be. I doubted it.

'He'll be back in a day or so,' Rosie continued, misunderstanding the concern looked on my face.

She handed me a cup of coffee, as we sat at the breakfast table.

'How are you parents?' Rosie asked, sipping her coffee.

'They're good, Dad seems to be doing a lot better. They're looking forward to seeing you and Sam this weekend.'

My parents, along with Paul and Sarah, were coming to the farm on Saturday for lunch, which would probably pan out into the evening.

There never were enough hours in the day when we all got together.

'I'm glad to hear that. We were so worried after your dad's heart-attack. They both mean the world to us and we would be devastated if anything happened to either of them.'

I was once again touched by Rosie's affections towards my parents and I reached out to squeeze her hand.

'I'm so happy you're in our lives, Rosie.'

She looked taken aback for a moment, before composing herself, and giving me a warm, loving smile.

'And we are truly blessed to have you in ours. I've noticed a difference in Grayson and Caleb since you've been around. They're becoming brothers again, and I'll be eternally grateful for that.'

Just as I was about to ask Rosie what she meant, about them becoming brothers again, the piglets decided that was the perfect time to wake up and start squealing for their formula.

'Sophie, be a honey and grab the bottles from the counter and give me a hand feeding these two, would you?'

Putting my questions to the back of my mind, I grabbed the bottles and we got to work.

Time seemed to slow, while I waited for Grayson to return home.

Finally, on Thursday morning, I overheard Rosie on the phone to him – he was on his way home.

My heart skipped a beat and I reminded myself that

what I had planned was only a very small gesture, he may not even like it.

Still, I couldn't help but feel jittery and I scolded myself for being so silly, then reminded myself that's exactly what life should be about, silly, happy moments that made you feel like a teenager again.

I was giving myself whiplash with all these emotions coursing through me, I thought, almost laughing out loud at myself.

Shaking myself off, I pulled myself back to the present.

I was mucking out the barn with Ava, one of our new volunteers, which, granted, wasn't the most glamorous job, but I enjoyed working with Ava. We'd become fast friends these past few weeks.

I guessed she was probably early to mid-sixties (although she could have easily passed for fifties).

She ran a small farm about half an hour from ours, growing and selling vegetables and flowers for events and to local florists.

I felt a kind of kinship to her. She awoke my inner hippie and I adored her carefree, easy going approach to life.

'Life is short, you've got to grab it by the balls while you can,' she'd said to me during one of our deeper conversations.

I couldn't help but laugh at her colourful analogies.

'Would you mind carrying on in here without me for a while? I wanted to get a few more pictures for the website and our social media accounts. The response has been amazing, but people want to see more,' I beamed, beyond happy by the response rate.

'Of course, sugar, I'll finish up in here then head over to feed the goats.'

'Thanks, Ava, you're a lifesaver. I'll meet you over there.'

With the new arrivals, there were more than enough photo ops.

This was by far one of my favourite aspects of working at the sanctuary, I loved being behind the camera and even more so when I was snapping pictures of all these wonderfully adorable animals.

After taken some great shots of Apollo in our clearing, I could already imagine them hanging up in the cottage, in black and white prints.

I'd also managed to sneak in a few shots of each member of the Danvers family working with different animals.

Although they loved all of the animals and cared for them equally, they couldn't help having their favourites.

Usually animals who held a special meaning for each of them, or a special place in their heart, the way Apollo did for me, and I thought they would make great Christmas gifts for each of them – if I could hold out until then that is.

For Rosie, it was Betty the goat, who always chewed on Rosie's skirt, or jeans or pretty much any item of clothing and I'd snapped a great shot of Rosie laughing in the sunshine, while Betty tugged at the hem of her skirt.

The way the sunlight filtered around them in the photo gave it a magical feel.

Sam was besotted with Buttercup, the sanctuary's cow

slash foster mom.

Buttercup had been ill-treated and Sam had been the one to rescue her and nurse her back to health. She loved Sam just as much as he loved her.

One afternoon I'd spotted Sam in the pasture with Buttercup. Just the two of them, hanging out like old friends.

Sam lovingly stroked her face, and anyone could see the love in both of their eyes in that one picture.

Caleb's had been a little harder to figure out, until the day I'd seen him in the pig barn with one of the fairly new members, Oliver.

Caleb had spent a little longer with Oliver and when I'd asked Sam about it, he'd told me a similar story to his own with Buttercup.

Caleb had been the one who found Oliver, abandoned in a cardboard box on the side of the road, so Caleb had brought him back to the sanctuary, only to find he had a problem with his legs and couldn't stand on his own.

With the help of the sanctuary's vet, and a lot of time and patience, Caleb had helped nurse Oliver back to health and the adorable pig was now able to walk on his own.

It was truly a heart-warming tale.

The picture I'd captured of Caleb and Oliver was one I loved.

Caleb had been kneeling down in front of Oliver, scratching his chin, a gentle smile on Caleb's face, as Oliver's snout almost touched Caleb's nose.

I'd managed to capture the look of joy in Oliver's sweet eyes, as well as the smile on Caleb's face and I looked forward to the day I gave it to him.

Grayson's was slightly more complex.

Many years ago, when Grayson was much younger, a mare had been brought to the sanctuary in rough shape.

Sam had taught Grayson everything he knew about horses and how to care for them, while they tried to nurse the mare back to health.

She was about to give birth, and though they cared for her as much as they could, in the end it hadn't been enough.

They'd lost her during the birth, but the foal had survived, and Grayson had vowed to take care of her foal. And he had, to this day.

She was a beautiful pale grey, almost white, horse named Oakley, and Grayson loved her as much today as I imagined he did back then.

His picture had been somewhat harder to capture, but after following him out to his spot by the lake, I'd managed to get two good shots.

The First showed them both by the water's edge, Grayson leaning down to scoop water in his hands for Oakley to drink from.

The second was more of a silhouette of them facing one another, with the setting sun positioned behind them through the trees, and although you couldn't see their features, you could feel the love emanating from the picture, with their heads bowed close together, almost as if they were saying a silent prayer together.

Speaking of Grayson, there he was. He must have just

arrived back at the farm.

He looked tired.

I started walking towards him, hesitating briefly when he let out a great big sigh, like he had the weight of the world on his shoulders.

Maybe he needed to be alone.

As I was about to turn back, he looked up and smiled, 'Hey, Sophie,' he called out and I continued towards him.

'Hey, is everything ok?' I asked as I got closer.

'Yeah, just a rough few days. The calves needed to be checked out so they're staying for overnight observation, but I think they'll be ok,' Grayson explained, running a hand through his hair.

'Well, whatever you need, I'm here to help, ok?'

'Thanks, Soph, that means a lot.'

I wasn't sure if this was the right time or not, but I thought the distraction might do Grayson the world of good, so before I could chicken out, I asked him if he would be around tomorrow afternoon, figuring today probably wasn't the best day for it.

He looked exhausted and I would bet anything that all he wanted was a shower, a homecooked meal, and his bed.

'Yeah, I will be, why?'

'Just wondered. Keep the afternoon free, will you?'

'Sophie, what's going on?' His eyes narrowed nervously.

'It's a surprise. Trust me, it's a good one. You'll like it, it's nothing to worry about. Now get some rest and I'll see you tomorrow,' I smiled and turned to head back to Ava to help her finish up for the day, leaving Grayson staring after me.

I wanted to make his life better, the way he'd done for me.

I wanted to make things easier and lessen his burdens, I just wasn't entirely sure how to do that, yet.

But I would figure it out.

The following morning, I was butterflies and jitters.

I had everything set for that afternoon and Ava was kindly covering for us, so I had a few hours to get as much done around the sanctuary as possible, before meeting Grayson in the barn.

'You seem very chipper this morning,' Sam commented while we were preparing for the calves to arrive in a few days.

They were progressing well so far, and would be coming home soon, but we had to section off a part of the barn for them while they healed.

'I'm just looking forward to this weekend, it'll be great having everyone here tomorrow,' I replied, which was true, it just wasn't the only reason for my good mood and Sam eyed me sceptically, seeing right through me.

I simply smiled and shrugged, before we continued working.

Sam was exceptionally easy to work with, we usually chatted easily while we worked, but occasionally, it was like he could sense when I was somewhere else, and he was happy to leave me to my thoughts while we worked in comfortable silence.

I wasn't sure why I felt so buzzed, or was I nervous? I didn't even know what I was feeling.

It wasn't a big deal at all. It certainly wasn't anything different from past experiences with Grayson. So why did I feel this excited buzz thrumming through my veins?

I brushed it off to the fact that it was probably because I was surprising him, and I wasn't sure if he'd like it or not, although I wasn't entirely convinced that was the reason, but I needed to stack it up to something.

When it was finally time, I raced back to my cottage, showered as quickly as humanly possible, grabbed everything that I'd prepared the night before and raced back out the door, having one more stop to make before meeting Grayson in the barn, and I needed to get moving if I was going to make it in time.

'Hey, there you are. Are you ok? You look a little flushed?' Grayson took in my flushed cheeks and I took a deep breath to slow my racing heart.

'I'm fine,' I tried to smile and calm my nerves.

You are being utterly ridiculous, Sophie, I told myself.

'Shall we?' I asked.

Grayson nodded, still eyeing me curiously.

We saddled our horses and once we were all set to go, I turned to Grayson with a wicked smile on my face.

'There's one more thing. You need to wear this,' I handed Grayson a blindfold and he looked at me as though I had two heads.

'You're kidding me, right?'

'Nope, it's all part of the surprise. Trust me, I won't let you fall in a ditch or anything,' I laughed and to my surprise he actually took the blindfold, although he didn't put it on right away.

'Is this really necessary?' He asked, looking from the blindfold to me after a short distance.

'Please? It would just make the surprise a lot better,' I pleaded.

After a few more moments deliberation, and one final look in my direction that said he thought I had officially lost it, he tied the blindfold around his head.

Taking hold of his horses' rains, I led the way.

Chapter 14

Given that we couldn't go very fast, we still made good time, and I was glad I'd gone with the blindfold.

As soon as we got there, I told Grayson he could remove it, and it made it all worthwhile, seeing him take in the elaborate picnic I'd laid out beside the lake, along with the fairy lights I'd hung up in the trees around us.

I'd spread out a blanket and filled it with as many of Grayson's favourite foods as I could, along with a chilled bottle of bubbly and bunches of wildflowers I'd picked from around the lake.

I had to admit that it looked good and given the expression on Grayson's face I think he did too.

'Sophie, you did all of this for me?' He asked, as we dismounted our horses, tethering them to a tree near the lake, where they could get to the water and with an abundance of grass, they would be set for as long as we were out here.

We stepped through the trees and I removed my shoes to sit on the blanket.

'I wanted to thank you for all you've done for me. I feel like you're either saving my life, or taking care of me, and I wanted to find some way to show you how much it meant to me,' I explained, suddenly feeling self-conscious.

'This is amazing, Sophie, thank you. I don't think anyone's ever done anything like this for me before.' Grayson looked truly shocked and I felt a wave of relief wash over me.

Popping the bubbly, I poured us each a glass, before toasting to Grayson.

I took a long drink, feeling my nerves settle.

'What? I was thirsty,' I replied in response to Grayson's raised eyebrows.

Setting my glass down, I plated up a little of everything and handed it to Grayson.

'Eat up,' I encouraged.

He took a long drink from his own glass, before placing it down and biting into a slider.

'Mmm, this is delicious,' he said between bites, and I smiled, glad that in some tiny way I could brighten his day.

We ate, we drank, we talked, for what felt like hours.

Grayson was lying back, his head propped up on his arm, watching me as I packed the food away, not wanting to attract bugs.

'Penny for your thoughts?' I smiled, thinking of the countless times he'd asked me that.

'I was thinking what an incredible woman you are,' he said, so serenely, like he was simply stating something as obvious as the sky being blue or the grass green.

I didn't know what to say and I felt my cheeks warm under his scrutiny.

'Let's go for a swim,' I jumped up, not wanting to be the focus of his intense gaze any longer.

'I'm not sure I can, I'm so stuffed I may just sink straight to the bottom,' Grayson replied, but lifted himself up onto his elbows.

'Come on, I'll save you if you start to sink,' I pulled off my shirt and threw it at him (I'd come prepared this time and wore a bikini under my clothes).

That was all it took. Grayson jumped up and pulled off his own shirt before stepping out of his jeans.

I was already in the water, enjoying the view.

The water felt amazing and I wasn't sure if it was the champagne, or the cool, soothing water, but I felt myself relax. The tension in my shoulders slowly melt away.

Grayson floated next to me and for a time neither of us spoke.

We didn't need to fill the silence, we were perfectly content in one another's company, lost in our own thoughts, while still enjoying having the other near.

'Tell me about your hopes and dreams for the future,' I eventually asked Grayson, suddenly curious about what he wanted from life.

'Wow. Where to start. Well, I'd love to grow the sanctuary, take in more animals, build more barns and enclosures. Ideally, I'd also want the entire farm to be completely self-sustaining. Growing our own fruit and vegetables. We're not too far off this, but I'd like to expand the veggie patch so we can provide local farmers markets and local shops. I want to invest in solar panels eventually too.'

'Not much then,' I teased, secretly impressed, but not

surprised that he had such big dreams. 'So that's all to do with the farm and the sanctuary, but what about you?'

'You mean do I want to get married, have two point five children and a white picket fence?' He laughed. 'Sure, maybe, one day.'

'I hope you don't let the woman you were engaged to put you off forever. It would be a shame to never let love back in because of one rotten egg,' I hedged, not wanting to open up old wounds.

'What about you? Are you ready to let love back in?' Grayson changed the subject, watching me intently.

'I might be open to it if the right person came along and the opportunity presented itself,' I tried to skirt around his question.

'You make it sound like a business deal. Not very romantic.'

'Sometimes there's more to a relationship than romance and being swept off your feet, you know,' I retorted.

I wouldn't have called my relationship with Luke a whirlwind romance, but we did nice things for one another and it was real. Our love ran deeper than superficial things and that had mattered more to me than romantic dinners or jewellery and flowers or being swept off your feet.

'And sometimes you deserve to be swept off your feet,' Grayson whispered.

He was so close the water rippled around me from his movements.

I found myself caught in his gaze once again, unable to blink, barely able to breath, as his piercing blue eyes bore into the very depths of my soul.

Searching for something, seeking answers to unspoken questions.

'You deserve to be told how special and beautiful you are, every day. You deserve to be treated like a queen every day of your life and know that you are truly, deeply loved,' Grayson went on.

I said nothing, hypnotised by the sound of his voice washing over me, taking me under with each word he whispered.

He reached across the surface of the water and tucked a strand of my wet hair behind my ear, sending involuntary shivers coursing through my entire body.

'You deserve everything you've ever wanted, Sophie,' he leaned in closer, his voice barely a whisper on the breeze.

In that moment there was only one thing I wanted.

It thrilled and terrified me.

I wanted him, all of him. I think I'd wanted Grayson Danvers from the moment I met him.

'Grayson…' I trailed off, unable to find the words, but he didn't need me to finish, he knew what I wanted.

Gently cupping the side of my face in his hand, he ran his thumb over my bottom lip.

The sensation setting off fireworks in the trail of his touch, as his hand continued down my neck, along my collarbone.

My eyes fluttered closed and I felt myself leaning into the arm that was now wrapped around my waist.

I didn't even know when he'd wrapped his arm around me, but it didn't matter.

All that mattered was his touch.

I never wanted it to stop, I wanted to be locked in this moment for all of time, but something was interrupting, something was piercing through the euphoric haze he had created.

My eyes opened and I realised it was his phone.

He scowled at it and a giggle escaped my lips as I realised that my expression mirrored his.

It finally stopped ringing and his eyes returned to mine.

My smile faded, replaced by a yearning I wasn't sure I'd ever felt before.

I ached to be in his arms, and I couldn't bear to wait any longer.

I traced my fingers up the length of his strong, muscular arms, memorising every line until my hands rested on his shoulders, only briefly, before I continued my ascent, entwining my fingers in his thick hair at the nape of his neck.

Just when I thought our lips would finally meet, it began again.

The incessant ringing, and I drew a ragged breath in.

'You should get it. It'll probably just keep ringing,' I reluctantly said, and I could see the war raging behind his eyes, sending thrills through me.

He didn't want to leave me either.

'I'll be waiting right here,' I assured him.

He sighed deeply and pulled me close, whispering, 'You better be,' before swimming off to answer his phone.

I couldn't gauge much from my position in the water, only that Grayson was pacing while on the phone and it looked serious.

It gave me time to breath and simply enjoy the warm sensation washing through me.

I dare say it was pure happiness.

Well, that and a few other things too; desire, hunger, raw attraction, just to name a few.

It felt strange, after so long, to feel this way again, but it was wonderful, and I wanted to cling on to the feeling for as long as I possibly could.

Apparently, mother nature had other plans.

A loud crack shattered my little bubble and the first few drops of rain started to fall from the sky before the heavens opened up and the rain poured down in torrents.

Of course it did. It always seemed to when we were together, I thought dryly.

I scrambled out of the water and started packing up our things while Grayson ended his phone call.

He grabbed the picnic blanket and remainder of the items I hadn't yet stashed into the saddlebags, before we both pulled our now soaking wet clothes back on.

We turned to leave, but I wasn't ready to lose this moment, not yet.

Besides, a little rain never hurt anyone.

Another loud crack from the sky made me second guess that. And then I stopped thinking altogether.

Just go for it, the little voice inside my head shouted.

I didn't need to be told twice.

'Grayson,' I called after him through the pouring rain.

When he turned back to me, I could see the need, the wanting, still in his eyes, and I smiled.

A questioning looked crossed his face for only a second, before I closed the short distance between us, wrapping my arms around his neck and pausing only briefly to capture this moment, and the look in his eyes – I wanted to remember everything about this moment.

Grayson seemed to understand, before the need grew too strong and our lips locked.

I lost myself in his strong arms and the urgency of that kiss.

The world fell away in that moment. No one, and nothing else existed, it was just the two of us, lost in time, sheltered by the pouring rain that soaked us through.

I didn't care.

All that mattered was his strong arms holding me tightly, one hand running down my back, sending shivers up and down my spine.

His soft lips moulding perfectly to my own and his intoxicating scent washing over me, sending me deeper into oblivion.

When I surfaced, I wasn't the same person I had been before. I would never be the same again.

I felt…alive. More alive than I ever thought possible.

My skin tingled from Grayson's touch, marked by this glorious man, while my lips cried out for more.

'We should go,' Grayson's voice was rough with emotion, and I shivered again as his lips brushed along my jaw line.

His eyes gave him away, they always did. The emotion behind them had been clear from that very first day in the barn, I just hadn't realised it back then.

He didn't want to leave, any more than I wanted to go.

'Ok,' I whispered against his lips, twisting my fingers through his hair.

He laughed, 'We need to get the horses back.'

That sobered me up.

I knew he was right. It wasn't fair to keep them out in this weather.

That shook my resolve and I started to remove my hands from his hair, but as I turned away, Grayson caught my hand and spun me back into his arms, kissing me more passionately, making my knees turn to jelly.

I felt high, or drunk, or somewhere completely otherworldly.

This was so different from what I'd shared with Luke. No worse, no better, just different.

It made my head spin in new and wonderful ways.

'Ok, we really need to go,' Grayson broke the kiss, resting his forehead against mine.

I smiled, kissing him one last time, a soft, chaste kiss that still somehow made every nerve ending in my body stand to attention, before we got on our horses and rode back to the barn.

After drying the horses and giving them a longer brush down than normal – we thought it only right after making them stand in the rain while we made out, Grayson walked with me to the main house.

I felt like a giddy teenager, riding the high of her first kiss. I couldn't stop smiling.

Sneaking a peak at Grayson, he appeared to share my feelings. A distant look clouded his eyes and a small smile curled up at the corners of his mouth.

As we neared the main house Grayson's pace slowed slightly and he turned towards me.

'Could we keep this quiet?' He gestured between us, 'Just for the time being?'

I hesitated, not liking the sudden feeling welling up inside me, making me feel like I was someone's dirty little secret and wondering where this was coming from, but not wanting to come across as insecure or needy I simply said, 'Sure.'

'Thanks, it's just that my folks have been wishing I would meet someone for a while now and I really don't want to make a fuss, you know? I want to explore whatever this is and I want to enjoy it, but most of all,' he looked around, before pushing me up against the side of the house and kissing me so deeply that I was certain this time my legs truly would give way.

They didn't, mainly thanks to Grayson holding me so tightly, sandwiching me between the side of the house and his body.

His warm, strong, insanely close body. A body that I wanted, no needed, to explore far more than I needed air to breath.

'Most of all,' he repeated before continuing, 'I want you all to myself.'

Before I could form a coherent word or sentence to respond, we heard movement from inside the house and Grayson stepped back, taking a deep breath, raking one hand through his damp hair (the rain had eased to a fine drizzle now), we walked into the house together, trying to act as normal as possible.

This was going to be im-possible!

To say I barely survived dinner would be the understatement of the century.

Not only had Rosie asked me if I was ok because I looked feverish, but every time Grayson's leg bumped mine, or his hand brushed against my own, as he passed the salad, I could feel my cheeks burning and my heart hammered in my chest.

This was going to be far more difficult than I thought.

I still wasn't sure how I felt about keeping things quiet, but I guess I could understand where Grayson was coming from.

I tried to put myself in his shoes and thought if it were my family, I may feel the same, given that we had no idea where this road would take us. If anywhere at all.

Suddenly something the fortune teller had said to me the night of the festival in Abingdon came back to me.

'You'll find yourself at a crossroads and you'll have to make the right choice for all, or it will cost you the thing you love most.'

I hadn't thought much of it at the time and I wasn't entirely sure why it had popped into my head when it did, but something told me I would find out soon enough.

Pushing the feeling down as far as I could, nowhere near ready to face reality yet. I would deal with whatever came when I needed to.

For now, curling up in my bed (sadly alone), but with the memory of Grayson taking up every corner of my mind, I drifted into a blissful, dreamless sleep. My only thought was seeing him again, in just a few short hours.

It wasn't such a hard price to pay when the prize was so worth the wait.

The weekend flew by in a blur of stolen moments and curious looks (on my part at least).

'Are you feeling ok?' My mom asked, touching the back of her hand to my forehead.

I knew I was flushed.

I had good reason for looking flushed, given the fact that I'd just been lip-locked in the upstairs hallway with Grayson.

It was becoming increasingly difficult to keep our hands off each other and if we weren't more careful, we were going to get caught. And soon.

Something I kept trying to remind him of, only to be pulled tighter against his chest and kissed more deeply – neither of which I was complaining about, by the way.

'I'm fine,' I lied to my mom, feeling giddy.

I felt happy, fulfilled and it took me completely by surprise.

I stood watching my family and the Danvers – who, for some time now, I classed as a second family, and I felt whole, complete.

I knew without a shadow of a doubt that I was home, that this is where I belonged.

It had been a long road getting here, but watching

everyone, I knew I was home.

It hadn't always been the easiest of roads travelled, but I didn't regret a single moment.

How could I when that same road had led me, first to Luke, and my life in New York, and now back to my own family, but to Grayson and his family too. And the sanctuary.

I'd known loss so great that I thought I would never recover from it, until now.

A piece of my heart would always belong to Luke and I would always miss him, but being here, being with Grayson, surrounded by family and friends, I knew that I was whole again.

They had put me back together when I'd feared I would forever be broken.

I smiled knowing that Luke was watching over all of us, and I hoped that he was happier and more at peace knowing that we were here now, together, looking after one another.

'You look so beautiful tonight,' Grayson's voice all but whispered, sending a trail of goosebumps down my arms, as his warm breath brushed my neck.

I turned to face him, draping my arms around his neck, admiring his beautiful face, so open and full of the same wonder I was feeling.

I wanted to memorise every line and curve of his perfect features, never forgetting these moments, or the way he looked at me and made me feel like I was the most beautiful woman he'd ever laid eyes on.

I stretched up and brushed my lips against his, the

butterflies in my tummy rejoiced, as my heart rate increased.

Grayson deepened the kiss, slipping his hands underneath the back of my shirt. A small moan escaping my lips.

This wasn't helping matters.

I wanted nothing more than to disappear into the night, just the two of us, and get lost in all that was Grayson Danvers, but I knew our families would soon start to wonder where we were.

Grayson must have been thinking along the same line, reluctantly pulling away.

'You're driving me crazy, Sophie,' he growled, sending my senses into overdrive yet again.

'Right back at ya,' I replied breathlessly.

'We better get back before someone notices we're missing, or before I decide to steal you away and never bring you back again,' Grayson pulled me in for one final kiss before he returned to our families.

I stayed where I was a moment longer, mainly to catch my breath, but I'd also wanted to get a few shots of everyone together, before Grayson had arrived and scrambled my brain.

Lifting my camera with slightly shaky hands, I did my best to steady them before clicking a few candid shots of everyone.

When I was ready, I joined the others, trying to avert my gaze from Grayson, knowing full well the chain reaction that would cause.

Chapter 15

In the weeks leading up to Kaitlyn's arrival, Grayson and I spent every spare, secret, moment together, which was becoming increasingly difficult.

Sam needed Grayson's help on a new project, leaving me to deal with Caleb, who wanted a second shot at dinner – something I suddenly felt very unsure of.

Did Caleb want more than friendship from me?

Usually I brushed his flirting off as Caleb simply being Caleb, but his more recent actions and comments had me wondering if maybe there was something more serious behind it.

Of course, he hadn't actually said anything to give me that impression.

It was just little things like when he'd hug me, holding on a little longer than necessary.

Or the possessive way his hand would linger on my lower back, as he let me walk into the barn first.

Or the way his eyes sometimes looked so intently into my own, so similarly to his brothers.

Not that anyone could match the fire burning behind Grayson's eyes.

It made me wonder if it had always been like this with

Caleb. Was I only now noticing it because I was with Grayson?

I didn't think so, but I couldn't be certain.

I was quickly using up all the excuses I could think of to avoid Caleb; I was busy working on the website or I was writing – both of which were true to an extent.

I had been updating the website and working on my new novel, which was coming along at a surprising rate, but most of my free time had been spent locked away in my cottage with Grayson.

Spent nestled together on the couch, or in the garden on balmy nights, talking for hours.

Ok, there may not have always been that much talking involved.

Don't judge! I doubt many women would be able to keep their hands off someone like Grayson Danvers for long.

No matter what we did, I was happy just being with Grayson.

Those simple evenings spent together, discovering one other, talking about everything and nothing and just being.

My only complaint, if you can call it that, was that Grayson was trying to be a gentleman, taking things slow.

Something I appeared to be struggling with far more than he was.

'Sophie, wait,' he said, on one such evening.

Having started out innocently enough, just talking on the couch, which led to kissing, which led to me on Grayson's lap, trying to remove his shirt.

I wanted to be with him in every possible way and it frustrated me to no end that he didn't seem to reciprocate my feelings.

Scrap that, his body seemed to reciprocate exactly the same feelings. His mind, however, did not.

'Remind me what we're waiting for, Grayson?' I huffed, exasperated.

'I just think we should take things slow. I want our first time together to be perfect.'

'Life isn't perfect, we both know that. It's about the spontaneous, messy, moments that we should grab with both hands, before they pass you by.'

He insisted that he simply wanted to take things slow, but I sensed there was more.

What I couldn't figure out, was why he wasn't telling me what was really bothering him.

Between the sanctuary, which was busier than ever, working on the website, writing the novel, sneaking in stolen moments with Grayson, it didn't leave me much time to linger on these thoughts.

Most nights I fell into bed, utterly spent.

So when I received a text from Kaitlyn, exclaiming how excited she was to be arriving tomorrow, I thought I was seeing things.

Tomorrow. How had that happened? Where had the time gone!

Grayson got to see a whole other side to me that night. One I wasn't sure he thought was completely nuts, or adorable. It could have gone either way, judging by the bemused look on his face, I thought with a chuckle, as I rambled on excitedly to him about Kaitlyn, unable to help myself.

She planned on spending a few nights with her parents and the remainder of her trip here on the farm with us.

I wished more than anything that we had more time together, but a few days was better than nothing. I would take what I could get.

When the day finally arrived, I was like a kid in a candy store, so hyped up with excitement that even Rosie and Sam found me amusing.

'How much coffee have you had already?' Caleb eyed me with more than just suspicion brewing in his eyes, and I was grateful that Grayson wasn't here.

I was certain he would pick up on these small changes and I wasn't sure how he would feel about it.

Then again, it was Grayson's choice to keep us a secret from his family. Things certainly would be a whole lot easier if he would just tell everyone.

Just then I heard a car pull up and dashed outside, just as Kaitlyn stepped out of her hire car.

'Kaitlyn,' I called from the porch, taking the stairs two at a time.

'Sophie, oh I've missed you so much,' she reached out to pull me into a hug, as I reached her, holding on so tightly, and for the longest time.

'I'm all for a little girl on girl action, but are you going to introduce us to your friend, Soph? Or should I just keep taking pictures of this with my mind?'

I turned, still keeping an arm around Kaitlyn, swatted

Caleb, before introducing her to everyone.

'It's so great to finally meet you all. Sophie's told me so much about you, and about the sanctuary. I feel like I know the place already,' Kaitlyn greeted them warmly, her eyes lingering on Caleb.

Suppressing a laugh, I remembered that I'd pre-warned her about Caleb's charms.

Fat lot of use that had done, she was clearly already swept up in his good looks.

'Nice to meet you, Kaitlyn. Now, if you'll excuse us, some of us have work to do,' Caleb jokingly stuck his tongue out at me.

Sam gave his son a disapproving look, but followed him to the barn anyway, telling Kaitlyn they'd catch up over dinner later.

'Come on in, I'll put a fresh pot of coffee on,' Rosie told us and we gladly followed her back inside.

'It's so great to see you, Soph. You look really good,' Kaitlyn squeezed my hand.

After coffee with Rosie, I'd helped Kaitlyn bring her bags back to the cottage.

Smiling at my best friend, who now sat next to me on the couch, I knew what she was really saying; I looked a whole lot better than the last time she'd seen me.

That felt like a lifetime ago.

How was it possible that it was only three months ago? So much had changed in those three months.

'You look tired,' I replied, knowing she wouldn't take offence.

‘I feel tired. Work has been exhausting. I just feel like I’m being pulled in too many different directions. I think Roger forgets there’s only one of me,’ Kaitlyn scowled at the mention of her boss.

‘Have you given any more thought to leaving, trying to find something else?’ I asked, sipping my green tea.

‘Yeah, I have. I’m just not sure I want to stay in New York anymore. It hasn’t been the same since you left either,’ Kaitlyn stretched, resting her head on the arm of the couch, her feet on my lap.

I tried to contain my excitement at the possibility of my best friend moving here, although I wasn’t even sure yet if that’s what she’d meant.

‘I just don’t know, Soph. I feel like I need a change, you know. Something different, whether that’s geographically or otherwise, I think it’s time for a change.’

‘I’m sure there are loads of opportunities out here,’ I couldn’t hide my smile.

‘I’ve been thinking about that too. I miss you, and I miss my family. How has it been for you, moving back?’ She asked seriously.

Where do I begin!

‘It’s been so great, Kay,’ I replied, staring off into space, my mind swimming with images of Grayson.

‘Sophie, what’s going on? You’re practically glowing. It’s Grayson isn’t it? Something’s happened,’ Kaitlyn’s enthusiasm grew, along with the grin on my face, and she threw a cushion at me, ‘Oh my God! Tell me everything!’

‘There isn’t a whole lot to tell. We kissed, we’ve been kissing, a lot. But no one knows, so you can’t say anything.

To anyone.'

'What's the deal with that?'

'He doesn't want to make a fuss yet. It's a really long story, but he wants us to figure things out for ourselves first, simply enjoy our time together and see where it takes us before we tell anyone.'

'I guess that makes sense. There's no point announcing it to everyone when it's still in the early stages. It is the early stages, right?' Kaitlyn raised an eyebrow.

'Yes, very early. Nothing's happened if that's what you want to know. But oh my, those kisses!' I swooned.

'Details, I want details,' Kaitlyn sat up, suddenly very much alert and enthused.

In the hours that followed, I told her everything from our time in Abingdon, where we'd gotten closer, to that first kiss in the rain by the lake, to the more recent stolen moments.

I got lost in telling our story.

It made me ache for Grayson in ways I didn't know were possible.

But, let's get back on track.

Wanting Kaitlyn to know there was more to Beaufort than just good-looking men, I tried my best to sell her on moving here and hoped, oh how I hoped, I'd done a good enough job.

This day just kept getting better.

Turns out a local radio station wanted to feature Willow Farm Sanctuary on their evening show.

'That's amazing news!' I wrapped my arms around

Grayson's neck, who'd just arrived back from meeting with them.

'It's all thanks to you, Sophie. We wouldn't have gotten this far without your help and the website,' Grayson brushed my hair off my face, his hand lingering there. 'I don't know what I would have done without you.'

Lifting my chin until my lips met his, he kissed me gently at first, quickly turning to urgent, insatiable need.

A sound came from behind me, but I was too wrapped up in Grayson to fully register what it was. It sounded again and I realised it was Kaitlyn clearing her throat, making Grayson jump and pull away, breathless.

'It's ok, Kaitlyn knows about us,' I told Grayson. 'Don't worry, she won't say anything,' I added quickly.

'So, this is Grayson Danvers. I've heard a lot about you,' Kaitlyn said, eyeing Grayson suspiciously.

I recognised the emotion behind her eyes; she was doing what a best friend did best, sizing him up. Looking out for me, not wanting me to get hurt again.

'Hi, Kaitlyn, it's great to finally meet you. I've heard a lot about you too,' Grayson replied warmly, albeit slightly confused by her seemingly hostile appearance. 'All good things, of course,' he added for good measure.

Kaitlyn smiled a little at that and I could see the slight change in her stance as she took us both in.

I wondered how we looked to her, from an outsider's perspective. Could she sense the intensity and intimacy between us? Was it as evident from the outside as it felt to me?

Thankfully it didn't take Kaitlyn long to come around, pulling a complete transformation, while the three of us sat in the garden, catching up over coffee.

I gathered she could tell Grayson was one of the good ones.

Sometimes you just knew, and with Grayson (once I'd gotten past his hard exterior, as well as my own denial over my feelings towards him), I'd seen that so clearly. He was good through and through.

It was fascinating to watch him with Kaitlyn.

He wasn't as guarded as he'd been with me at the start, always seeming to be holding back, and I wondered if it could maybe, just maybe, have anything to do with his feelings for me.

I wondered if one day he would tell me about those first few weeks, our first encounter especially. Why he had seemed to standoffish.

That felt like a distant memory now, and I realised suddenly that that version of him – the closed off Grayson, hadn't been around for quite some time.

He seemed lighter in recent days, happier, more carefree.

This made me so happy and I smiled, watching him, feeling my heart swell, when Kaitlyn's hand flashed in front of my face.

'Earth to Sophie.'

'Huh? Sorry, what were you saying?' I asked, coming back down to earth.

'Are you ready to head over to the main house for dinner?' Grayson must have repeated.

'Yeah, I'm ready,' I smiled in response to the looks they were both giving me, not offering any explanation for my behaviour.

I mean, what could I say? Don't mind me, I'm just swooning over my ruggedly good-looking, kind-hearted boyfriend.

Boyfriend.

Did I just say boyfriend? Hmm, I wasn't sure if I could even call him that when we were in a secret, whatever this was.

Well, that was a problem for another day. Tonight was about Kaitlyn being here, anything else could wait.

Dinner was… Interesting.

Kaitlyn hit it off, right off the bat, with Rosie and Sam, which had been a given really, she was just as laid back and easy going as they were, and I'd yet to meet someone who didn't like her.

My parents had come over too, equally as thrilled to see Kaitlyn again – they'd always loved her like she was part of the family.

Caleb had been the wild card and didn't fail to disappoint, turning up in full flirtation mode, and I groaned internally, not wanting my best friend to have to endure his wicked ways.

But what surprised me the most was that she appeared to enjoy his silly jokes and flirtatious comments. Almost encouraging him, fluttering her eyelashes at him and flicking her hair occasionally.

I watched in utter disbelief.

Later that night I cornered Caleb in the kitchen, as we put the dishes away. I had a bone to pick with him.

'Lay off Kaitlyn, would you,' I warned, 'She's leaving in

a few days for New York and I don't need her going back broken hearted because you've made her fall for you, just to leave her high and dry.'

'Would I ever do such a thing?' Caleb asked innocently.

I simply narrowed my eyes at him.

'You're not jealous, are you, Soph?' He asked, lounging against the counter, giving me a brooding smile.

'What! No, Caleb, I most certainly am not jealous!'

I didn't think I was.

I didn't feel jealous.

I was only worried about Kaitlyn.

But it was too late. Caleb had planted the seed of doubt, honing in on that as soon as he saw the waver behind my eyes.

He stepped towards me, handing me another plate, leaning in closer than necessary and whispered, 'Don't worry, Sophie, you'll always be my best girl.'

I wanted to smack that cocky smile off his face. What game was he playing at?

'Do you need a hand with anything?' Grayson's voice made my head snap up.

Oh God, that must have looked bad.

'Here, you take over bro, I've got work to do,' Caleb winked at me before leaving the kitchen and a few minutes later I heard Kaitlyn laughing, more than likely at one of his lame jokes.

'What was that about?' Grayson asked cautiously.

'Nothing. Just Caleb being Caleb,' I replied as convincingly as I could muster but all I felt was annoyance, mainly at Caleb's inflated ego.

Thinking I was jealous.
How ridiculous.

As the night drew to a close, we said goodnight to the Danvers, before making our way back to the cottage. The moonlight our only guide.

Kaitlyn looped her arm through mine, 'What a beautiful night,' she sighed, content, and my fears came flooding back.

'Oh no. Please tell me you haven't fallen for Caleb's charms already?'

'I don't know what you mean. Can't a girl simply enjoy the country air,' I could hear her smiling.

'Just be careful, ok? Remember what I told you about him.'

'I know, I know, the perpetual bachelor, ladies' man, and all-round flirt. Relax, Soph, I'm only having a little fun.'

'I'm sorry, I don't mean to rain on your parade or anything, I just don't want to see you get hurt.'

'I had all the same concerns for you, so I get it. That was until I saw the way you two were looking at each other. You're like the cover of a Hallmark card. It's kind of gross, Soph,' Kaitlyn laughed, 'But I'm really glad you're happy,' she added.

'Thanks Kay. Now we just need to find your Grayson. How are things with what's-his-name by the way?'

Kaitlyn had a bad habit of going for dead beat guys who were going nowhere slowly.

Her latest project was a struggling artist, as he referred to himself, which I translated as someone simply wanting somewhere to crash where he didn't have to pay rent or contribute to food or bills.

'Things didn't work out with Sebastian,' Kailyn replied.

I knew she wanted to meet someone, but she needed to change the type of guy she went for, before she would find anything serious.

'You know, guys out here are a lot better than the majority of the guys we've met in New York. Just another pro to add to the list of reasons you should move here,' I nudged her playfully.

'You're doing a pretty good job of selling me on that.'

We spent hours talking and laughing, late into the night, just like we used to, and I realised how much I'd really missed her.

Nothing could beat nights like this, catching up with your best friend, eating ice cream at midnight, and I made my mind up to spend the next few days showing Kaitlyn how wonderful it was here and just what she was missing out on.

Thankfully Ava had agreed to cover for me at the sanctuary, giving me more time with Kaitlyn.

For the most part, it was just her and I, but occasionally Caleb or Grayson (or both) would join us.

One particular evening, as the four of us sat in my garden, had me feeling particularly on edge. Mainly because of the way Grayson would, every so often look over at me like he wanted to devour me right there and then.

'We should all go out this weekend, one last blow out

before you have to leave,' Caleb announced, and I tore my eyes away from Grayson's.

'That sounds great!' Kaitlyn replied, a little too quickly and I suppressed a smile.

I couldn't believe my time with her was almost up. I was dreading her leaving, but we still had a few more days.

We planned to make a night of it, dinner before hitting some of the bars.

How much things had changed since we were last there, I thought idly.

I had to admit, Kaitlyn wasn't the only one looking forward to the night out. It seemed ages since I'd gotten dressed up.

'What am I going to wear,' Kaitlyn grinned, once Grayson and Caleb had left later that night.

She rummaged through her suitcase, sending clothes everywhere.

'Did you bring your entire wardrobe?' I laughed, picking up after her.

'You know our golden rule. Always pack just in case outfits,' we repeated the latter together.

'I think you have more than enough just in case outfits here to supply every boutique in Beaufort.'

'Stop laughing and help me finding something to wear,' Kailyn complained, continuing the hunt.

Another hour later and we'd narrowed it down to three choices, and after almost falling asleep on my feet, I told her we could have a fashion show the next day, long before we were due to leave, but that my body clock was no longer on New York time and I needed sleep.

'You've turned soft,' she said, hugging me goodnight.

'You won't be saying that when I'm waking you up at five o'clock tomorrow morning,' I teased and got an item of clothing thrown in my general direction.

Laughing, I collapsed into bed, relishing in the softness that enveloped me, as I drifted off to sleep.

'You look beautiful. Would you stop fussing!' I told Kailyn for the umpteenth time.

Having finally settled on a black sequin dress, that hugged her slim figure perfectly and showed just enough of her long legs, paired with a pair of black stiletto heels, she looked amazing.

I'd opted for a shorter (well, shorter than I would usually wear) red dress with a fitted bodice, that flared out slightly from the waist down.

We both wore our hair down, in loose waves, and applied a little make up, without overdoing it. We looked pretty good by the time we were done, I had to admit.

After a few selfies, we were just about to leave to meet Grayson and Caleb at the main house when we heard a knock at the door.

Apparently, they had both decided to be chivalrous men and walk with us. I opened the door to find them both similarly dressed, in dark jeans, and button up shirts, only Caleb's was a much darker blue than Grayson's.

He looked so handsome, it had my stomach doing flip flops already.

It was going to be a long night!

'You look beautiful,' Grayson said quietly, his eyes

travelling the full length of me.

I was fairly certain my cheeks were turning the colour of my dress right about now.

'I'll second that,' Caleb made no attempt to be discreet as he looked at me, until Kaitlyn appeared by my side.

Then his eyes were devouring her and I smiled, thinking yep, we were definitely in for an interesting evening.

After a mouth-watering seafood dinner, we stayed at the restaurant a while longer, finishing our drinks and swapping stories – which mainly consisted of Caleb wanting the dirt on our wild New York party days.

'Sophie was quite the wild child. Don't let her sweet, innocent act fool you,' Kaitlyn smiled sweetly at me.

'You weren't all that sweet, or innocent back then either, if I recall,' I replied, thinking back to our college days.

We had so much fun together! So many frat parties. So many hangovers.

'Ok, now we're getting somewhere. Tell us about these wild days and please tell me they included doing shots off each other and scantily clad pillow fights,' Caleb rubbed his hands together.

Kaitlyn and I burst into laughter.

What was it with guys imagining girls having half naked pillow fights?

We learned a lot about each other that night – like the fact that Caleb had been on the chess club, before taking part in what was considered cooler sports, like baseball and basketball.

Turned out he'd been really good at the latter, making it

to college on a basketball scholarship.

And that Grayson had gone through an exceptionally awkward phase in high school, to the point where he almost couldn't get a date for prom.

I struggled to imagine that, looking at him now, sitting back in his chair, long legs stretched out in front of him. He was like the epitome of cool. And gorgeous, of course.

But there was so much more to him than that. He was kind and considerate, caring and passionate.

'You're doing it again,' Kaitlyn whispered, while the guys were paying the bill.

Kaitlyn and I meandered along the water's edge on the promenade.

'Doing what?' I asked.

'That whole love-struck, staring at Grayson dreamily thing. I'm all for it, but you may want to tone it down if you still don't want to give up the ghost.'

'I can't help it,' I sighed.

I was tired of keeping things a secret. I wanted our families to know. Heck, I wanted the whole world to know.

'You're completely head over heels in love with him,' Kaitlyn stated, not asking.

Was I? I cared deeply for him and I was unbelievably attracted to him. And yes, I wanted to spend every waking moment with him....

Oh boy, she may be on to something.

'It's way too soon for that. Right?'

'Soph, if there's one thing I know about you, it's that when you know what's right and what your heart wants, time is irrelevant. It's one of the things I admire so much about you, I love the way you go for something with every fibre of your being, no holding back, no doubts.'

'Is that really how you see me?' I was taken aback.

'That's not how I see you, that's how you are. I wish I was more like you. I probably would have quit my job ages ago.'

'You're one of the strongest, most courageous women I've ever known, Kay. Don't forget that. There's nothing wrong with taking calculated risks. Do you want to know something?' She nodded. 'I always wish I was more like you in that way.' We laughed at each other and at ourselves, but I suppose this is what makes true friendships, admiring each other's qualities; the good and the bad, and encouraging each other to be the best versions of ourselves.

Chapter 16

Grayson and Caleb caught up with us then and we followed them to a nearby bar, which turned out to be packed, so we ordered a round of drinks and made our way outside.

It was surprisingly warm for the end of summer. Not that I was complaining. The warm night and the salty sea air were always welcome.

'You look incredible tonight. If we were alone...' Grayson whispered in my ear.

Kaitlyn and Caleb were so engrossed in their own conversation, I doubted they would have heard anything else around them.

The shiver that ran through me had nothing to do with the breeze and everything to do with Grayson's words and his proximity to me.

I tried to pull myself together.

'If people knew about us, we wouldn't have to whisper and hide, I could be kissing you right now,' I whispered back, not sure if this was coming from me, or my third drink.

Either way, I was glad to have said it. I'd been thinking it long enough.

'We'll tell everyone soon, ok? I promise,' Grayson's hand grazed the side of my leg.

'That's not fair, don't think you can distract your way out of this conversation,' I said with far less conviction than I felt.

'I would never do such a thing,' he replied innocently, continuing to run his hand up my thigh, under my dress.

'Do you guys want another drink?' Kaitlyn called over Grayson's shoulder.

He removed his hand and turned to face the others.

I inhaled a ragged breath.

'We'll get this round,' I grabbed Kaitlyn's hand and pulled her towards the outdoor bar.

'Everything ok?' Kaitlyn asked when we reached the bar.

'Yeah, just needed a breather,' I sighed.

My head still swimming while we placed our ordered, making sure to include a few waters with our round of drinks. I didn't want to drink too much when I felt the way I did.

Combining alcohol with emotion generally didn't end well.

I couldn't focus for the rest of the night, unable to shake the bad feeling that had been creeping into my bones. Like there was another reason Grayson didn't want to tell everyone about us, I just couldn't figure out what it was.

'Where are you tonight?' Grayson asked me some time after midnight.

We had just been on the dancefloor when I'd stepped off for a break.

Watching Caleb twirl Kaitlyn around while Grayson had tried to do the same with me just hadn't been working.

My head was all over the place.

'I'm right here,' I replied half-heartedly.

'No, you're not. Talk to me, what's going on?'

'I'm just trying to understand why we're keeping this a secret and I'm coming up blank.'

'It's like I said, I just wanted to take things slow. To figure things out between us, just us, without anyone else getting involved.'

'See, that's what I don't get. I can't imagine your parents, or even Caleb, interfering or butting in. And as for the rest, I know how I feel about you Grayson. This isn't just a passing phase for me.'

I was trying to tell him how serious I was about him, about us, without actually saying the words out loud.

'If there's something else, or someone else, or if you're not that interested, I'd rather know now,' I added.

Something that looked like anger, or frustration, flashed in his eyes.

'Do you really think there could be someone else, or that I'm not that interested?' Definitely a bit of both.

My own frustrations flared.

'I don't know what to think, Grayson. All I know is that I don't like being treated like someone's dirty little secret,' I snapped back.

He didn't seem to know what to say to that and just glared at me for a moment before muttering something about getting another drink and storming off.

Ugh! Infuriating!

I walked back on to the dance floor in an attempt to salvage what was left of the evening, joining Kaitlyn and Caleb before Caleb went off looking for Grayson.

A few shots (so much for not drinking too much) and another few songs later, Kaitlyn and I swayed around the dance floor.

Or the dance floor swayed around us, I wasn't sure which.

'Hey there, can we join you?'

Someone placed their hand on my lower back, and I turned to see a sandy blonde haired, brown eyed, cutie and his friend.

'Sure,' I beamed, moving back to make some space.

Kaitlyn gave me a curious look, which I promptly ignored.

'I'm Sophie, this is Kaitlyn,' I introduced us to our new friends.

'I'm Damon, this is Jamie,' the sandy blonde said with a broad smile, showing off a set of perfectly straight pearly whites.

We didn't do a whole lot of talking after that, but we sure danced our asses off.

Until Grayson spotted us, that is.

His hulking form appeared next to me and I could feel the anger emanating from him.

'Sophie, can we talk?'

'Sorry, I'm dancing,' I replied flippantly.

'What are you trying to prove?' Grayson demanded, making Caleb and Kaitlyn look up in surprise.

'Careful, Grayson, don't let the cat out the bag,' I whispered.

Ok, maybe slurred. And definitely didn't whisper.

'Is that what this is about? You're being ridiculous!'

'Am I though?'

'You know you are. This isn't you, Sophie,' Grayson frown deepened.

'And how would you know what's me? Do you think you know me so well?'

'I know you well enough to know that you don't want to do something you'll regret tomorrow.'

I hated that he was right.

I suddenly looked around, confused. We were on the beach. How had we gotten here?

I looked back towards the dancefloor where Caleb was twirling Kaitlyn around and our new friends, what were their names again? Whatever they were, they were nowhere to be seen.

'Don't even think about it,' Grayson growled in my ear, his hands on my waist, holding me in place.

'Let go of me, Grayson, you don't own me,' I tried to wriggle out of his grasp, but it was pointless.

'Please just let me explain, Soph. I want to tell you everything.'

Something in his voice made me stop wriggling and look up at him. His eyes were filled with something I couldn't quite place. Fear?

'Grayson, what is it?' I asked, suddenly scared of the answer.

'There you two are,' Caleb boomed over the sound of the

waves. 'How are you holding up, Soph? Too many shots, huh?' Caleb sounded like he'd had a few too many shots too.

'Caleb, give us a minute, would you,' Grayson said, not taking his eyes off mine.

'Awe come on bro, don't be like that, let's get another round of drinks,' Caleb hauled his brother away, leaving me rooted to the spot.

What had Grayson been about to tell me? Was I sure I was ready to hear it? It must be bad, given the look in his eyes.

'Soph, are you ok? Why don't we sit for a bit,' Kaitlyn said, leading the way to a nearby table. 'Here, have some water,' she handed me a bottle of water. I took a long drink from it.

'Better?' she asked.

'Yeah, a bit.'

'What's wrong? It looked pretty serious between you two back there.'

'I honestly don't know, Kay. I just have this bad feeling in the pit of my stomach that he's keeping something from me. I think he was about to tell me when you guys came over.'

'I'm so sorry, I tried to get Caleb to stay with me on the dancefloor, but he wasn't having it once he'd spotted you guys.'

'It's ok, it's not your fault,' I reassured her, when I was the one who needed reassuring.

It didn't take the guys long to get back with another round of drinks, but I had had enough for the night, so

Caleb downed mine before demanding we all hit the dancefloor again.

He grabbed mine and Kaitlyn's hands before I could protest, dragging us behind him.

Grayson stayed at the table.

I was starting to feel a little ill and I didn't think it had anything to do with the alcohol.

Bright sunlight woke me the following morning and I groaned.

I must have forgotten to close the curtains last night.

Hearing movement in the kitchen, I dragged myself out of bed and padded my way down the hall to find Kaitlyn putting a fresh pot of coffee on.

'Morning,' I croaked.

'Morning,' she replied through a yawn. 'Coffee won't be long.'

'Thanks,' I said, flopping onto the couch.

'So, that was some night, huh?' Kaitlyn followed suit, sitting cross-legged next to me.

'I'm so sorry, I didn't mean to bring the drama,' I replied, cringing at my performance last night.

'Don't be silly, it really wasn't even that big a deal. Are you ok though? You were so quiet on the ride home.'

'Yeah, I just have a bad feeling, Kay. Something is up with Grayson and I swear he was on the verge of telling me last night. Part of me hopes he never tells me, after seeing the look in his eyes, but part of me needs to know the truth.'

'Then you should go find him and ask him. You deserve

to know the truth.'

'You're right. I may need caffeine first though. And a shower.'

'Definitely a shower,' Kaitlyn scrunched her nose.

'Hey,' I laughed, ouch, that hurt my head.

After finishing my coffee and a quick shower, I walked over to Grayson's house, not knowing what to expect, but preparing myself for the worst.

My hand trembled as I knocked on his door, remember the silence on the drive home last night. Caleb had apparently been oblivious to it all, he'd barely come up for air.

The door opened and I jumped.

'Morning,' I said.

'Morning,' Grayson replied.

He wore an old pair of jeans, which hung enticingly low on his hips and I tried not to ogle his bare upper body, much.

This is serious, Sophie, I reminded myself.

'Can we talk?' I asked hesitantly.

'Sure, come on in,' he held the door open for me before grabbing a t-shirt, pulling it on as we moved into the living room.

I realised that I'd never been in his home before. We just always seemed to end up at my cottage instead.

Despite it being very masculine, it was surprisingly warm and inviting.

The living room was mostly greys; large charcoal grey couch, with matching armchair, lighter grey shaggy rug, pale grey curtains, although different shades, which worked perfectly with the wooden features.

A chunky rustic wooden coffee table sat in the middle of the room, along with the wooden wall unit, which held a TV, a number of books, and a few plants, which I could only assume were Rosie's touches.

'Would you like something to drink?' Grayson offered and when I shook my head, he gestured for me to sit down, as he did the same.

'I'm sorry about last night. I know I acted like a spoilt brat who wasn't getting her own way. I just had this awful feeling that something was off, and I let my insecurities, and possibly the alcohol, get the better of me. But Grayson-' I didn't get the chance to ask him what he was going to tell me last night, before he'd closed the gap between us, gently angling my face until our lips met.

This kiss was so different to any other we'd shared. It was urgent, rough, and it caught me completely off guard.

My mind went blank.

All thoughts of last night now a distant memory. All I could think, all I could breath, all I was, in that moment was Grayson Danvers.

Nothing else mattered. Whatever it was he was afraid to tell me, it didn't matter.

He'd just confirmed what I needed to know, that I was all he wanted and needed.

His longing echoed through the very core of me and as I wrapped my arms around his neck, I knew that things wouldn't be the same after this.

I wouldn't be the same again.

I would be forever changed, with the whispers of his soul burned into my own.

'Hi,' Grayson said when we finally resurfaced.

'Hi,' I replied, unable to hide the giddy smile that broke across my face.

We lay facing each other, legs and arms entangled in the sheets of his large four poster bed.

I hadn't noticed much on the way in and if I was being honest, I wasn't that interested at this present moment in time either.

Wanting nothing more than just to lie there, staring into the depths of his blue eyes, letting them carry me away to faraway places where it was just the two of us.

'What are you thinking?' He asked, his full lips turning up at the corners into a small, content, smile.

'How happy I am and how I want to stay right here, just like this, forever,' I replied without hesitation. 'What are you thinking?'

'Along those same lines. With just a few additions,' he moved in closer, running his hand over my face, down my neck, down the length of my bare back and I shivered involuntarily, a small moan escaping my lips.

'That being one,' he ran his hand up my back again and my eyes fluttered closed.

I could sense him moving closer, tilting my head in anticipation before feeling his soft lips against my own while his hand continued to explore, moving over my ribs, to my stomach, my hip, 'And this,' he went on with his torture until it was too much and I pulled him closer as we lost ourselves in each other all over again.

When I eventually floated back down to earth, I sighed, in a state of pure bliss.

'You are going to be the death of me, Grayson Danvers,' I rolled over, so my chin rested on his broad chest.

'I aim to please ma'am.'

'Oh, trust me, you succeed!' That was the understatement of the century!

Suddenly all joking left his breath-taking face and he touched his hand to my cheek, running his thumb over my lips.

'I love you, Sophie,' he whispered, and my eyes flew opened. 'I know it's soon, but I think I've loved you from the moment I met you. You were infuriating and stubborn and I wanted to tame the wild streak in your eyes. Instead, you brought my heart back to life.'

'I love you, Grayson,' was all I could say.

I couldn't find the words to tell him everything I longed to. To tell him just how much he meant to me and how he had mended my own broken heart and soul.

Instead, I pulled his face to mine and kissed him deeply, trying to show him all the things my unspoken thoughts couldn't yet say.

'I'm guessing that went well,' Kaitlyn's eyebrows shot up when I walked back into the cottage.

I sighed and leaned against the door, staring dreamily into the distance.

Leaving Grayson had been one of the hardest things I'd ever done. I could have stayed there, in his bed, locked away from the rest of the world forever.

But when I realised how late it had gotten, I jumped up, knowing Kaitlyn would be leaving soon, I had to get back.

Reluctantly getting up, I got dressed – trying to find my clothes was something else, they had been scattered throughout the house on our way from the living room to the bedroom.

Grayson was no help at all, naturally, lying in bed enjoying the view, as he's said, watching me search frantically for every item of clothing.

He'd finally gotten up and walked me to the door to say goodbye, where he'd pushed me up against the door, before opening it, kissing me so deeply I thought I'd never make it back to my cottage.

'Oh my God, Sophie, you little minx! You slept with him!' Kaitlyn accused with a great big smile on her face.

I couldn't say anything. I didn't need to say anything. It was written all over my face.

'I want details, don't leave anything out,' Kaitlyn dragged me onto the couch and made me give her a play by play.

Of course, I left out any, shall we say, personal details, but I gave her the overview.

'Oh my!' She lay back fanning herself dramatically.

'You have no idea!' I leaned back too. 'He told me he loves me,' I added, watching Kaitlyn's face for her reaction.

Her eyes grew wider momentarily and then she nodded, 'It's soon, but no surprise really. It's pretty obvious that you two are in love with each other.'

'I'm going to miss you,' I leaned over to hug her.

I wished more than anything that she could stay.

'I'm going to miss you too.'

Once we'd all said our goodbye's to Kaitlyn, I walked back to Grayson's house with him.

'Would you like to stay for dinner?' He asked, opening the door for me.

'I'd love to,' I replied, making myself at home, curling into a ball on his couch.

'I'm going to take a quick shower,' he trailed a line of kisses from my forehead, nose, lips, jawline, neck. 'Feel free to join me,' he called from the bathroom, leaving the door open a crack.

As tempting as that offer was, I was intrigued to look around Grayson's house.

I wanted to take everything in, learn everything there was to know about him. I preferred thinking of it this way, rather than snooping.

A few pictures dotted the walls and the wall unit, mostly of Grayson and Caleb in their younger years, some with the four of them, some were of the animals.

It gave me a snapshot into the things he held most dear. Not that I didn't already know.

I looked over the books that scattered the shelves around the TV, a few travel books, some of wildlife, a few poetry books – that was a surprise.

And then I found a photo album and my curiosity peaked.

I desperately wanted to see a younger Grayson. So, I pulled the album from the shelf, sat back down on the couch and started flipping through it.

His baby pictures were beyond adorable! He was all dark curls and big blue eyes and had the chubbiest cheeks.

There were a lot of the brothers growing up and some with a younger Rosie and Sam. They looked so happy and in love. Then again, they still did all these years later.

I then came across one or two photos of what I could only assume were Grayson's awkward years, as Caleb had referred to them, but they didn't look so bad.

I could still see Grayson's handsome features beyond the slightly goofy looking teenage phase. But I supposed I was bias.

The photos then moved on past high school, to college I guessed. There were a few of Grayson and his friends at parties, some of him working on the farm and then my heart stopped beating and I couldn't breathe.

In one of the photos of Grayson on the farm, just outside the main barn, he had his arm draped casually around a shoulder that I knew well.

It was the same shoulder I'd fallen asleep on countless nights, the same shoulder I'd rested my cheek on while curled up watching a movie.

Luke's younger, smiling facing stared back at me.

Grayson next to him.

How was this possible?

My whole world shifted. I felt like I was going to pass out, or be sick, or both.

'Sophie, what's wrong?' I barely registered the alarm in Grayson's voice.

I looked up at him slowly, eyes wide, just as he looked down to see the photo album in my lap.

'I can explain,' he said, but I had my own questions to ask.

'How did you know him? Did you know that he was my husband?' I demanded, not recognising my own voice.

'I realised at the hospital in Abingdon. At least I thought there might have been a connection. That was when I found your next of kin details and your surname. I'd stupidly given the hospital your maiden name, but then found your driver's license. I didn't know how to tell you-'

'What was all of this, us? Some sick game? Or was it out of pity? Has any of this been real?'

I could feel my eyes burning, my breath coming in short, sharp bursts. My head reeled with every different possibility.

'Of course it's real. I've meant everything I've ever said to you. I've tried to tell you, so many times, I just didn't know how. Sophie, I love you, more than I ever thought possible after everything I went through before, and I know you feel the same,' Grayson reached out for me and I jumped up, snapping my hand away.

The photo album tumbling to the floor in the process.

I needed to get out of there! I stumbled past Grayson in an attempt to make it to the front door, but he was faster, standing in my way.

'Get out of my way, Grayson,' I yelled at him.

'Sophie, please, don't go. Just stay and we can talk about it. I'll tell you everything,' he tried to reach out to me again and I finally snapped.

'Don't touch me!'

I could see the hurt in his eyes, but I couldn't think straight, I needed to get away from him, away from his pleading eyes that were so full of love for me.

I pushed passed him and ran as fast as my feet could carry me, I ran past my cottage and kept on running, not sure of where my feet were taking me, but I didn't care.

All the while I was moving, I wasn't feeling or thinking.

I just had to keep going, keep moving.

Chapter 17

When I fell to my knees, out of breath, only partially from the run. Sobs raked through me, breaking my chest open all over again.

Wrapping my arms around my shoulders, I tried to hold myself together, while the tears flowed down my cheeks, landing on the earth beneath me.

The picture haunted me. Grayson's eyes haunted me.

He'd looked so hurt before I'd brushed passed him.

Was it all a lie, was he faking it? Was he truly hurt? Did he truly love me? Or did it have more to do with knowing Luke?

So many questions raced through my mind as I sobbed amongst the trees.

When my tears ran dry and my breathing slowed, I looked up, keeping my arms wrapped around myself, nearly coming undone all over again.

I was in the wooded area next to the lake where Grayson and I had shared so many special moments.

They had felt so real, so true, but now, knowing what I knew, and looking back on those moments shared with him, I saw things differently.

Had it all simply been out of pity for me? The widow of

someone he once knew.

Had they been friends? They looked like they had known each other for years, old friends posing for a photo.

I stood on shaky legs and walked over to a rock next to the lake.

I felt cold to the bone and suddenly exhausted.

I wasn't sure how long I sat there, lost in my thoughts, but when I looked up again the sky had turned dark, casting shadows across the lake.

I glared across the now darkened water. What a fool I'd been, thinking it would be that easy, that we would fall in love and live happily ever after. We barely even know each other.

But the little voice in my head whispered, you know that's not true.

And she was right. I knew Grayson, at least I thought I had.

Then again, we could all get swept up in the fairy tale. Maybe I was living proof of that. Wanting to believe what we had was real, when, in fact, it was all a lie.

My mind and heart had never been so conflicted.

My heart was telling me to believe him, but my mind was putting up a wall. Heck, it was putting up an entire fortress.

How could I deny what I'd felt these past few weeks?

But if he could keep something this big, this important, from me, what else could he be hiding?

I didn't want to think about it anymore, I didn't want to feel anymore, so I got up, dusted myself off and walked back to my cottage.

I probably shouldn't have been surprised to find Grayson there, but I was.

My heart hammered in my chest as I looked at him, sitting on the porch, looking like a beaten man.

It broke my heart seeing him like that, but then I reminded myself what he'd kept from me – not that I needed reminding.

'Grayson, I don't want to talk,' I walked right to my front door, hands trembling on the handle.

'I didn't come to talk. I came to apologise. I owe you an explanation, Sophie.'

My hand froze on the door handle, but I didn't turn to face him.

'I met Luke while working for a charity during our college summer break – we happened to join the same one and we became friends almost right off the bat, but we lost touch over the years. I should have told you the moment I realised the connection, I'm sorry I didn't, but when you woke up, in the hospital, I was so relieved. There's no excuse for it, I know that, but I got scared, I couldn't bring myself to say the words to you. And then you told me what happened, and you seemed so....' He trailed off, taking a long breath.

'I just knew I couldn't tell you then. I didn't want to cause you any more pain. So, I decided to try back off and give you space, but my feels only grew stronger for you and our connection deepened while we were away. That's when I knew for sure that I was falling for you. I didn't know what to do. I know I was a coward, but I didn't want to lose you, so I kept telling myself that I would tell you when the time was right, but the timing was never right. And then I started telling you last night, just before Caleb interrupted us. I had never come that close to telling you before and I was so angry with my brother for interrupting. But a part of me was relieved. I was so afraid of what telling you would do, what it would mean for us. Like I said, there's no excuse, I should have told you and I'm sorry for that, I'm sorry for so many things, Sophie, but I'll never be sorry for what happened between us. You've made me feel whole again. Happier than I've ever been, and I think you feel the same. I can't be sorry for that. I just hope that one day you can forgive me for keeping this from you.'

I couldn't move. I just stood there, rooted to the spot, hand still on the doorhandle.

I heard Grayson walk away.

I wanted to run to him, to wrap my arms around him and tell him that I loved him and that I did forgive him, but I couldn't forgive him that quickly.

I wasn't sure if I ever could.

The weeks that followed I kept myself busy and out of Grayson's way, or perhaps he was staying out of mine, I wasn't sure, but the longer I went without seeing him, the worse I felt and the more the ache in my heart grew.

A storm was due, and the county had been put on high alert, so in the days leading up to the storm, the farm was a bustling hub of workers and volunteers alike.

We had to make sure every building was secure and sealed up.

Sam and Rosie had seen their fair share of storms in the past, so they were well prepared and tried to assure me that the animals would be ok.

I was, undeniably, concerned for the wellbeing of the animals, but they misunderstood my dark mood.

In successfully avoiding Grayson, I had inadvertently avoided all of them too. Sam, Rosie, Caleb. But with my head and heart still at war, I couldn't risk being around him.

I still had no idea how to feel or what to think of the whole situation.

Grayson had kept a huge secret from me, a secret about one of the most important aspects of my life.

I had tried on numerous occasions to see things from his perspective, I tried putting myself in his shoes, and sure, maybe a part of me understood why he hadn't told me. I would have been afraid of losing him if the roles had been reversed.

But I'd like to think I would have told him, no matter how afraid I was.

Then again, how could I judge when I hadn't actually been in his shoes.

I believed that Grayson loved me.

What I wasn't sure about was what those feelings had stemmed from. Were they his true feelings, or had he simply felt pity for his friends' widow?

These were questions I couldn't answer and the more I ran them over in my head, the more confused I became.

If I was being honest with myself, I'd started developing feelings for Grayson long before Abingdon, but had he?

I'd like to think so, given the moments we'd shared before he found out my surname.

Then again, he'd told me he knew he was falling for me while we were in Abingdon, so what did it all mean?

It didn't help that I bumped straight into Grayson (literally) earlier that day, while I was hammering boards across the pig pen with Sam.

Being in close proximity to him did nothing to help me figure things out, it only added to my confusion.

My body always responded the same way – wanting him.

I hadn't been paying enough attention to where I was going, although in my defence, I could hardly see over the wooden board I was carrying, and I'd walked straight into him.

'Oh, I'm sorry-' I stopped dead when I saw Grayson's face appear over the top of the board.

'Here, let me,' he took the board from me.

'Thanks,'

Following him to the side of the pen, he held the board up for me to hammer into place, and that was it, he spoke to his dad briefly before leaving the pen.

I had ached to touch him, to talk to him, but couldn't bring myself to do either.

He could barely look at me and it killed me. But what could I say?

'Almost done, Soph?' Sam called from inside.

'Yeah, Sam, I'm done out here,' I meant in more ways than one.

'Everything ok, honey?' Sam asked as we gathered our tools.

I wanted to pour my heart out, to tell him that I was in love with his son, even if we weren't speaking at the moment and I wasn't even sure if his feelings for me were real.

Instead I forced a smile and told him I was fine.

It didn't look like he bought it.

'Aren't you staying for dinner sweetheart?' Rosie asked later that day.

I was checking in on the piglets (knowing that Grayson was helping Caleb – at the other end of the farm).

'No, thanks, Rosie. I'm sorry to miss dinner, again,' I replied.

I'd made any excuses I could think of in the past weeks; battening down the hatches at the cottage (something I still hadn't actually done by the way), writing, working on the website, a call with my editor, absolutely anything that came to mind.

'Ok, well, take a plate back with you, I'll feel happier knowing you've had a home cooked meal.'

'Thanks, Rosie, I really appreciate it.'

'You know I'm always here if you want to talk about anything,' Rosie said, as she piled a plate far too high.

I would never get through all of that food tonight, but it would keep just fine for a day or two.

I wondered if Sam had been talking to Rosie, or the other way around.

'I'm ok, Rosie, but thank you.'

I felt awful for conflicting my mood on them, which was a part of the reason I had dinner in my cottage most nights.

The main reason being Grayson of course.

'Mmhmm, well the offer will always stand,' she replied, much like Sam, unconvinced.

Kissing her cheek, before thanking her again for the food, which smelled amazing. I walked back to my cottage with a heavy heart.

I wanted to be having dinner with Grayson, I wanted everything to go back to before I'd found the photo.

A deep rumble sounded in the distance and I looked up at the dark clouds, mirroring my mood.

I really did need to board up the windows on the cottage, especially since I'd said I'd been doing it already.

The worst of the storm was due to hit tomorrow and may continue into the weekend, which meant we may need to cancel the annual autumn fundraiser grill that the Danvers hosted every year for the sanctuary.

My parents, along with most of Beaufort, had been due to attend. Now it was down to mother nature.

I wanted to go home to help my parents board up the house, but my mom had convinced me to stay on the farm, saying it would make them both feel better knowing that there was an extra pair of hands helping on the farm, adding that my brother was helping them board up the house.

I felt better knowing that Paul would be there to help out.

I woke up to the sound of rain splattering against my bedroom window the following morning and stretched out like a starfish.

I felt utterly exhausted, I hadn't been sleeping well, for obvious reasons, and after another night spent tossing and turning, I woke feeling more tired than when I'd gone to bed the night before.

Rolling out of bed, I poured a cup of coffee before getting dressed and going to the main house to meet Sam, needing to do a few last-minute checks today across the farm.

I only hoped I could get back in time to board up the windows at the cottage.

'Morning beautiful, ready for the storm?' Caleb asked, pulling on his boots.

'As I'll ever be,' I replied, not wanting them to know about the cottage.

'You can always hunker down with me,' Caleb winked, and his mom scoffed.

'I'm sure I'll be just fine, thanks.'

'You can always stay here with us if it gets too rough,' Rosie offered.

'Thanks, Rosie, I'll keep that in mind.'

If I was being honest, I was looking forward to locking myself away from the world and being alone in my misery.

'Let's get going,' Sam appeared, pulling his jacket on. 'You two take the west side,' Sam indicated to Caleb and I. 'Grayson and I will cover the east side, he's already out there, so we'll meet back here in a few hours.'

'Yes sir,' Caleb grabbed his jacked and I followed him out into the rain.

It wasn't quite a downpour yet, but the low ominous clouds promised it would be soon enough.

We checked every possible window, door, roof that we could, and when we were certain that we'd done all we could, we parted ways.

I raced home to start on the windows, wishing, yet again, I'd done it last night.

The rain was now torrential, and thunder and lightning lit up the sky, making me jump every time a loud crack shattered through the air.

As I got closer to the cottage, I could see movement, but it was all a blur through the pouring rain.

Squinting, I wondered if it was Sam. Had I forgotten something?

As I got closer, I recognised the figure on the roof.

'Grayson, what are you doing?' I called through the rain.

'I thought you were all set?' He yelled down, my temper flaring.

He was angry with me? Seriously!

'I've been a little busy, ok,' I yelled back.

Picking up a board to hammer onto one of the windows, then moving onto the next and the next.

By the time the windows were done, Grayson was about done on the roof.

Luckily too. The heavens had opened up and rain poured down on us in torrents. It was like standing under a waterfall, I could barely see a few inches in front of me.

A gush of water streamed off the roof and a loud crack sounded a little too close for comfort.

I heard it before I saw it or even registered what was happening.

Grayson was falling – off my roof.

'Grayson!' I called out, but it was too late, there was nothing I could do.

He hit the ground with a loud thud and didn't move.

I froze for a second before racing towards him.

'Grayson! Grayson, can you hear me?' I touched his face gently, noting the blood coming from his forehead. 'Grayson?' I waited.

Time stopped.

In that moment I cursed myself for being such a fool. I loved this man, with all my heart and soul.

Sure, he'd made a mistake, but hadn't we all, at one point or another in our lives made big, stupid mistakes?

We were only human after all and I vowed that if he was ok and if we made it through this storm, I would love him with every ounce of my soul for as long as he would have me.

'Grayson, I love you, please don't leave me,' I cried, tears pouring down my face, washed away by the rain.

'You…' he croaked. I froze. 'You love me?' His eyes fluttered open.

'Of course I do, you idiot. I love you so much.'

He tried to sit up and swayed.

Putting my arm around his back and mustering all the strength I had left in me, I helped him to his feet.

'Come on, we need to get inside.'

I put his arm around my shoulder and let him lean on me as we stumbled our way to the front door.

Once we were safely inside, I placed him down as gently as I could on my couch before racing around for towels and the small first aid kit I'd seen under the kitchen sink.

'Are you ok?' I asked, sitting next to him, wiping the blood from his head, trying to see how bad it was.

'I love you, Sophie. I'm so sorry about everything. I would never do anything to hurt you, you must know that?' His voice was faint.

'I know you wouldn't. I was just upset, I'm sorry too, but let's talk about it later. I need to make sure you're ok first.' The wound on his head didn't appear to be too deep, but he had a gash on his arm that was worrying me.

After cleaning him up as best I could, and bandaging up his cuts and scrapes, I gently removed his wet clothes and wrapped a blanket around him, before making us both a cup of tea.

My hands still shook from the shock of seeing him fall.

It brought back memories of Luke, along with a fresh wave of fear, so strong it threatened to do far more damage than the storm raging on outside.

The windows rattled and I only hoped I had done a good enough job in boarding them up.

'Here, drink this,' I instructed, placing the tea in Grayson's battered hands.

I wasn't sure if the cuts were from the fall, or from working on the roof in the storm, or a combination.

'What on earth were you doing up there?' I asked when I couldn't hold it in any longer.

'I came by to check on the cottage. The roof had been damaged in the last storm, so I wanted to make sure it was boarded up. Imagine my surprise when I got here to find nothing was done,' Grayson gave me a disapproving look before continuing, 'I needed to make sure you were safe.' He took a long drink of his tea before placing his cup on the table.

Sitting down again, I gently squeezed his hand, 'Thank you, Grayson.'

He looked up, the storm raging behind his eyes mirroring the one lashing against the windows outside, and in the next second his lips met mine, telling me everything I needed to know.

He loved me. He wanted me, needed me, as much as I did him.

But as much as I wanted all of him right now, making sure he was ok took priority.

Reluctantly, I gently pulled away.

'Grayson, you might have a concussion. I think you should take it easy.' My voice lacked the conviction I felt.

'Sophie, I'm fine. I've missed you so much.' He pulled me in close, his eyes burning desire into my soul, and my resolve crumbled into a million pieces.

My lips brushed against his, gently, longingly, and I knew I'd never stood a chance.

The world around us melted away, as I let go. Giving in to my love for Grayson, my need for him, as I blissfully let the whirlwind that was Grayson Danvers take me under.

'Good morning, sleeping beauty,' Grayson smiled, curling his arms around me, pulling me against his side.

'Good morning,' I grinned back. 'How are you feeling?' I asked, remembering the events of the night before.

'Never better,' he replied, kissing the top of my head.

Despite the confidence in his tone, I checked him over. He did seem ok, despite noticing the start of what would probably be pretty bad bruising.

'I still think you need to get checked out. By a doctor,' I added quickly, before he could volunteer me for the job.

I knew him well enough.

'Sophie, I'm fine, honestly, I've had far worse falls before,' he stretched out like a lazy housecat, allowing me full view of his toned torso.

He was a magnificent specimen of a man and I wondered how I'd gotten so lucky.

As much as I wanted to stay right there with the man I loved, I knew we had to get up and check on the farm, and everyone else.

Grayson clearly had the same idea, as he reluctantly got up and pulled his jeans on.

'I better go check on my parents and Caleb, and then do the rounds throughout the farm,' he said, pulling his shirt on awkwardly, clearly feeling stiff.

Not that he would admit it.

I got up, pulling on an old t-shirt and gently wrapped my arms around him.

'Give me five minutes and I'll come with you,' I said before kissing him deeply.

We pulled away, slightly breathless, and I grinned up at him like a giddy teenager.

Grayson took a long breath, before planting a kiss on my forehead and letting me go.

'You'll be the death of me woman,' he called after me, as I disappeared into the bathroom, still grinning.

'Good morning you two. You made it through the night I see,' Sam greeted us in their kitchen fifteen minutes later.

'We sure did,' Grayson winked at me, making my cheeks burn.

'How were things here?' I asked Rosie, trying to ignore Grayson.

'Oh, just fine honey, we've seen worse storms. We were far more concerned about you,' Rosie looked at Grayson, 'Your dad came out to check on you, but you weren't there.'

'I went to check on Sophie,' was all Grayson said in return.

As Rosie turned away, I thought I caught a great big smile appearing on her face, having a rather strong resemblance to the one I'd been wearing all morning. Odd.

'We should go check on the animals,' Sam said to Grayson, and I sensed something brewing beneath his calm exterior, so I thought better of going with them.

'Is everything ok?' I asked Rosie once the boys had left.

'I wish I knew,' Rosie sat down opposite me at the breakfast table. 'I think Sam and Caleb had an argument, but Sam won't say a word about it. He tries to protect me, but I'd rather know what's going on.'

'Well I'm sure it's nothing to worry about. How about we go and check on the horses?' I asked, hoping to take Rosie's mind off things.

'That sounds perfect,' Rosie smiled, finishing off her coffee, before following me out to the barn.

Thankfully there didn't seem to be much damage around the farm, only a few fence posts knocked over, or the odd leaky roof, but on the whole, we came out of the storm a lot better than I'd expected.

Rosie was far happier about the fact that the fundraiser grill could go ahead, and when it came around, so was I.

It was exactly what we all needed.

Chapter 18

'You look beautiful,' Grayson eyed me head to toe when I opened the door.

It was a beautiful sunny day with only a hint of the cooler autumn air rustling through the leaves, sending a few spiralling towards the ground.

Autumn in North Carolina was something to behold. The vast contrast between the rusty coloured leaves was breath-taking.

Despite the cooler weather, I'd opted for skinny jeans with ankle boots and a teal blouse, paired with my favourite brown leather jacket, just in case the temperature dropped once the sun went down.

'You don't look too bad yourself,' I replied, wrapping my arms around Grayson's neck, kissing him. Enjoying his smell, his taste, his touch.

'We better get going, or I might just change my mind and keep you locked away here forever.' He pulled me closer, nuzzling my neck.

'Mmm you won't hear any arguments from me,' I smiled, knowing full well we needed to attend the grill.

It was important, not just to the Danvers, but to the sanctuary.

'How about we come back here after the grill? I can make us some hot chocolate, you can pick a film, and we can have a quiet night in?'

Grayson nodded and I smiled to myself as we left the cottage, thinking if this is what the rest of my life consisted of, spending my nights wrapped in Grayson's strong arms, I would be happy forever.

This man, this place, had captured my heart and soul. Bringing me back to life when I'd thought I would never truly be whole again.

Grayson made the rounds with his family at the grill, leaving me to mingle.

I already knew a lot of the people who were here, but I was still happy to see my parents arrive, with Paul and Sarah in tow.

My dad looked well. It filled me with so much joy to see the improvements over the past few months.

When I'd first arrived, he'd looked pale, and older than his years, but watching him now, the colour in his cheeks and twinkle in his eyes were back again.

I'd seen the tension gradually fall away from my mom's shoulders, as her own expression had become lighter, happier, at seeing the Dad's improvements.

'You look happy, honey,' my dad smiled, as he twirled me around the makeshift dancefloor a few hours later.

'I am, mainly to see you looking better,' I beamed at him, remembering when he'd taught me to dance in our living room, by letting me stand on his feet while he shuffled us around.

'I don't think I'm the only reason for the change in you,' my dad winked, and looked over at Grayson, who was currently dancing with his mom.

Rosie's laughter filled the air at something Grayson was saying, and I smiled, watching with happiness and pride at the change in him.

He seemed so much lighter and happier, less guarded.

'No, definitely not the only reason,' my dad smiled knowingly.

We had yet to announce to everyone that we were together, but I doubted anyone needed to be told, by the knowing looks Rosie and my parents had been given me all night.

I guess the cat was out the bag.

'Mind if I cut in,' Caleb appeared, looking pretty wasted, placing a steadying hand on my shoulder.

My dad gave us a concerned look before leaving the dancefloor, only once I nodded, mouthing it was ok.

'Caleb, don't you think it's time we get you home?' I asked, smelling the alcohol on his breath as he pulled me into his arms, attempting to sway to the music, not entirely succeeding.

'Awe come on, Soph, it's a party,' he slurred.

'What's wrong? Do you want to talk about it?'

I could only assume his current state had something to do with whatever was going on between him and his dad.

'Now why would you think anything's wrong? Lighten up, have some fun.'

Caleb attempted to spin me, but stumbled, almost

pulling us both down.

'Ok, come on, let's get you to bed,' I put my arm around his waist, trying to steady him.

'Oooh now that's an offer I can't refuse,' Caleb leaned into me and before I knew what was happening, his lips were on mine.

A second was all it took.

A second for my eyes to widen in shock. A second for my body to freeze.

A second for Grayson to witness what was happening, and in the blink of an eye, for his fist to connect with Caleb's jaw.

'Grayson, don't!' I tried to pull him away, but it was pointless.

He gripped his brother by the shirt, 'What is wrong with you?'

'Don't be like that bro, you didn't mind sharing before,' Caleb wobbled, rubbing his jaw.

I wasn't sure what he was talking about, but before Grayson could land another right hook on his brother, I managed to get between the two of them.

By then Sam had arrived and was pulling Grayson away.

'I'll get him home. You need to cool off,' I ordered Grayson, before near enough dragging Caleb away by the scruff of his neck.

After what felt like the longest walk of my life, trying to hold Caleb up right most of the way, we finally made it to his house, where he proceeded to kick off his shoes in different directions, once I was able to get us both through the front door.

He then started removing items of clothing, throwing them wherever he pleased.

I had to stop him when he reached for his briefs.

'Whoa! I've already seen far more of you than I care to for one evening,' I said, helping him to his room, where he flopped onto his bed.

'I'm such a mess,' he mumbled.

I was taken aback by the ache in his voice, making him sound on the verge of tears.

It broke my heart.

I wanted to help him, but I had no idea how, when I had no idea what had happened.

I tucked him in and turned to leave, but a gentle hand caught my own.

'Please don't leave me alone. I don't want to be alone,' his voice was so sad in the darkness, I couldn't stand it.

'I'm right here, I'm not going anywhere,' I assured him, sitting on the edge of the bed next to him.

He clung onto my hand as though it was his only lifeline, as his eyes closed.

Once his breathing was steady, I reached into my pocket with my free hand and sent Grayson a text letting him know I was going to stay with Caleb.

I knew it wouldn't go down well, but he would have to deal with it. Caleb was in no state to be alone and he was more to me than just Grayson's brother, he was my friend.

A friend I wasn't prepared to abandon when he needed me the most.

Opening my eyes, I blinked, not recognizing where I was.

Nearly having heart failure when I rolled over to see Caleb fast asleep next to me, until the events of last night flooded my brain.

I groaned internally, realising I'd fallen asleep next to Caleb, who was still sound asleep, gently snoring.

As quietly as I could, I swung my legs off the bed, freezing when it squeaked under me.

Evidently, Caleb was a heavy sleeper, simply rolling over, oblivious to anything going on around him.

Making my way to the kitchen, picking up his discarded clothes along the way, I put a fresh pot of coffee on, before scrummaging through his fridge to find eggs and bacon, that was the best hangover cure I knew of.

The smell must have woken him because about ten minutes later a very sleepy, very hungover looking, Caleb appeared at the breakfast counter.

'Good morning,' I said, handing him a cup of coffee.

'Morning,' Caleb croaked, sipping the coffee. 'Why are you in my kitchen, cooking?' He added, frowning.

'Do you remember much of last night?'

'Not really. What happened?'

'Well, for a start, you got completely wasted at the grill. You then seemed to think kissing me in front of everyone would be a good idea, which landed you a punch in the face from Grayson.'

'Sounds like a stellar night,' he rubbed his jaw, wincing when he touched the spot where Grayson's fist had connected.

'Caleb, what's going on? What really happened?' I

pushed a plate of food in front of him, giving him a minute to eat a few bites.

'I'm really sorry, Soph. I didn't mean to kiss you, or ruin anyone's night.' He sighed when he knew I wasn't going to let up until he talked to me, 'I told my dad about wanting to open up my own place on the beach and, well, it didn't go down very well.'

I'd suspected as much.

'What did he say?' I asked quietly.

'You mean between the disapproving, "how can any son of mine want to open a beach bar", looks?'

'Caleb, I'm sorry,' I felt wracked with guilt.

I'd been the one to push Caleb to tell his dad about his dreams, so certain Sam would want his son to follow his heart.

'It's not your fault, Soph. If anything, I should be thanking you. If it wasn't for you, I would never have had the courage to tell him in the first place.'

'I wish I'd been there, maybe I could have helped. Told him what a wonderful cook you are.' I wondered if it would have made any difference.

Leaving Caleb to finish his breakfast, I washed up and checked my phone, again.

Still no reply from Grayson.

I knew he'd be mad at Caleb, but he was drunk (not that I thought that was any excuse) but he's going through a lot. It took a lot of guts to open up to their dad, only to be shot down.

It was only natural that he was taking it so hard.

I needed to see Grayson, to explain everything. I knew

he'd understand once he knew the full story.

First, I needed a shower and change of clothes, so after I'd washed up, I told Caleb I was leaving but I'd be back later to check on him.

'Hey, Soph,' Caleb called as I opened the door. 'Thanks for staying with me, and I'm sorry if I've caused any problems with Grayson.'

'You haven't, and you're welcome. That's what friends are for right?'

He hugged me tightly before I left, and I couldn't help feeling my heart break a little.

He might act like nothing phased him, but he felt deeply, and hurt even deeper.

One final squeeze and I left Caleb's house, trying Grayson's cell, but no answer.

Where was he?

There was no sign of him at his house, or my cottage, so I jumped in the shower and changed before heading to the main house where I found Rosie in the garden, stacking the last of the chairs from last night.

'Morning, Rosie. Here, let me help with those.'

'Thank you, honey. Are you ok, after last night?' Rosie asked, concern creasing her forehead.

'I'm fine, thank you, but I was wondering if you'd seen Grayson? I haven't spoken to him since, well, you know.'

'No, I'm sorry, I haven't seen him since last night. He left after you took Caleb home. Thank you for doing that, by the way. It was very kind of you to look after him. I would have done it myself, but Sam and I really needed to stay with the party,' Rosie explained.

'Of course, it was no trouble at all.' I hoped.

Rosie and I continued clearing up and when we were done, I tried Grayson again. Still no answer.

My stomach twisted in knots. Something was seriously wrong.

I tried not to let my imagination run away with me on the walk back to Caleb's, wondering where Grayson was and why he was ignoring me.

Trying to convince myself it had nothing to do with me, he was just mad at his brother, which, if I ever found him, I could explain what had happened with Sam and clear this whole mess up.

Try as I might to convince myself, there was no ignoring the bad feeling that had settled in the pit of my stomach, telling me it was something far more.

As I neared Caleb's house, I heard voices inside. Raised voices. And although a part of me wanted to barge in and stop them, something made me slow down.

'How could you! Hasn't the past taught you anything?' Grayson's voice was filled with anger.

'I'm sorry, I didn't know you two were so serious. Why haven't you told anyone?' Caleb fired back, echoing my sentiments.

'Don't give me that, Caleb, you knew damn well how I felt about her, you must have known something was going on. And after everything we've already been through. What were you thinking!'

'I wasn't thinking, ok. I was upset and got wasted and acted like an idiot, I know, and I'm sorry,' Caleb's voice lowered, and I took a few steps closer.

'Well, whatever the hell is wrong with you, I hope it was worth it.'

I heard footsteps and quickly backed off, so I wasn't caught eavesdropping.

'Grayson, where have you been? I've been looking for you everywhere,' I didn't have to act surprised when he left Caleb's house, he nearly pulled the door off its hinges.

'That explains why you're here, on my brother's doorstep,' he snapped back.

'What is that supposed to mean?' I crossed my arms, my own temper flaring, but I really didn't want to get into this with him. Not here.

'Nothing, never mind, I'm out of here,' he fumed, storming off without another word.

'Grayson,' I called after him, but he ignored me, as though I hadn't even spoken and carried on blazing a trail away from me.

What is it with these Danvers men!

I spent the rest of the afternoon with Caleb, mostly because he was like a sad puppy dog and I still felt partially responsible for causing this mess, but also because I figured it was best to give Grayson and I both time to cool off before we spoke again.

'So, what are you going to do?' I asked Caleb.

We were sitting in his garden, sipping hot chocolate, something Grayson and I should have been doing the night before, I thought ruefully.

'I'm going to do it. I'm opening my own place. If my dad

can't support me or be happy for me then so be it, but I'm doing it, Soph. I don't want to look back on my life in ten-years' time and regret not following my dreams. If it doesn't work out, I'll find a new dream.'

'Good for you, Caleb. You'll make it work, I know you will.'

I was happy for Caleb. I just wished I could change Sam's mind. I was certainly going to find a way to try, I just had to fix my own problems first.

I offered to help Caleb with his business plan and putting the website and promotional packages together and anything else he may need help with.

I vowed to help him and support him as much as possible. He was going to need it from someone after all, if he wasn't going to get it from Sam or Grayson.

'I really should get going, I need to find your brother. If he isn't still being an idiot,' I said, once we finished our drinks and had spent a little more time talking things over.

'A little advice?' Caleb asked. I nodded. 'Cut him a little slack. He's been through the wringer, but he's worth it if you can see past his many, many flaws,' Caleb laughed.

'Good to know. For what it's worth, I think you're doing the right thing. Give your dad time, he'll come around, it was probably just a shock to him. He'll understand how important this is to you when he sees what you create, just give it time.'

'I guess,' Caleb didn't sound overly convinced, but he thanked me anyway and we said our goodbye's.

Taking a deep, calming breath, I slowly started in the direction of Grayson's house.

'Hi,' Grayson opened the door wearing an old pair of jeans and t-shirt.

'Hi,' he replied, his eyes guarded.

'Can I come in?' He simply stepped back to let me pass. My blood started to boil. 'I don't know what you think I've done wrong, but your brother is dealing with a lot and I'm his friend and I wanted to be there for him, that's it, nothing more, nothing less. As his brother, I would have thought you'd be doing the same.'

Grayson sighed. He looked tired.

'Why don't we sit down. There's something you should know.'

All the frustration I'd been feeling instantly vanished at the seriousness in Grayson's expression.

'Grayson, what is it?' I asked, sitting beside him.

'Do you remember I told you about the woman I was engaged to?'

I nodded.

'Well, there's more to that story, but I'm going to need a beer for this,' Grayson got up, grabbing a beer from the fridge before pouring me a glass of wine without asking if I wanted one.

He handed it to me, and I took a sip to settle my nerves, waiting for him to go on.

'Catherine won us all over in no time at all when I brought her home to meet my family. She was good at that, at getting what she wanted and swaying people to her will. It worked all too well. She played me, and she played Caleb. She fed us both so many lies I still have no idea how she kept up with them all. She was seeing Caleb while she was engaged to me,' Grayson paused briefly, taking a long drink of beer before continuing.

I sat quietly, barely breathing, remembering the night out, hearing April and Paige talking in the bathroom about Catherine and history repeating itself.

So many pieces fell into place.

'She had Caleb and I both wrapped around her finger. She kept telling Caleb that she was in love with him and she was going to end things with me when the time was right. That we were practically over already anyway. I'm not excusing what my brother did, but having been under her spell myself, I can understand why he got caught in her web so easily. She was a master of manipulation. Things eventually came to a head one night when I caught them together. I told her to leave the farm, leave my family, and never come back. It nearly destroyed Caleb and I. It's taken us a long time to move past that, so seeing him kissing you last night brought back all of those old feelings,' Grayson finished, running a hand through his hair.

I reached out for Grayson's hand, 'I don't know what to say. I'm so sorry you had to go through that, but I'm not Catherine, I would never do that.'

'I know, I'm not mad at you or blaming you, it just dredged up the past and it's something I need to deal with, but Caleb,' Grayson stood and walked over to the patio doors, looking out into the garden. 'I don't know what to do about Caleb.'

'Grayson, I'm here and I'm not going anywhere. I'll do whatever I can to help fix things with your brother, you don't have to go through any of this alone, but I think you should talk to Caleb, he could use his brother right now.'

My Grayson would have pulled me close and kissed the top of my head. My Grayson would acknowledge what I'd just said.

This new Grayson simply stood, unmoving, staring out into the darkness and that feeling of dread started to creep back under my skin.

The days that followed were uneasy, unnerving. You could cut the tension in the air with a knife.

Things between Grayson and Caleb seemed worse than ever and things between Grayson and I hadn't been the same.

I felt torn, wanting to be there for Grayson and fix things for the brothers as well as be the friend that Caleb needed, but it was impossible.

Either way I would be letting someone down and no matter how hard I tried, the wedge that had come between Grayson and I grew day by day and it killed me.

As the days drew into weeks, I stopped trying to talk to Grayson about it, it only seemed to make things worse, but I knew I couldn't go on this way either.

I needed to do something, we needed to do something, to move past this, so I asked everyone to meet me in the main house one autumn evening and to my surprise everyone turned up.

Although Caleb and Grayson both nearly turned and walked straight back out when they arrived to find the rest of us sitting waiting.

'Sophie, what is this?' Grayson asked, anger flaring, as I

watched his eyes turn icy once again.

It was heart-breaking to see those beautiful, warm, loving blue eyes turn gradually harder, more guarded, reminding me far too much of the first time I'd met Grayson, in the barn.

I thought I'd melted the ice caps that engulfed him, but Catherine's deceit had hurt them, to the very core of their relationship.

I was determined to fix that.

'Please don't go,' I said to both of them. 'We need to talk things through, we can't go on like this, any of us, it's not healthy and it won't end well.'

'This isn't your concern,' Grayson shot back.

It was like a slap to the face.

I swallowed hard, fighting back the tears that threatened to spill over.

'This affects all of us, including me, so that makes it my concern,' I replied sternly.

Grayson tried to stare me down, but I wasn't going down easily and when he realised as much he sighed and sat in one of the armchairs.

The five of us spent the next few hours talking, yelling, sitting in silence, arguing, talking again and finally, exhausted, Caleb stood, announced that he would see out the rest of the month on the farm, after which he would be moving to Beaufort where he would be working on his beach bar restaurant.

The room fell silent and for once I didn't know what to say.

I'd been such a fool to think I could fix things. They were

both so stubborn. Heck, all three Danvers men were as stubborn as each other.

And with Grayson and Caleb so stuck in the past, they would never be able to move forward until they could forgive and forget.

After Grayson and Caleb had left, Sam quietly excused himself, leaving Rosie and I alone.

'Thank you for trying,' Rosie said, her voice barely a whisper.

Hearing the sadness in her voice was more than I could take, and I burst into tears.

'I'm so sorry, Rosie, this is all my fault, I'm so sorry,' I sobbed uncontrollably for so many reasons.

I cried for the distance that had grown between Grayson and I.

I cried for the brothers who would probably never talk again, for father and son whose relationship appeared beyond repair, for Rosie whose family was falling apart.

'Now, now, it'll be ok, these things have a way of working themselves out, you'll see, don't fret,' Rosie soothed and I wondered how she could be so strong, so certain, when everything was crumbling down around us.

That night I lay in bed, alone, thinking of the events of the past few weeks and of everything Grayson had told me about Catherine.

I wondered if I was like her, deep down. Was I being as selfish as her, wanting both brothers?

I wanted all of Grayson and until recently I'd had all of him, as he had had all of me, but had I enjoyed the attention from Caleb too?

I never thought I encouraged it, but what if I had? What if I was just like Catherine and I had been the cause of everything?

If I hadn't come here, nothing would have changed. The family wouldn't be falling apart. Was I the problem?

I tossed and turned, eventually giving up completely, I was never going to get any sleep with this much on my mind, so I got up, took a hot shower, wrapped up warm and took a slow walk towards the barn to see Apollo and check on the other horses.

It must have been some time after five in the morning when I neared the barn and the crisp autumn air nipped at my cheeks.

The barn lights were on and I could hear voices as I approached.

'I've said I'm sorry a hundred times, I don't know what more you want from me.' I recognised Caleb's voice.

'I want to know why her, why Sophie.' That was Grayson.

'We're just friends, nothing's going on and you know that,' Caleb replied, sounding exasperated.

I thought my heart actually stopped beating. How could Grayson think anything was going on with Caleb and I?

'Why did you kiss her? After everything that's happened between us and knowing full well how I felt about her!'

'I told you, I was wasted and wasn't thinking. Hell, it could have been anyone, Sophie just happened to be in the wrong place at the wrong time. Why can't you believe me? Is it so impossible to trust me again? I made a mistake with

Catherine, but I thought we'd moved passed that. I guess I was wrong.'

'I guess so,' Grayson replied before storming off.

I slipped up the side of the barn so that he didn't see me.

I didn't want either of them to see me. I needed to get out of there.

I couldn't do this anymore.

Chapter 19

Once again, I found myself staring out over a gloomy New York autumn day.

Or maybe it wasn't that the day was gloomy, but my mood. My heart sank further into darkness.

'Morning,' Kaitlyn appeared, pouring herself a cup of coffee.

'Morning,' I replied, my voice sounding hollow and empty, even to my own ears.

It had been two months since I left the farm. Left Beaufort and my family, left my heart, left…. Grayson.

I could barely think his name without wanting to fall to the floor in sobs. But no more tears, I'd vowed. I had to pull myself together and move on with my life this time, this couldn't be a repeat of what I'd gone through after Luke.

I wouldn't survive it a second time.

Grayson had tried calling me every day, sometimes several times a day after I left, but I could never bring myself to answer, or even listen to the voicemails he left.

He tried texting and emailing but I deleted them as they came in, without reading a single one.

I knew I wouldn't be strong enough to stay away, if he

asked me to come back. Ha, why would he be asking me to come back, I thought bitterly.

Hearing that last argument between Grayson and Caleb in the barn had been the final straw for me.

I had been so hurt hearing Grayson implying something was going on between Caleb and I, but beyond that, I could no longer pretend that I wasn't the problem, or that I could fix things between them.

My being there was only making things worse and I refused to be another Catherine and come between the brothers, and their family.

I wouldn't, I couldn't, do that to the people I'd come to love with all my heart, so I'd raced back to the cottage, packed my bags and left.

I'd cried the entire drive to my parents' house and when I arrived, when I thought there was nothing left, a whole new wave of sadness had crashed over me and the sobs began again.

My parents were beside themselves with concern, seeing me in such a state, but when I'd managed to pull myself together to tell them what had happened they had assured me that none of it was my fault, but it was too late.

I knew I had done too much damage and refused to return to the farm.

Later that day my phone buzzed, first Grayson's name had appeared, then Caleb, and finally Rosie's home number.

I ignored them all and as I lay in bed, tears soaking my pillow, hearing my parent's phone ring as I held my breath.

I'd made my mom and dad both swear to me that they

wouldn't tell anyone I was here, but I couldn't help eavesdropping anyway.

'No, Rosie, she's not here, but she's ok, please don't worry. I'll ask her to call you as soon as she can.'

I let out a sigh of relief.

I hated asking my parents to lie for me and I knew they hated doing it, but I couldn't face any of them.

I needed to put some space between us for a while and get my bearings.

After a week hiding out at my parents (mainly because Grayson had turned up a few times and I was too scared to leave for fear of bumping into him), I made the decision to go back to New York.

'Honey, we don't think that's the best option,' my parents both looked at me, concern clear in their eyes.

I knew they were worried I was going to end up back where I'd started after I'd lost Luke.

'I'll be ok this time, I promise, it won't be like before. I just need to move on with my life, get back on track with writing and my old life in New York,' I assured them.

It had taken a lot of convincing but eventually they knew they couldn't stop me, so they made me promise to call if I was down or just needed to talk, and to come home as often as possible.

'I promise, I will,' I replied to all of their requests.

Leaving, again, was so much harder than I had prepared myself for and I knew the main reason was because I was leaving my heart behind this time.

It would forever belong to Grayson and wherever he

was, that's where my heart would be. But I held it together until I arrived in New York (I was getting better at keeping it in than I had been before).

Until I saw Kaitlyn and went to pieces all over again.

My best friend truly was my saving grace.

We spent my first night back in the city in her apartment with a bottle of wine (ok, maybe two), I cried far more than I thought possible – seriously, I was going to end up completely dehydrated at this rate.

Kaitlyn listened, hugged me when I cried, held my hand while I told her everything that had happened and most importantly, topped up my wine as soon as I finished the glass.

'I have to agree with your parents, I don't think any of it is your fault. Yes, they had issues because of Catherine, but Soph, you are nothing like her. You've proven that, you've sacrificed your own happiness for them, all of them.'

'I just don't think they could have gotten passed everything that happened and moved on while I was still there, a constant reminder of what had happened with Catherine and what, it appeared to Grayson, was happening all over again.'

'That doesn't sound like Grayson. Are you sure he thought something was going on between you and Caleb?' Kaitlyn asked, sipping her own wine.

'Trust me, I could hear the accusation in his voice.' Remembering the conversation I'd overheard all too well.

'And you haven't spoken to any of them since you left?'

'No,' I replied sadly. 'They tried calling, Grayson even

turned up at my parents' house a few times, but I couldn't face him, Kay.'

'I know it's not what you want to hear, but Soph, I still think you should talk to him.'

'I can't. It's too hard and hurts too much. I know I'm stronger than I was after Luke, but I need time to heal, I just can't face talking to him now.'

Maybe ever, I thought.

Two weeks later (two weeks of continuous phone calls and me contemplating changing my number), I finally sat down on a Friday afternoon, having decided to write letters to the Danvers.

I wanted to, at the very least, explain why I'd left so suddenly and apologise for everything I'd done.

I needed to try make them understand, if I could, and hope that they could one day forgive me, so I sat at Kaitlyn's desk and started with Rosie and Sam's.

Dear Rosie and Sam,

I don't know where to start, other than by apologising for what I've put your family through.

Meeting all of you and being a part of your lives has been one of the biggest blessings of my life and it came at a time when I needed it more than you will ever know.

I only wish I could have found a way to repay you for everything you've done for me.

I'm so sorry for the problems I've caused with Grayson and Caleb and between Sam and Caleb, but please, don't let that come between you.

Caleb is a wonderful man, he only wants to follow his dreams and to know that he has your love, support and approval in doing so.

If my time on this earth has taught me anything, it's that life is far too short and precious to let a difference in opinion come between you, so Sam, please try to understand that Caleb isn't trying to hurt you, he just doesn't want to look back on his life one day and regret not taking a chance on his dream.

He's a wonderful cook and I know his beach bar will be a success, but it won't mean anything to him if he doesn't have his family there to celebrate his success with him.

I would also like to add that Caleb and I have only ever been friends, nothing more.

I care so deeply about him, about all of you, but my heart has only ever truly belonged to Grayson.

After I lost Luke, I never imagined I would find love again, I certainly wasn't looking for it, but I fell for Grayson from the start, without even realising it at first.

I'm truly sorry for causing Grayson pain and making him doubt me in any way, that was never my intention and it kills me to think I've hurt him.

I will always love him, and my heart will forever belong to him, but I won't be like Catherine. I won't come between your sons, or your family, you mean too much to me to let that happen.

All my love, always,

Sophie

Then came Caleb's letter.

Dear Caleb,

I'm so sorry I had to leave so suddenly, without saying goodbye, but I knew if I had to face any of you, saying goodbye wouldn't have been possible and it's what had to be done.

I care about you and your family so very much. It kills me knowing that I've come between you and your brother and Sam.

I had no other option but to leave. I only hope you can forgive me for that, along with everything else.

If I had known what happened with Catherine, well, honestly, I don't know what I would have, or could have, done differently, but I would have tried.

I never would have come between you and Grayson the way she did. Family is too important, which is why I believe you should try talking to your dad again.

I know it didn't go down well the first time around, but give him time. Time to come to terms with you leaving the farm and then please try talking to him again, make him see, make him understand, because to lose one's family is one of life's biggest tragedies.

As for Grayson, I don't know where to begin, or how to fix things, but I promise you Caleb that I will try to find a way.

Until then, remember these words that a wise friend once told me, 'Cut him some slack, he's been through the wringer.'

You both have, so cut yourself some slack too, ok? You deserve to be happy and to follow your dreams and I know, in time, your dad will see this too.

Your family loves you, remember that.

My only hope is that they are there to share in your success (because you will be a success – believe that and believe in yourself and your dreams will become a reality).

You have been a true friend and I wish you all the success and happiness this world owes you, Caleb.

All my love,

Sophie

When I came to write Grayson's, I found myself staring

at a blank page for what felt like an eternity.

I started writing, tore the page out, crumpled it up and tossed it in the bin.

Tried again and did the same. Then a third and fourth time and eventually gave up entirely.

I would post the first two letters before trying again with Grayson's, but I would need time to find the right words.

In the meantime, I felt an overwhelming desire to document everything that had happened since I left New York.

I never wanted to forget my time at home, with my family, with the Danvers, and as much as it hurt to think about, my time with Grayson too.

So, pulling out my laptop, I started writing. I wrote and wrote until the lighting changed and I heard the front door open.

'Hi, Soph,' Kaitlyn called and then looked up to see me writing and beamed. 'It's about time.'

I smiled back at her before saving my work and shutting the laptop off for now.

We made dinner together that night and although I would never be completely whole, I knew I was going to be ok.

'I have some news, but you're not going to like it,' Kaitlyn announced after dinner.

'What is it?' I asked, putting the last of the dishes away.

'I had been planning something, but it was before everything happened and you came back here. I was planning on surprising you actually. Then you turned up here and, well, the surprise was on me I guess,' Kaitlyn laughed nervously, and I felt anxious.

'Kaitlyn, please just tell me what's wrong.'

'I'm moving to Beaufort.'

Ok, I hadn't seen that one coming.

I sat down on the couch next to my best friend and stared at her as though she'd just grown a third eye.

'I know, the timing is awful, I'm so sorry. I'll stay here as long as you need, but I wanted to tell you sooner rather than later.'

'When?' I croaked out.

'I was planning on being there by Christmas.'

I felt faint. Christmas was just over two months away.

'I'm sorry, I shouldn't have said anything,' Kaitlyn fussed.

'No, no, I'm sorry. I'm just surprised. What brought this on?'

'After coming out to see you, and my family, and seeing how happy you were on the farm, it made me rethink my own life. The goal was always to go back home anyway, so I figured I'd just make it happen a little sooner. I haven't been happy here lately and it only got worse after you left...' Kaitlyn trailed off.

'And then my life fell apart, again, and I came crawling back,' I half smiled at my best friend.

Life certainly was easier with her by my side. She was like my sister after all – which made me think of my parents and Paul and Sarah and my niece or nephew who would be here in a few months' time.

Did I want to spend the rest of my life so far from my family?

I had loved being home again. Being able to see them whenever I wanted to and spend more time with them.

I'd spent enough time away from home and it was time to go back.

'I want to come with you,' I said aloud, realising it was exactly what I wanted.

'What!' Kaitlyn exclaimed excitedly. 'Are you sure?'

'Yeah, I really am. I came back here because I thought being in Beaufort would be too difficult but being away from my family has been the hard part. I want to be there when Paul's baby is born and for birthdays and Christmas and you already know that you're like a sister to me, you're part of my family too. Being away from all of you would be far worse than facing my fears of bumping into Grayson, or his family, which probably isn't very likely to happen in any case, so yes, I want to come with you. I want to go home, for good this time.'

After that night, Kailyn buzzed around the apartment, making arrangements for us to be home by Christmas.

We were going to surprise our parents and if I was being honest with myself, Kaitlyn's enthusiasm and excitement was rubbing off on me and I couldn't wait to go home, with only a hint of nerves fluttering in my belly at the thought of seeing certain people.

Kaitlyn had everything planned, so that left me as much spare time as I needed to write. Which I did, day and night.

Some chapters were harder than others (mainly those that revolved around Grayson), but it was cathartic, in a way, to express my emotions this way, to get it all out on the pages.

How I felt about him, how much I loved him, how he'd changed my life and mended my heart.

The hard part was remembering he was no longer in my life, no longer there to hold me tight, no longer there to kiss me and send butterflies fluttering through me.

Those were the difficult moments, the moments I tried not to dwell on.

So, I focused on finishing the book, that was the goal. Focus on one thing at a time, take it one day at a time.

Baby steps, I reminded myself.

I didn't have to worry about keeping busy and distracted – Kaitlyn had big plans for the move. Plans that required my help.

She was going to open her own studio in Beaufort (it was about time, her work was amazing) and she'd asked if I would set up the website.

'The farm website was such a success. I was hoping maybe you could do mine too?' She asked excitedly.

'Of course, anything I can do to help, you know I'll do it.'

Thankfully between writing, packing (or repacking) and creating the perfect website, it didn't leave me much time to wonder how Grayson was, or if he thought of me, or even missed me.

Maybe he was relieved I was gone, one less reminder of Catherine and one less complication in his life.

That thought cut me like a knife and I hoped it wasn't true.

Evenings were usually the hardest part of my existence, so I spent them writing (often until past midnight), when I'd fall into bed, utterly exhausted, and (usually) into a dreamless sleep.

But some nights, dreams of piercing blue eyes haunted me, and I'd wake up feeling like my heart had been ripped right out of my chest.

On those occasions I wondered if I was doing the right thing, writing this book, reliving the past, the best and worst moments of my life, but in the end I always came back to the same conclusion, it absolutely was the right thing.

Our love deserved to be remembered and although I was writing it as a fictional novel, I would always know that it was ours, the story of us, how we'd begun, how we'd found one another.

One thing I was still unsure of was the ending.

It probably wouldn't sell if I ended the book to mirror my own life.

People generally wanted a happily ever after ending. To escape real life in those moments, getting lost between the pages of fiction.

So, I would give them a happily ever after, one that should have happened.

The happily ever after I'd imagined for Grayson and I.

'How did Roger take the news?' I asked Kaitlyn.

We were meeting up with some friends for dinner on a particularly chilly November evening.

'Not well, but in true Roger fashion he somehow made

me feel like I was the one in the wrong and that I wouldn't last without him, or the magazine,' Kaitlyn replied, sipping her cocktail.

She was better off without her slave driver boss.

'I would love to be around to see his reaction when you blow everyone out of the water with your very own studio and beautiful photographs,' I encouraged.

'Thanks, Soph. I'm so happy, and a little relieved, you'll be there with me. This is a huge step for me, and I can't imagine doing it alone.'

'I'll be there every step of the way. It's going to be great, Kay, you just wait and see.'

'Maybe we could start up our own magazine. You could do the writing and I'll take the pictures. I'm serious,' Kailyn added, in response to my dubious look. 'We could write about local events and promote local. We could write feature pieces about local people and things that really matter, not just stick thin models with no personalities.'

She may be on to something, but we didn't have time to delve into it, when we noticed our friends arriving.

We'd known Cooper and Amanda for years and it was great to see them again.

Cooper had brought along her latest boy toy, who she introduced as Hudson and I assumed Chase was Amanda's new flame.

I assumed wrong.

Shortly after they arrived, Ty joined us (apparently, this was Amanda's new boyfriend).

Chase, it would seem, had been brought in especially for me. At least that's how it seemed, as he invaded my personal space a few too many times.

'You have beautiful eyes, I'd love to draw them sometime,' Chase stated dramatically, lightly brushing the back of his hand over my cheek.

Oh my God! Get me out of here!

I caught Kaitlyn stifling a laugh and wanted to lob my bread stick at her.

I waited as long as I possibly could after dinner, before announcing that I needed to get some work in before the night was through, saying goodnight to my friends, who pleaded with me to stay.

'Sorry guys, duty calls,' I feigned disappointment.

'Call me,' Chase called after me as I practically ran from the restaurant.

Arriving home, alone, was a surprising relief.

I kicked my high heels off (missing my cowboy boots, I thought glumly), stripped out of my dress and stepped into a hot shower, washing away the disastrous evening.

As the hot water ran over my skin, my mind drifted to Grayson, as it always did, and I wondered what he was doing right now.

I missed him so much.

I had picked up the phone to call him so many times these past weeks, chickening out each and every time.

I just couldn't bring myself to do it. What would I say? What could I say? Sorry just didn't seem to cut it.

Words couldn't get me out of this, as I'd come to realise when I eventually gave up altogether trying to write his letter.

The more time went on the less I knew what to say or do.

I hadn't heard back from Rosie, Sam or Caleb since posting their letters and my parents had been vague when I spoke to them.

Although that wasn't unusual. They didn't usually mention the Danvers when I spoke to them (which was most days), either to prevent upsetting me, or because the Danvers were upset with me for everything that had happened, and then for my sudden departure on top of everything else.

They had every right to be angry with me, I thought miserably.

Naturally, I worried about bumping into them when we got home but couldn't imagine it. They had only gone into Beaufort on a few, rare occasions when I had been there, so the chances were slim.

At least that's what I told myself, trying to convince myself all would be ok and I wouldn't have to face them.

I had been so lost in thought, I hadn't heard Kaitlyn get home and I jumped as she walked into the living room.

'Sorry,' she chuckled.

'It's ok, I was a million miles away,' I replied, closing my laptop.

'So, that was fun,' Kailyn laughed, flopping onto the couch next to me.

'It was awful. What were they thinking!'

'They just want to see you happy again.'

'I know. It's just too soon. Actually, even if it wasn't too soon, it still wouldn't have happened, he was just...' I trailed off trying to think of a nice way of putting it.

'A weirdo,' Kaitlyn laughed.

'It's not funny.' But I laughed despite myself and threw a scatter cushion at her.

'So, how's the book coming along? I don't suppose I could read some of it?'

'I'm actually nearly done and no, you definitely cannot ready it. Yet,' I added.

I felt, well, I suppose I felt embarrassed about this one.

It was the first book I'd written that stemmed from my own life. It had felt more like writing in a journal than writing another novel.

'Well I can't wait to read it once it's done,' Kaitlyn said before hugging me goodnight and disappearing into her room.

I opened the laptop again, staring at the draft that was almost done, wondering how the story would end. Imagining how our lives could have panned out.

Feeling the familiar pang of my heart, I continued typing, determined to figure out the perfect ending as it neared.

Chapter 20

One thing I would definitely miss about New York was Christmas time. It truly was a winter wonderland, I thought, wandering through the bustling streets.

I had been out shopping and found some wonderful gifts for Kaitlyn and my family.

I couldn't wait to see their faces when I turned up on Christmas Eve and even more so when I told them I would be staying for good.

I hoped it would be a good Christmas present. One they wanted.

Lately, I had been worrying that they were disappointed in me, after everything that had happened with Grayson and his family.

Of course, they both assured me that none of it had been my fault and there was nothing I could have done about the situation, but I couldn't help wondering if they felt even a hint of disappointment.

They certainly hadn't shown it if they had.

I felt my phone buzzing in my pocket and my heart stopped, as it always did whenever my phone buzzed.

Pulling it out, hoping to see Grayson's name, even though I probably wouldn't have answered if it was him calling.

Hey, I never said I had everything figured out.

I breathed out when I saw my editor's name appear on the screen instead.

'Brian, hi.'

Brian had been with me from the start.

As an assistant all those years ago, he'd been the one to discover my very first novel and although he'd worked his way up in the company, he still insisted on working with me directly, instead of one of the junior assistants.

We worked well together, and I trusted his advice and opinions.

'Hi, Sophie. I'm glad I caught you, I've read your novel and I think it's great. It's unlike anything you've done before. It's raw and emotional and I think it would appeal to the vast majority of readers. I'm just finishing up for the holidays, but I'm taking it with me to highlight any possible changes. Nothing big, just tweaks to polish it up, you know the drill. Anyway, I'll get back to you in the new year, but I have a good feeling about this one.'

'That's amazing, thank you. I hope you and Hayley have a wonder Christmas with the kids.'

'Merry Christmas, Soph.'

I hung up the phone, feeling elated.

Standing there, in the middle of New York City, surrounded by people, on the verge of another novel, my heart suddenly sank when I realised that I couldn't share this with the one person I wanted to more than anything.

Stop feeling sorry for yourself, I scolded myself.

I had so much to be grateful for in my life, so I put my big girl panties on and got over my pity party.

I sent Kailyn a text to tell her the news and continued on my shopping spree.

'I can't believe this is it, I can't believe we're leaving.'

Kaitlyn and I were sitting on the floor of her apartment, eating Chinese takeout.

It was our last night in New York.

'How are you feeling?' I asked between mouthfuls.

'Nervous, excited, terrified.'

'I think we're making the right decision and I believe that everything will work out,' was what I said, but deep down I had the same reservations as Kaitlyn, which I guess is only natural when you're uprooting your whole life.

I had wondered if we were making a mistake, but I knew it was the right choice deep down.

New York didn't feel like home anymore. But I worried that Beaufort wouldn't either.

I wasn't sure anywhere would feel like home again since leaving the farm.

But I had made my choices and now I had to live with them, so the following morning we hopped in the removal van we'd hired and took turns driving the long road home.

Only stopping briefly along the way for lunch and of course a few coffees.

Kailyn had rented a cottage for the two of us, but we would of course be spending the holidays with our families.

I would then be helping Kaitlyn set up her studio and once she was up and running, we were going to start planning our magazine.

It felt good to have something to look forward to, to have a plan.

I was sure I had a few more novels left in me, but I was excited about this new chapter and a new challenge.

I loved writing, in any shape or form, so I was looking forward to trying my hand at writing articles for the magazine, especially about real people, no more fictional characters, at least for a little while.

Perhaps it was because there were two of us this time, but the trip hadn't felt all that long when we saw the sign for Beaufort.

Excitement started to bubble up inside me (and the same longing that had been with me since I left the farm, the longing that only one person could satiate), but all my fears and doubts faded away and I knew I was home.

We both were, I thought, smiling at Kaitlyn who looked just as excited as I felt.

'We're almost home,' she said, squeezing my arm.

'We're almost home,' I repeated happily.

The cottage wasn't hard to find and we got everything unpacked shortly after arriving, which turned out to be far more draining after the long drive than either of us anticipated.

Around ten o'clock we called it a night, wanting to get a good night's sleep before seeing our families the following day, which had been the best decision.

I slept better that night than I had in ages and woke up feeling refreshed and ready to face the day.

After saying our goodbye's and wishing one another a

happy Christmas, we hopped in taxi's and left our new home.

I was thrilled that I'd left my car with my parents. It would be one less thing to worry about and it meant Kaitlyn and I had our own transportation, although Kaitlyn assured me she was planning on getting herself a car as soon as we were settled.

Even though I had my own key, I decided to knock on my parent's door, wanting to surprise them, not give my dad another heart attack by having them think someone was breaking in.

'Sophie! What are you doing home?' My mom asked excitedly. 'George, it's Sophie, she's home.'

My dad came to meet us, 'Hi, honey. Were we expecting you?' He asked, looking confused, but happy to see me nonetheless.

'No, I wanted to surprise you,' I beamed at them.

'Well come in, come in. Are you hungry? When did you arrive?' My mom asked.

'Last night, with Kaitlyn.'

'Oh, how wonderful, Kaitlyn's parents will be so happy to have her home for the holidays,' Mom replied.

'Actually, it's a little longer than just the holidays,' I said as we all made our way into the living room. 'I have some news,' my parents looked worried. 'I'm home to stay.'

'Are you serious? Honey, that's fantastic news!' My dad replied, a smile lit his face.

'This is the best Christmas present ever,' my mom said, emotion clear on her face.

'Are you sure it's ok?' I asked them, not wanting to face the elephant in the room.

'Of course, why wouldn't it be?' My dad asked, oblivious.

'Well, I made such of mess of things, with the Danvers, I wasn't sure if me being here would make things worse,' I replied awkwardly.

'Oh, honey, you need to move past that, you didn't do anything. You helped them more than you know,' my mom said.

'How do you mean?' I couldn't possibly fathom how I had helped them when I'd left everything in such a mess.

'Rosie called me after she and Sam received your letter. She was beside herself, she felt terrible that you thought any of what had happened was your fault. They think so highly of you, Sophie, they think of you as family and the only thing that upset them was knowing that you were hurting. Anyway, Rosie said that after readying your letter, it was like a wakeup call for Sam, he went to see Caleb and they talked everything through. Sam was never disappointed in Caleb, he was just surprised and he was disappointed in himself for not realising sooner that his son had other dreams and aspirations. He'd always just assumed that Caleb was happy working on the farm.'

'So, they're ok now?' I asked in disbelief.

'They're more than ok, they're closer than ever. Sam's even helping Caleb with his restaurant,' my mom explained.

I wanted to cry, from relief, from joy, from the fact that some good had come of the mess I'd made.

'But what about Grayson and Caleb?'

'They're working through their issues, but Sophie, those issues were there long before you came along. If anything, you brought them closer together.'

'Before tearing them apart again,' I looked down at my hands, unable to face my parents.

'You did nothing of the sort,' my dad interjected.

'You didn't hear them arguing the day I left the farm. Grayson was accusing Caleb and I of, well, having feelings for each other, or worse. You guys were there the night of the grill, you saw how angry Grayson was when Caleb kissed me. I know Caleb was being an idiot and that he shouldn't have done it, but maybe I gave him the wrong signals or something.'

I didn't really want to be opening up old wounds, but sometimes it was good to talk about things and get them off your chest.

'Honey, we know you, and we've seen you with both of them and anyone would have to be blind not to see that you only ever had eyes for Grayson. Heck, we knew it the first time we saw you two together. So trust us when we tell you, you did nothing wrong. Grayson and Caleb have to work through their issues together. Rosie and Sam are helping them with that, but none of those issues have anything to do with you,' my dad told me.

Sometimes in life that was all one needed, to see the pride and love in your parent's eyes and know that everything would be ok.

'Thank you both. I feel better knowing that, but it doesn't change the fact that I just up and left them all,' I said after a moment.

'No, it doesn't, but Rosie and Sam understand why you felt you had to leave. They know you were only trying to make things better,' Mom reassured me.

I did feel better after talking to my parents, but I still wasn't sure I could face Rosie or Sam any time soon. Or Caleb for that matter.

And Grayson, well, I wasn't sure I'd ever have the strength to face him again without it breaking me apart.

But for now, I put all thoughts of Grayson out of my mind and enjoyed this time with my family.

Christmas morning

I'd always loved Christmas. It was by far my favourite holiday.

I loved the magic it brought, watching Christmas films, curled up on the couch with a hot chocolate.

I loved decorating and putting the Christmas tree up, but mostly I loved spending it with the ones I love.

I raced downstairs, still in my pyjamas, to find my parents in the kitchen.

'Merry Christmas,' I hugged them both and my dad chuckled.

'Merry Christmas,' they both replied.

'I'm glad to see not much has changed when it comes to Christmas,' my dad winked at me.

'Nope, I'm still a kid at heart,' I grinned back. 'When will Paul and Sarah be here?'

‘They’ll be here around eleven so that they can spend a few hours with us before they go to Sarah’s parents,’ Mom said.

I picked up my phone to text Kaitlyn and noticed an email from Brian. Publication of my book would be going ahead in the new year.

‘Oh my gosh!’ I squeaked.

‘What is it?’ Dad looked up from his coffee.

‘My new book is going to be published in the new year.’

‘Honey, that’s wonderful news, congratulations. I didn’t know you were writing again,’ Mom looked hopeful. Like I was finally getting back to myself again.

‘I felt inspired,’ I replied, not entirely sure if inspiration was the word for it, but whatever it was, I was glad I’d run with it.

As most Christmas days went, we ate too much, laughed a lot, shared old stories, exchanged gifts and the day went by far too quickly.

After saying our goodbye’s to Paul and Sarah, I flopped down on the couch.

‘I’m so full, I don’t think I can move,’ I sighed.

‘Likewise,’ my dad agreed.

‘Thank you for an amazing lunch, Mom.’

‘You’re welcome, it’s been great having you home,’ my mom smiled.

It really was a wonderful Christmas. And as sad as I was for the things (or one particular thing) I was missing out on, I was truly blessed and grateful for the things I did have and the amazing people in my life.

New Year's Eve

Ordinarily, I loved New Year's Eve. Almost as much as Christmas, but this year, after everything, I was looking forward to staying in, ordering takeout and having an early night.

'Not happening! Get your cute butt up, we're going out,' Kaitlyn instructed.

'Not happening! Staying put, in my pyjamas,' I replied with a cheeky grin.

'Soph, come on, this year has been crazy, but we have a second shot, let's start the new year off with a bang! Come on. Pleeeease.'

'Ugh,' I groaned, I couldn't say no to her.

'Yay,' she squealed, jumping up to dig through our unpacked boxes for something to wear.

An hour later, we were primped, preened and ready to go.

'I can't believe you talked me into this,' I grumbled on the way into town.

'We're going to have fun, that's an order,' Kaitlyn attempted a serious look, failing miserably, looking way too excited.

'Yes ma'am,' I couldn't help but laugh.

As usual, Kaitlyn was right, we did have fun.

We had a few cocktails (yes, only a few this time, no more overindulging) and watched the fireworks and danced the night away.

It was almost midnight when I saw him, across the dancefloor. I froze on the spot.

I swear my heart actually stopped beating. I could feel the blood draining from my face.

'Soph, what's wrong?' Kaitlyn asked, but I couldn't respond.

My mind was going a million miles an hour. Who else was here with him? Had he seen me?

I was about to turn and run. Too late!

'Oh,' I heard Kaitlyn say, 'Caleb.'

'Sophie, hi,' Caleb said, after he'd pushed his way through the crowded dancefloor to get to us.

'Hi,' was all I could say.

'Hi, Caleb, how are you?' I heard Kaitlyn say beside me, but my eyes were scanning the room. Was Grayson here? I didn't want to stick around to find out.

I waited for Caleb and Kaitlyn to stop talking before announcing that I was leaving.

'He's not here, if that's what you're worried about,' Caleb guessed.

'It's not that, I was getting ready to go anyway,' I lied.

'Please stay Soph, it's almost midnight,' Kaitlyn pleaded.

I hugged her tightly and whispered, 'I'm sorry, I can't, but you stay and have fun, ok?'

'Ok,' she squeezed me back, 'Happy New Year, Soph.'

'Happy New Year, Kay,' I waved them off and battled my way through the crowd.

The cool air washed over me, and I welcomed it, needing it to clear my mind, but a strong hand on my arm stopped me from putting the much-needed distance between myself and the bar.

'Caleb,' I whispered when I turned to see who the hand belonged to. I should have guessed.

'Soph, you don't have to leave. I wish you'd stay, we have a lot to catch up on. I thought you were in New York by the way?' He asked curiously.

'Rain check?' I purposely ignored his question about New York, nowhere near ready for him to know I was back for good. I tried to smile, but he saw right through me, 'I'm sorry, I just feel so bad about everything that happened, and then for leaving.'

'I'm the one who should be sorry. I messed everything up and made you feel like you had to leave. Which you didn't by the way. You could still come back you know. He misses you.'

I didn't know what to say to that.

I didn't think I could find my voice to say anything at all.

After a moment to compose myself, I forced a smile on my face.

'I really should be going, but you have fun tonight and look after Kaitlyn, ok?'

'I will. Happy New Year, Soph,' Caleb leaned over and kissed my cheek before disappearing back into the bar, leaving me standing in the street, feeling numb.

Three words repeated in my head the entire way home… He misses you. He misses you. He misses you.

What was I supposed to do with that? How could he miss me? I'm pretty sure he thought I was cheating on him with his brother!

This was not how I wanted to start the new year.

Alone, memories of the past haunting me, unable to move forward, but not wanting to be stuck in the past, I hung there, in limbo, and when the clock struck midnight I closed my eyes and wished that things would be ok, that somehow, I would be ok and maybe just maybe, I would find my way back to him.

I knew it was a silly wish, some may have thought it a wasted wish, but I made it anyway and went to bed feeling determined to shake myself from this state of limbo.

Good things were coming, I told myself.

The new book, the new venture with Kaitlyn, starting our new lives. I would make the best of this life I'd been given, and I remembered a night long ago (at least it felt long ago – it felt like a different lifetime) when Grayson had toasted to living life to the full.

My last thought before I drifted off to sleep was of Grayson, I wondered if he was keeping his word, was he living his life to the full?

Chapter 21

By the time Valentine's Day rolled around (one holiday of which I was not a fan, I might add), my book had been published and was doing better than I could have hoped for.

I had attended a few book signings, mostly in and around Beaufort, although I made one appearance in New York at Brian's request.

Kaitlyn and I were about to launch our magazine and Kaitlyn's studio had been a huge success.

A few local artists had even asked if they could show their work in her studio.

All in all, the year was starting out a lot better than last year had ended.

After bumping into Caleb on New Year's Eve, he'd tried calling a few times, but I had ignored each call.

One particular call had sent my heartrate through the roof and it hadn't been Caleb's.

About a week after seeing Caleb, Kaitlyn and I were sitting on the small cottage porch when my phone rang.

Looking down, I half expected to see Brian's name appear, before almost sending my tea flying in every direction when it wasn't Brian's name that popped up.

'What's with you?' Kaitlyn eyed me curiously.

'It's Grayson,' I croaked.

'So answer it,' Kaitlyn's eyes lit up.

'I can't,' I sat frozen, staring at the screen.

I literally couldn't move to answer it, even if I wanted to – which I absolutely did not.

What would I say after all this time?

I was sure Kaitlyn was about to reach out and answer it herself when it stopped ringing.

He hadn't called again.

My parents had eventually given up mentioning Grayson to me altogether, although I think deep down, they still wished that we could work things out.

Deep down, so did I.

They were briefly distracted by being proud parents when my book hit shelves in Beaufort, making sure all their friends bought copies, just as they had.

They always insisted on purchasing one of my books, even though I'd always offered to send them a free copy, so it caught me completely by surprise when my mom asked if she could have a few copies.

Of course I'd said yes, but when I asked who they were for, she'd acted pretty shady. Like we were doing some dodgy drug deal.

The thought of my mom being involved in any kind of dodgy deal had me chuckling to myself, so I brushed it off as nothing more than them finally coming around to receiving freebies.

A further distraction came in a truly wonderful form not long after Valentine's day.

Our family welcomed my beautiful niece into the world.

Baby Olivia Jane Preston was born in the early hours of a particularly warm morning in February.

'She's perfect,' I cooed, holding her, simply blown away by her perfect, tiny features.

She had my brother's big brown eyes and long lashes, with her mom's delicate nose.

She was the loveliest baby I'd ever laid eyes on.

Granted, I was biased, but I wasn't the only one who thought so. She already had my brother wrapped around her little finger and I smiled, picturing her growing up, getting her own way at every turn.

They were going to have their hands full with this little heartbreaker.

My parents weren't much better, fussing and cooing and cuddled.

It warmed my heart. They had wanted grandchildren for ages, and I was so happy that they finally got their wish.

This precious baby girl was going to be so loved and so spoilt, I thought, as we said our goodbyes for the night.

I had spent a lot of time with my family since arriving back in Beaufort and I was once again reassured that I had made the right choice in coming home.

Family was the most important thing in this life and I had hit the jackpot when I'd been born into mine.

I was going to make the most of every moment I had with them.

As much as I enjoyed being around the people I loved, I was also rediscovering that I was ok in my own company.

In fact, I was quite enjoying my newfound solitude.

I spent many afternoons wandering the waterfront, watching fisherman sit beside lifelong friends and reminisce about days gone by, or along the Shackleford Banks with the wild horses.

I loved Beaufort at this time of year, there weren't many tourists around and this felt like the Beaufort I knew and loved, the authentic Beaufort.

No matter where I went, I always had my camera in hand, ready to take the perfect shot for a possible article in the magazine, or simply for the joy of capturing a moment in time.

Freezing that moment when something brought a smile to the face of a child playing in the sand, or an elderly couple walking hand in hand along the waterfront, having shared many happy years together, and still so in love.

Life was about these moments and I loved being able to capture them. It made me feel like I was a part of something bigger.

My heart still ached for Grayson and I accepted that it probably always would, but I also took comfort in knowing that there was hope.

There was always hope if we looked for it.

My hope was that he would be happy again someday, even if that meant meeting someone new and falling in love.

If that meant forgetting about me and moving on with his life, it would be ok. I would be ok, knowing he was happy.

And so, my life settled into a tranquil flow, like the gentle trickle of a stream, flowing between spending my time working on the magazine, starting a new novel, spending time with Kaitlyn and my family and of course spoiling my adorable niece, but most importantly, making time for myself too.

Finding time to do yoga and meditate. To run and to take photos and immerse myself in nature. To be free and wander, as I believed we were meant to do.

The world wouldn't be such a beautiful, fascinating place if we weren't meant to discover its hidden secrets.

It was truly freeing, letting oneself go and to simply be at peace with yourself, be at one with nature, be true to yourself.

Allowing ourselves time to stop and smell the roses, instead of blazing full steam ahead, like so many of my friends in New York.

It was times like this I was once again grateful for my new life. This second chance at life.

As winter turned to spring and the flowers started to bloom, so did the magazine.

Things were good, and my life was getting back on track. I simply took it one day at a time.

This particular day, I was perched on the swing chair on the porch watching the world go by, sipping camomile tea.

'Did you have anything in mind for your birthday?' Kaitlyn asked, joining me a short while later.

My birthday was a week away and I hadn't really given it much thought.

'Not really, maybe just a nice dinner out somewhere.'

'Oh! There's a new place I've heard about it, it gets really good reviews, shall I book it?'

'Sure,' I replied, happy to let Kaitlyn take control, it was what she loved to do after all, so why deprive her.

Besides, if I was being honest, I wasn't really feeling my birthday this year, so if we could treat it like a normal night out, all the better.

Kaitlyn went into full planning mode, booking a table, arranging a taxi and even picking out my outfit.

'Kay, as much as I appreciate all of this, you didn't have to go to all the fuss.' I didn't have the heart to come out and say that I didn't actually want the fuss.

The week had flown by and my birthday had come around before I could even catch my breath.

'Nonsense, it's your birthday. Besides, you deserve to be pampered and fussed over,' she winked at me and I noticed she was even more hyper than usual.

What was she up to, I wondered as my suspicions peaked.

'Come on, we don't want to be late,' she ushered me into the bathroom so I could get showered.

By the time we left the house, my spirits were lifted, and I was looking forward to our night out.

Girlie time and having your hair and makeup done sure could turn things around, I thought, smoothing over my dress.

Kaitlyn had picked out a beautiful strapless mint green dress with an embellished bodice, it was surprisingly comfortable and understated.

Modest elegance, Kailyn had said.

Her own dress was a simple black, figure hugging, knee length dress. She looked beautiful.

'We clean up pretty well don't we,' she'd replied when I complimented her.

'Where is this place?' I asked as we drove past the outskirts of town.

'Oh, it's not too far, it's a little place off the beaten track, you're going to love it,' Kaitlyn assured me.

I suddenly had a bad feeling I was in for a surprise party, but Kaitlyn kept me distracted, showing me ideas for the magazine that she'd stored on her phone and before I knew it the taxi stopped and I looked up.

'Kaitlyn, where are we?' I asked, looking around.

It looked like someone's house. It looked familiar.

Were we picking anyone else up?

'You'll see,' she replied, paying the taxi driver and stepping out.

We were just about to walk through the front door when she spun on her heal, 'I left my scarf in the taxi, you head on in, I'll be right behind you.'

Ok, weird, but I opened the front door, half expecting to see my family jump out to surprise me, but it was empty.

It definitely looked like someone's house. Was this the new way of dining, in a stranger's house.

'Hello?' I called.

Nothing.

Maybe they were outside, I thought, making my way through the cosy house.

There was something oddly familiar about the inside

too, but I couldn't quite put my finger on what it was.

Finding the back door, I stepped out into the garden.

It was beautiful. Oak trees lined the perimeter, draped in Spanish moss, and as twilight settled upon the day, I could see just a hint of fairly lights wrapped around their branches.

A table with two chairs had been placed in the garden under the trees, set with cutlery, crockery, champagne and candles, but still, I saw no one.

As I approached, I saw a note on the table and picked it up.

Put me on, had been written in neat handwriting on the note which sat on top of a blindfold.

Ok, this was weird.

I looked around, hoping to see Kaitlyn, or my family, but still no one.

I was tempted to head back out front to see if Kaitlyn was even there, but curiosity got the better of me and I picked the blindfold up, pausing momentarily to question my sanity, before placing it over my eyes and securing it in place.

And waited.

Suddenly without my sight, my other senses kicked in.

I listened to the leaves gently rustling above me and the birds tweeting, settling in for the day.

I smelled the sweet scent of the flowers that grew around the garden and despite the pleasant weather I felt goose bumps rising on my arms.

And then I heard the faint hum of music.

It was close and I turned around, reaching for the blindfold, but a gentle hand stopped me from removing it.

'Kaitlyn?' I asked, but somehow knowing it wasn't her.

No answer.

Instead, a steady hand took hold of mine, while another hand was placed on the small of my back and we started to sway to the music.

I wasn't sure if I should be flattered or freaked out, but as my muscles relaxed and I placed my free hand on the strangers' shoulder, heat flooded my body.

I knew the feel of these shoulders, of the hand holding mine, the wonderfully familiar clean, almost earthy scent that flooded my nose and for a moment I let myself get lost to my senses, swaying to the music, imagining myself in the arms of the man I loved and before my brain could fully comprehend what I was doing, my lips brushed his and I knew.

'Grayson,' I whispered.

As soon as his name left my lips, he pulled me in close and kissed me deeper and I knew, without a shadow of a doubt, it was him.

I blinked, my eyes readjusting to the light as the blindfold was carefully removed.

'Sophie,' was all he said, those beautiful blue eyes only slightly guarded.

'Grayson, what are we doing here? I don't understand?'

'I read your book,' he replied.

Although he had released me, he was still close enough that his breath washed over my face and I breathed him in.

How was it possible to miss so much of someone? Their smell, their touch, the sound of their voice.

'Oh,' I replied, a million different chapters, paragraphs, words, running through my mind.

'There was one particular chapter that perplexed me though,' he continued.

I'm sure there were many, I thought, but I tried to keep it casual.

'And which one was that?' I asked.

'The big fight between the two brothers, which is overheard, and I believe completely misunderstood.'

Oh boy, no skirting around this then, he clearly wanted to cut straight to the chase.

I cringed and took a step back at the thought of hearing Grayson and Caleb arguing in the barn the day I had left the farm.

'How so?' I asked. Keep it casual, I chanted to myself.

'Well you see, your leading man is a bit of a hot-headed buffoon and he was so angry at his brother that it may have been interpreted as an accusation, when, in fact, that couldn't be further from the truth. He knew full well that the love of his life would never do anything to hurt him, but he was too focused on the past and worrying about history repeating itself that he lashed out at his brother.'

I stared. Was Grayson saying what I thought he was?

'Sophie, I'm sorry,' he took a step closer. 'Truly sorry if I made you think, even for a second, that I didn't trust you. I love you,' he reached out to touch my cheek and I closed my eyes at the feel of his skin on mine, trying to clear the zillion thoughts rushing through my brain.

'But it sounded like you were accusing Caleb and I of....' I trailed off, unable to finish that sentence.

'I was angry with Caleb for doing what he did, but Sophie, I swear, I never thought for a second that anything was going on between the two of you. I know you, and I know you would never betray me like that.'

The emotion I'd been trying so hard to bottle up for the past few months came bubbling to the surface suddenly and I threw my arms around Grayson's neck, feeling tears burning my eyes.

'I'm so sorry Grayson, I'm sorry for everything. For leaving, for causing problems with your family, I wish I could take it all back.'

'Sophie,' he gently pushed me away, still keeping me close, but wanting to look at me. 'You beautiful, sweet, kind, ridiculous creature. You have nothing to apologise for. You didn't cause any problems, the problem was already there, if anything you helped fixed it. Things with Caleb and I are better than ever, even Caleb and my dad are in a far better place. Our family is no longer broken, and we have you to thank for that.'

I couldn't comprehend what he was saying. How had I fixed anything? I had ruined their perfect family.

'But I'm no better than Catherine,' I looked down at the floor, ashamed.

Grayson's hand pulled me in again and I rested my head on his chest.

'Sophie, you are nothing like Catherine. She manipulated us, she wormed her way in and then played us off against one another. There's been a rift between

Caleb and I ever since, as much as we tried to pretend everything was ok, it wasn't, but after everything that happened, you leaving, your book, your letters to my family, we hashed everything out. We went into the early hours of the morning, but once we were done and once everything was aired, we were finally able to move on. If it hadn't been for you, that never would have happened.'

'I didn't come between the two of you?' I said, as I tried to process everything he was saying.

'No, you brought us back together.'

'And you weren't accusing Caleb of having an affair with me in the barn the day I left?'

'No. I was just angry with him, but more than that I was angry with myself and I let my stupid pride and old wounds take over. I love you, Sophie, I always have, and I never want to be apart from you again. Come home to me.'

I looked up at the man who had owned my heart from the moment I'd encountered his stubborn ass in the barn and the only words I could form, weren't just words, they were a promise, 'Always, and forever.'

One Year Later

'You look very… calm,' Kaitlyn said, eyeballing me suspiciously.

'I feel very calm,' I replied with a broad smile. I felt elated.

So much had happened this past year.

It turns out that Kailyn and Caleb had kissed at

midnight on New Year's Eve and had continued kissing ever since.

They were perfect for each other, I only wished I'd seen that from the start, but then again, everything happens for a reason and when it's meant to.

Kaitlyn was the happiest I'd ever seen her, and she had mentioned that her and Caleb were moving in together.

Her studio was blooming and although we were both busy, we kept the magazine going and had even featured Caleb's now very popular beach bar and restaurant.

It had been so heart-warming not only to witness Caleb's success, but to see the relationship between him and Sam grow so strong, and how proud both Sam and Rosie were of their son.

As for the Danvers brothers, their relationship was better than ever.

They were becoming friends again and had been a huge part of one another's lives and successes this past year.

My parents had finally taken a vacation, and then another, and another. Travelling to Morocco, India, Bali and many road trips through the States.

Dad was doing well, although I had to keep reminding him to eat healthy and exercise.

My beautiful niece, Olivia, was getting cuter by the day and I was so proud of the father Paul had become.

I had a feeling baby number two would be on the way soon, from the brooding looks Sarah got every time she saw a new-born baby, or when Olivia looked up at her lovingly.

Sam and Rosie, who had joined my parents on their trip

to Morocco, were starting to wind down and leave the day to day running of the farm, for the most part, to Grayson and I.

I couldn't have been happier.

The day Grayson had come back into my life was one I still thought of most days.

We had spent hours talking and when he had finally convinced me that I hadn't been the one who had torn his family apart, it dawned on me that I had no idea where we were or who's house we had been in.

'It's ours if, or when, you're ready,' Grayson had said and then laughed at my blank expression.

He had bought the house for us.

Turns out it was the farm that Grayson had told me about the first time we'd gone swimming in the lake.

The elderly couple who owned the farm had decided to sell and move closer to their children, so Grayson had bought it, given it some TLC and transformed it into our now beautiful, warm, welcoming home.

We spent long summer days making it our own, buying bits of furniture and artwork for the walls.

I didn't think life could get any better than those days, but on a balmy summer afternoon, Grayson packed a picnic basket for us, and we took our horses for a ride to the lake – our lake.

After a dip in the cool water, Grayson got down on one knee and proposed to me, amongst the still water and wildflowers of our little piece of heaven.

So here I was, on my wedding day, feeling surprisingly calm, overjoyed and beyond grateful for this life I had been given and all the people in it.

'Come on, we need to get ready,' Kaitlyn, who was of course my maid of honour, ushered me into a chair to have my hair and makeup done.

Grayson and I had both wanted a small, simple wedding. Opting for having the ceremony and reception here at our home, on the farm.

It would all take place at the lake, which was decorated with wildflowers and fairy lights everywhere to give it a magical, whimsical feel.

Finding my wedding dress had been far simpler than I would have thought possible.

Kaitlyn, Rosie, my mom and I had all gone into Wilmington for a girlie day and I had no expectations. I simply wanted to enjoy a day out, just the girls, trying on dresses and having a little fashion show of wedding dresses, maid of honour dresses and of course outfits for Rosie and my mom.

Imagine my surprise when the first dress I tried on (at first dress shop we'd been in), turned out to be the one.

Kaitlyn insisted I try on a number of other dresses, just to be sure, she had said, but I ended up going back to that first one, loving it's simple, romantic feel.

It had the most beautiful, intricate lace detail over the fitted bodice, spilling over onto the skirt, which was slightly flared but not overly poofy – I had no desire to resemble a Disney princess.

Delicate off the shoulder lace straps draped softly over

my upper arms, with a row of little white buttons trailing up the back of the dress.

It was perfect.

After a few happy tears, we spent the rest of the day shopping for accessories, finding a dress for Kaitlyn, along with outfits for the moms

Everything seemed to be falling into place.

Caleb was catering the wedding, although I wasn't sure how he was going to juggle being best man and catering too, but he assured us he had everything under control, and I believed him.

I'd never been much of a bride-zilla type anyway, so perhaps that was the reason things seemed to flow so well and part of the reason I felt so calm when the day finally arrived.

Of course, I was nervous, and I had an excited buzz thrumming through my veins, but this is what I wanted, and I couldn't wait to start our lives together.

The ceremony was beautiful, with our closest family and friends attending, all seated amongst the trees next to the lake.

Grayson and I stood in front of the beautiful arch our dads had made for us, which had been decorated with fairy lights and wildflowers (picked from around the lake).

It was more than I could have hoped for.

After the ceremony, and having a few pictures taken, we ate and danced and cut our beautiful rustic wedding cake (also courtesy of Caleb), which I took great pleasure in mushing into Grayson's face.

That was, until he returned the favour.

Our wedding pictures were going to be comical.

'Are you happy, baby girl?' My dad asked when we had our first dance together.

'So happy,' I beamed.

'That makes me incredibly happy too, honey,' my dad kissed my cheek before stepping aside for Grayson to step in.

'Hello, Mrs Danvers,' he grinned at me.

'Hello, Mr Danvers,' I grinned back.

We were like two teenagers, which only made me smile wider.

'Have I told you how beautiful you look?' Grayson asked, leaning in to whisper in my ear, his warm breath causing a shiver to run through me.

'You have, but feel free to tell me again,' I giggled.

Grayson pulled back, looked deep into my eyes, 'You are the most beautiful woman I have ever laid eyes on, Sophie Danvers.'

The intensity in his beautiful, warm, baby blues made my knees go week and when he leaned in to kiss me, I felt the world melt away and in those moments, the moments when only Grayson and I existed, I felt so happy I thought my heart may burst right out of my chest with joy.

'Mind if I cut in? I'd like to dance with my sister-in-law,' Caleb asked Grayson, who hugged his brother and thanked him again for the amazing job he'd done helping us with the wedding, before leaving Caleb and I on the dance floor.

'Welcome to the family, sis,' Caleb pulled me into his arms in his easy going way, before spinning me around, sending my dress swirling around me.

I couldn't help but laugh. We sure had come a long way, all of us.

'Thank you for everything, Caleb. We couldn't have done this without you. The food was amazing and that cake! If things don't work out with the beach bar, you could always get into catering weddings,' I teased, knowing full well the beach bar and restaurant would be around for a long time to come.

'There's only one more wedding I'll cater for.'

For the first time, possibly ever, Caleb was serious, only a small smile played at the corners of his mouth and it took me a moment to register what he was saying.

'Oh my-' I squealed, only for Caleb to shush me, looking around for a moment to make sure no one was close enough to hear. 'Are you serious? You're going to propose?' I wanted to cry with joy all over again – seriously, when did I turn into such a crier?

'I bought the ring a few weeks ago and I've booked a beach house for the weekend. Do you think she'll say yes? I don't think I've ever been so nervous about anything in my life.'

'Oh, Caleb, I've never seen Kaitlyn so happy. She is so in love with you, of course she'll say yes. I'm so happy for you, for both of you, that you found each other.'

'Me too, Soph, me too. But don't worry, you'll always be my best girl,' Caleb gave me a squeeze before disappearing to find Kaitlyn.

'What are you so giddy about?' Grayson asked me later that night when he was able to pull me away from our guests, to twirl me around the dancefloor.

'It's my wedding day I'll have you know, I'm entitled to be as giddy as I like,' I laughed at how much I sounded like a five-year-old girl. 'Can you keep a secret?' I asked, a glint in my eye.

Grayson frowned, but nodded.

'Caleb is going to propose to Kaitlyn,' I whispered to him.

'Seriously? Wow. Good for him, he deserves to be happy.'

'I'm just happy that the two of you are getting along so well.'

'So am I. I don't want anything to come between my family again. They're the most important thing in this life.'

'Besides your wife of course,' I corrected.

'Of course. What's that saying, happy wife, happy life?'

'And don't you forget it, Mr Danvers.'

'I wouldn't dare, Mrs Danvers.'

'Hi, Mom. Are you having a good time?' I asked, when I finally managed to catch up with my mom later that night.

'Oh, honey, it's been a magical night. I'm so happy for you. I was so worried after you left the farm and went back to New York, but sometimes we have to fight through the darkness to find our way back to the light and no one has fought harder than you. I'm so proud of you, of the woman you've become, the woman you've always been.'

'I wouldn't be the woman I am today without you.

You've always been my rock, my home, my best friend, my confidant and an incredible role model. You've given up so much for Paul and I. My only hope is that one day I'm as good a mom to my own kids as you've been to Paul and I.'

'You will make a wonderful mother, Sophie. You have so much love in your heart, your children will be truly blessed.'

'Ok, you're going to make me cry,' I sniffed back more tears, only this time, it was for a whole different reason.

'No more tears tonight, only happiness and smiles and dancing, definitely more dancing,' my mom hugged me tightly before taking my hand and leading me to the dancefloor, where we joined the rest of our family and friends and danced far into the night.

When most of our guests had left and only a small group remained, Grayson found me sitting on a rock by the lake, simply watching our loved ones and soaking up the most wonderful night of my life, not wanting to forget a moment of it.

'May I have one last dance, Mrs Danvers?'

'You certainly may, Mr Danvers,' I laughed, taking his hand, letting him pull me close as we swayed under the moonlight, the crickets serenading us as we moved.

'Was today everything you hoped it would be?' Grayson asked, my head resting on his chest, I was exhausted but never more exhilarated, all at the same time.

'Everything and so much more, Grayson. I love you with all my heart.'

'I love you too, Sophie.'

'You know, you never did tell me what the fortune teller said to you that night in Virginia?' I asked, not sure what had made me think of that.

I felt Grayson chuckle and pulled back to look at him.

'What's so funny?'

'She said that history would repeat itself unless I stopped it and if I could find a way to prevent it, life would take me down a much sweeter path. She was right, Sophie, it brought me back to you, which is the only path I ever want to walk, the one with you by my side.' Grayson kissed me, before asking what the fortune teller had told me.

I smiled at the memory.

'She said I would come to a crossroad in my life, which at the time I thought was such a cliché, but she also said that I would have to make the right choice for everyone, which is partially why I thought leaving was the best thing for everyone, I thought that was what she'd meant. I didn't think for a second that staying was the right thing for anyone. If only she'd been more specific, it would have saved a lot of heartache,' I half joked. 'She also said that if I opened my heart up to love again, I would be complete and whole again. You've fixed me too, Grayson, you put my heart back together again when I didn't think that was even a possibility. I don't know what lead me to you, whether it was fate or destiny, or something bigger than all of us, but whatever it was, it's been the best part of my life so far.'

'So far, huh?' Grayson's breath-taking smile reached his blue eyes.

'Well, there might be one thing to top it,' I couldn't wait

any longer.

'Oh yeah, what would that be?'

I reached out for his hand and placing it on my belly, I simply smiled at him, sending one precious thought his way.

He looked confused for a moment and then looked down at his hand on my belly, looked back up at my face, back to his hand again, before picking me up and spinning me around and then abruptly, but very gently, placing me back down on the soft ground, fussing over me.

'Grayson, I'm pregnant, not made of glass,' I laughed as we sat down together on our rock.

'I'm going to be a dad,' he sounded happy, and a little stunned.

'How do you feel?' I asked hesitantly.

We hadn't really spoken all that much about having kids.

We knew we both wanted them, but I guess I thought it would probably be another few years before we started trying.

Grayson took my hands in his. 'I thought this day couldn't get any better, but Sophie, you've made me the happiest man alive twice in one day,' he pulled me close and showered me in kisses.

I tried to pull away, laughing as I pushed him gently.

'I love you, you goofball,' I said, still laughing.

'I love you, Sophie, I love you and our unborn child, always and forever,' he placed a gentle hand back on my belly, his eyes full of love and expectation for the future.

'Always and forever,' I repeated, immersing myself in this moment.

This perfect, blissful moment that wasn't the end of our story.

It was just the beginning.

The End